THE EMIGRE

Joan Brady won the 1993 Whitbread Book of the
Year Award – as well as France's coveted Prix du
Meilleur Livre Etranger – for her second novel *Theory
of War*, which became an international bestseller and
has been translated into eight languages. She is also
the author of short stories, a highly acclaimed auto-
biography, *Prologue*, and most recently *Death Comes
for Peter Pan*. She lives in Devon.

'Dazzlingly fantastic…The densely packed narrative ranges over continents and decades, unravelling the ties of love and hate that bind a bustling cast of vividly drawn grotesques. At its centre is the enigma of Nikolas Strakhan, musician, chess-player and fraud. Impervious to morality and irresistible to women, he sweeps like a whirlwind through precariously ordered lives…A compelling picture of jealousies and betrayals, of the dangers that menace even what seems most safe'

The Times

A Whitbread-Prize winner who has conjured up a wonderful character and an absorbing tale…Sex is at the very core of this novel, and Brady's fabulous metaphors shine a new light on this oldest of subjects…it's never easy to be certain about what is real in the rather sinister world Brady depicts …Hilariously farcical situations…race toward a chillingly funny conclusion. Brady has embroidered a rich fabric with intricate and intriguing patterns…Amazing'

Literary Review

'An exotic cocktail, shaken in Paris and stirred in Hampstead…Brady has a good eye and a good ear, too, which enable her to plot her way through countless international locations…she conjures atmospheres enhanced by colourful, fluent dialogue. Like a musician who has spent a lifetime honing her talent, Brady has at last found in this new, more comic form an instrument on which she can play happily in any key she chooses'

Observer

'The story unfolds with a fine, confident swagger…In the cauldron of conflicting emotions, there is exquisite dramatic irony… Nikolas is a fascinating character…Brady never lets us lose sight of the dreamer who really does believe he is a musical genius and will stop at nothing to find a platform for his talents. The arch villain is also a holy fool…There is plenty here to keep readers on their toes'

Sunday Telegraph

'Fascinating…related to us by an admiring but appalled associate of the protagonist whose strength of feeling serves to fire the reader's imagination…Mysterious…flamboyant…Brady cleverly plays with our understanding of truth…the reader is seduced…Set pieces deliver pure delight…A fine novel that is ambitious in scope and captivating to the end'

Spectator

Joan Brady

THE EMIGRÉ

V

VINTAGE

Published by Vintage 2000

2 4 6 8 10 9 7 5 3 1

Copyright © Joan Brady 1999

The right of Joan Brady to be identified as the author of
this work has been asserted by her in accordance with
the Copyright, Designs and Patents Act, 1988

First published in Great Britain in 1999
by Secker & Warburg

Vintage
Random House, 20 Vauxhall Bridge Road,
London SW1V 2SA

Random House Australia (Pty) Limited
20 Alfred Street, Milsons Point, Sydney
New South Wales 2061, Australia

Random House New Zealand Limited
18 Poland Road, Glenfield, Auckland 10,
New Zealand

Random House (Pty) Limited
Endulini, 5A Jubilee Road, Parktown 2193,
South Africa

The Random House Group Limited Reg. No. 954009
www.randomhouse.co.uk

A CIP catalogue record for this book
is available from the British Library

ISBN 0 7493 9503 6

Papers used by Random House are natural, recyclable
products made from wood grown in sustainable forests.
The manufacturing processes conform to the environ-
mental regulations of the country of origin

Printed and bound in Great Britain by
Cox & Wyman Limited, Reading, Berkshire

For Kira
who tells such wonderful stories

CONTENTS

The year referred to below is 1984

TECHNICAL CONSULTANTS

The Viscountess Chaplin
Harold C. Schonberg, principal music critic (and occasional chess correspondent) of the *New York Times*
Gavin Henderson, who played with Sviatoslav Richter
Anthony Phillips, who accompanied Richter on his American tour in 1960
Jolyon Kay, Commercial Attaché, British Embassy, Paris
Dr Tim Manser
Kira Strakhova, principal dancer, Ballets Russes
Lynda Kinzey, physicist
Toby Gilbert, Parisian
Kevin Vinsen, Director, Canary Green Computers

QUOTES

The verses on page 39 are from 'A Thought' by Mikhail Yuryvich Lermontov and 'Autumn' by Alexander Sergeyevich Pushkin. Both were translated by Max Eastman; they appeared in *An Anthology of World Poetry*, edited by Mark Van Doren (Albert & Charles Boni, New York, 1928).

ACKNOWLEDGEMENTS

A lot of people helped with this novel, and I'm deeply grateful to them all.

Several of my technical consultants worked on the manuscript itself. I'd like particularly to thank Rosemary Chaplin, who not only explained the intricacies of an aristocrat's way of life but also contributed a charming scene in the life of the child Priscilla and clarified banking practice in the 1960s; Harold Schonberg, who put order into Nikolas's chess as well as his music and created a game for him to win; my oldest friend Toby Gilbert, who found a place for Nikolas to live and to lunch, cleaned up his French and his drinking habits, and contributed invaluable comments on the structure of the book; my school friend Lynda Kinzey, who not only taught me about explosives but helped me work out escape routes (and listened to my endless complaints); and Tim Manser, who diagnosed Nikolas and corrected his various symptoms, both physical and mental – as well as my spelling. I owe special thanks to Kira Strakhova, to whom this book is dedicated. She's the source of many of the stories that make up Nikolas's background; without these – and her encouragement – the book would have been a far fainter thing.

I'd also like to thank Laura Morris and Geoff Mulligan, whose suggestions contributed so much; Rosemary Buckman, without whose support there would have been no book at all; Ann Kimber, Angela Lambert and Diana Athill, for help when help was needed and for helpful comments; Jules Preston, who told me how *not* to ride a motorcycle; his mother Nettie, who told me about the town of Brighton; Wellington Jewellers of Totnes, who told me about diamonds and the Illusion setting; and dear Al Hart, who said years ago that he thought I was a fabulist.

PART I

The First Week in September

CHAPTER 1

Reality? What's so good about it? Where's the structure in it? Nobody wants it. Nobody buys it. Myth is better. I love myth. Make-believe and fairy tale too: impossible quests, fantastic riches, the devil raised from hell, dragons and magical creatures. But who would have thought this advertisement in *The Times* – oh, how discreet it is – could be the start of such a story?

Harry let out a whoop of glee when he saw it and reached for the telephone. The upshot was that on the morning of the concert we took the train from Brighton to London and arrived at Nikolas Strakhan's house in Swiss Cottage just before noon. As Harry raised his hand to the knocker, the door flew open.

A huge man stood there. 'What have you got on your face?' he demanded. No greeting.

Harry touched his beard tentatively. 'You don't like it?'

The house was Georgian, ivy-covered, as huge for a house as the man was for a man; it opened on to the street, and we stood outside, awkward on the pavement. The man cocked his head this way, then that. 'I used to think of you as my handsome nephew.'

'It's really that bad?'

'You must shave it off at once.' He patted Harry's cheek. 'Upstairs. To your left. I'll entertain Eve while you're busy.'

'Now you just wait – ' Harry began.

'This isn't Eve?' The massive face scanned me. 'Who is she then? You've switched girlfriends in the last week? Without telling me? I like this one.'

'Of course it's Eve. Why do you say these things? Who else could it be?'

'Well, introduce us.'

'Eve Holland, this is Nikolas Strakhan.'

I took the hand he offered me. 'You're right about the beard, aren't you?' I said, delighted at the thought. 'It makes him look – I'm not sure. What do you think? What *is* wrong with it?'

'No, no, Harry,' Nikolas said. 'Not that way. All that sea air is addling your brain. What do you want to live in Brighton for, anyway? I've already told you: up the stairs and to your left. Eve, you come with me.'

'Nikolas, I'm not about to – ' Harry began again.

'Go on. Go on. You can't wear a thing like that to lunch. Think of the children.'

'Goddamn you, Nikolas,' said Harry, who (like his father) never, never swears. 'You leave me and my beard alone.'

Nikolas shrugged and turned into the marble-tiled entrance hall. 'Mickie went all the way to Harrods this morning to get us something edible,' he said, 'but the English are constitutionally incapable of understanding food. Even at Harrods you can't get a raw truffle to save your skin, and preserved ones have no taste at all. Why would they do something like that? Nobody can beat a good Stilton, though, not the French themselves. Don't you agree, Eve? Lunch is in the garden at the back. Follow me.'

He was fat – fifty years old, give or take a year or so. His trousers rounded up over a heart-shaped bottom that wobbled as he walked ahead of us. There was no carpet in the vast living room; the floor was a mosaic of woods, a little cold, but so richly textured that the coldness didn't seem to matter much. Against one wall hung a mobile. Harry told me later that it was an original Calder; the size of the thing alone oozed money. No carpet. No pictures. Next came a studio: two grand pianos and a wall of mirrors. Then a solarium with a bank of French windows that led on to a raw wood porch, where a cedar of Lebanon rose up through the boards and arched over a table partially laid for the lunch to come.

September is such a variable month. The day was sunny, warm, languid, too hot for the time of year, but perfect for a picnic in the shade of a cedar of Lebanon.

'Sit down,' Nikolas said, seating himself in a large wooden chair with a plush cushion on it. The other chairs were smaller. They had no cushions. 'Sit. Sit. Does your enchanting Eve drink wine? I wouldn't ask if she were French, but since she's American . . .' He let his sentence trail off, addressing it to Harry but looking at me. His eyes were wide-set; his face lit up here, then there, appraisal, disdain, surprise – was that a shade of contempt? was it a threat? – a quick-change artist who sometimes wears all his costumes at once.

The hand Harry ran over his beard was protective. Yet I knew he'd shave it off as soon as we got back to the safety of Brighton;

I couldn't repress a smile. 'She doesn't usually drink at lunch,' he said, a little sheepish, noting the smile, knowing its meaning. 'You'll have to ask her yourself.'

'What intimacies you allow me, Harry. You'd better be careful. I've already taken quite a fancy to this girl. I might press my advantage. Will you drink wine this noon, Eve?'

'I'd love a glass, if it's on offer,' I said.

'I'm offering it.'

I bowed a mock bow. 'Then I'd love it.'

He poured out wine into water glasses, better wine than I was used to – far better – but it was the water glasses that caught my eye. Could they be a flaw in the exquisite taste of the household? Was it possible? I doubted it – and began to feel uneasy about the wine glasses Harry and I had bought only the day before.

And there was a simplicity of line to Mickie, who appeared just about then, that seemed of a piece with the water glasses. Harry had told me a little about her: half-French, half-American, English-educated, about my age – twenty-three – something like a quarter of a century younger than Nikolas. She bustled on to the patio with a platter of sliced tomatoes covered in herbs and a basket of bread. She wasn't good-looking; there was a heaviness about the jaw, and her features were too irregular. But she brought to mind the homely strengths of a bygone age, starched aprons and broth on the back burner. Nothing saccharine, though: a smart slap on the backside if you didn't wash behind your ears. She had dark hair, grey-streaked despite her youth.

I turned in my chair and smiled up at her. Harry rose and held out his arms. And Nikolas? Nikolas ignored her. He turned his back on her and said to me in a loud voice, 'I've been wanting to ask you, Eve: do you bleach your hair?'

'Oh dear, is it so obvious? You don't think it's as bad as Harry's beard, do you? My Aunt Peggy hates it. She says – '

'Shut up, Nikolas,' Mickie said, swinging out of Harry's embrace. 'I'm damned if I'll take the grey out of my hair just to satisfy some paedophile whim of yours.' Her accent was definitely English, but it had other sounds in it too. I wasn't sure just what. I figured she and Nikolas spoke French when they were alone. 'Pay no attention to him, Eve. It's me he's getting at.'

Nikolas laughed and patted her rear.

I can't remember what we talked about over the tomatoes, although I do remember that the tomatoes were as good as the wine – and when it comes to food I know what I'm talking about – as good as the ones my uncle and aunt grow in their back yard in California. The new wine glasses would have to go. There is something – I could see it now – well, effete, about wine glasses, something over-complicated, unnecessary.

While Nikolas uncorked a second bottle, Mickie brought in a rack of lamb and a platter of brilliant green broccoli. She carved the meat, pink slices, a fine blackened glaze on the outside. At the end of the table the salad waited its turn, red-tinged leaves glistening in the sun.

'What's on the programme tonight, Nikolas?' Harry said, taking the plate Mickie handed him.

There was a moment's silence – odd, I thought – then Nikolas shifted his vast body to face away from Harry. 'Music,' he said.

'I got that much from the ad in *The Times*.' Amusement twitched at the corners of Harry's mouth.

'Did you indeed?'

'I like Britten – but not very much. Is it all Britten?'

The vast body turned back. 'No.' Mickie handed him a plate. He waved his hand. 'Nothing for me, Mickie. The meat's too fat.'

'Hey, come on, tell me,' Harry persisted. 'What other music are you conducting?'

'Harry, I spend my days and nights at this. I'd like to be the one to choose whether we talk about it or not. Surely you can indulge me today. Tell me about politics. I don't understand politics.'

Harry took this slap in the face with an adman's roll – he writes advertising copy for a living – and laughed. Besides, he loves political talk. All his Madison Avenue gloss slides magically left when it comes to politics; he believes in the common weal and the rights of the downtrodden. 'What is there to say? Every time that orange-haired movie actor appears on the box I squirm for my country.'

'Movie actor? What movie actor?'

'Don't be absurd,' Harry said sharply.

He told me later that he was never absolutely certain Nikolas was lying when he said things like this. Why pretend not to know what *everybody* knows? The year was 1984. Ronald Reagan was running for his second term. Of course, explanations of the obvious do make an idiot of the explainer, and Nikolas's face glowed with anticipation.

'Is he nervous?' I whispered to Mickie.

'Nikolas? Nervous? Why?'

'Richter's a very famous pianist, isn't he? Even I've heard of him, and I've never heard of anybody.'

Mickie shrugged. 'You know Nikolas.'

'Do I? Is he so easy to know?'

'It depends on what you want.'

I wasn't sure how to answer this, so I said, 'Do people ever get used to appearing on stage?'

'Nikolas hasn't conducted in public before. What's Harry been telling you?'

'I just assumed – ' I began weakly, then went on in a rush. 'He *must* be nervous. There's hardly any fat on this lamb. It's perfect – so simple. I don't know how you did it, and the broccoli – He can't mean he doesn't like the look of the meat.'

She glanced at him (not, I thought, a particularly friendly

glance). 'Last week he wouldn't have anything else in the house.'

'Why won't he eat it today?'

'Oh, he'll eat all right.' She gave a short laugh. 'Just wait. Won't you have some more bread? More bread, Harry?'

'. . . corrupt, foolish, vacuous,' Harry was saying. He took another chunk of bread, bit into it blindly and continued to rant while he chewed. 'Reagan's ill-educated, vain, preening. He's a fascist of – '

'Why do you concern yourself with such a person?' Nikolas interrupted. 'Why not put him out of mind?'

'Not even you can be this irresponsible.'

'If I thought the way you talk, I'd have to act, and I'm not prepared to act. As long as I don't think about it, I can comfortably carry on doing music.'

'Nikolas, the guy's already slashed the arts budgets. So has Thatcher, for that matter. Suppose – you aren't going to pretend you haven't heard of Thatcher, are you?'

Margaret Thatcher had been Prime Minister for five years, but Nikolas looked blank. 'What's he do?'

'She's a woman, Nikolas.'

'No! Another American? Why are you – ? That looks good.' Nicholas peered down at Harry's plate. 'Is it good? Now that I see it up close, it looks almost French. English meat is too fat. Can I change my mind, Mickie?'

Mickie gave me a wry smile, heaped meat and broccoli on a plate and put it down in front of Nikolas, who attacked it as though he hadn't had a decent meal in weeks.

We drank two more bottles of wine at that sunny table and talked about people in Harry's family, which was large and diverse, and about famous musicians I know I should have heard of. Nikolas's two small daughters came out with their nanny, kissed Harry dutifully, shook my hand, disappeared for a trip to the park. Nobody said anything more about the concert to come. Not a word. But I was becoming distinctly uncomfortable; from time to time Nikolas looked at me much as he'd looked at his lamb before he'd swallowed it down in a single gulp. Nobody had ever looked at me quite so hungrily before, and I didn't like it. I leaned my head on Harry's shoulder. I reached out and took his hand. God knows what he thought I had in mind. My contribution to bedroom negotiations was as half-hearted as his own.

By four o'clock the cedar tree no longer shaded the table, and the air was too hot to be comfortable. Nikolas left us to rest. Harry and I staggered up the stairs after Mickie, who showed us where we were to sleep that night. We flopped on the bed and fell into a drunken torpor.

I'm supposed to be a scientist – a deliciously grand title for a one-time research assistant at Edison Laboratories, don't you agree? Not that I started out to be a scientist. Long before I graduated from high school, I'd decided on a PhD in literature. Professors McKinley and Buchanan put a stop to that; they were the leading lights in the English Department of the University of California at Berkeley when I went there, and somehow my Freshman year got split between the two of them.

McKinley came first: a dapper dresser, blazers with brass buttons, tall and thin, wry, sarcastic. I took detailed notes on Milton, Blake, Shelley. On the final exam I wrote down the Professor's best thoughts. To my horror, I got a C.

Eve Holland? a C? Never. It was a mistake. It had to be. I made an appointment and went to see the man himself.

'I don't want to read my own opinions on an exam paper,' he said. 'I know them all already. Can't you tell me something new?'

Nobody in high school had wanted to hear anything new. 'I'll do so another time,' I said.

Then came Professor Buchanan, who recited whole passages of Eliot and Auden in a grand, resonant voice like a Methodist preacher of old. With McKinley's training behind me, I knew better than to study my notes for the final; I pored over textural analyses instead. The exam asked exactly the questions I wanted.

I got a C.

'You think I deliver lectures to amuse myself?' Buchanan sighed. 'Can't you remember any of what I've been trying to drum into you?'

Well. So. And what, pray, is the point of studying a discipline like that? Is it a discipline at all? What are you supposed to get at the end of it? A degree in academic caprice? I spent a week drifting in and out of one kind of haze or another – whatever I could buy until my money ran out.

'What do you expect?' said my Uncle Phineas, when I arrived on his doorstep, shivery and tearful. 'Try mathematics or physics – something solid. Find out what makes a rocket go up.' I'd always loved fireworks. 'Find out why a Catherine wheel is beautiful. Why should you waste your time pitting one fool's opinion against another's?'

So the next term I enrolled in a calculus course under the direction of a graduate student who smelled of soap and milk.

'I can *almost* understand this,' I said to him; it was Newton's Method, I think. 'Almost. I have the feeling that if I could just –'

'What do you want to understand it for?' he said.

I figured he was putting me down. 'Understanding will help me do it,' I said testily.

'No it won't.'

I couldn't hear sarcasm in his voice, so I glanced up; his smile was self-deprecating, friendly. 'It won't?' I said. 'Are you sure? Why not?'

He sat next to me and wrote corrections over my scrawl. 'It's a trick.'

'But – '

Then came the moment of revelation. 'Best of all, it's a trick that works. If you find a trick that works, don't look any further. Just use it.'

11

I inhaled this lovely thought along with the graduate student's milk and soap. My university years laid themselves out in front of me for the taking; I got straight As, and not just because a friendly graduate student marked my paper either. My answers were right because they were right, and they'd have stayed right all the way down the hall from Professor McKinley's office to Professor Buchanan's.

There's more, though. This stuff isn't just tricks and techniques: there are serious surprises, serious excitements. I hadn't even guessed. Every once in a while – See that? What could it be? only dark? only confusion? No, no, children. Look closer. See it now? Who could mistake it? It's a wild elephant and, as the old adage has it, she who mounts the wild elephant goes where the wild elephant goes. A ride like this – some unexpected proof, some long-sought-after pattern – is visceral, in the heart, in the gut, a beauty so abrupt, so exhilarating, so fierce you're not sure you can bear it. 'Yes,' you cry. 'That's how it is. That's the truth of it.'

And then, what the hell, I was head-hunted in my Senior year. Nobody head-hunts literature students. Edison Laboratories, manufacturers of arms and explosives, offered me an amazing salary. As Uncle Phineas noted (noting too that it was about time I earned my own living), where is physics more powerful than in an explosion? One tiny, clean equation and – wham! Fire and destruction everywhere. But despite my academic record and my salary (despite the years I'd spent in love with fireworks), the personnel manager said to himself, 'She's only a girl.' He stuck me in front of a VDU, where I calculated error margins all day long, not so much as a Catherine wheel in sight.

And no hint – not the faintest, most remote whiff – of a wild elephant anywhere to be found.

I was deep in despair by the time Aldrich & Rheinholt of Madison Avenue sent Harry to help the lab put a new gloss on its corporate image. Harry toured the plant, spotted me and designed the ad. There I sit, propped on a high stool in a tiny skirt and a white coat, backed by a fearsome array of chemical junk, vials, glass tubing, bubbling liquids in blues and reds – as close as I'd ever come to real research. The blonde hair that outrages Aunt Peggy (and provokes inquiry from Nikolas Strakhan) partially covers my face. Beside me, a sign says

> QUIET
>
> SCIENTIST at WORK

Harry took me out to celebrate the ad's first appearance – and my elevation to the title of 'Scientist' from the lowly position of 'Research Assistant'. I'd almost forgotten what a delight enthusiasm can be. Harry was enthusiastic about everything – the Chinese restaurant I suggested, the dumplings and wine the waiter brought us, the waiter himself, every comment I made. Nobody at Edison had much interest in anything.

Harry said he loved advertising. I laughed. He laughed – and said it again.

'Toothpaste and tampons and soap powder?' I said, truly puzzled. 'How can *love* come into it?'

He saluted me with his chopsticks and skewered a dumpling. 'Hey, you say I dip this into the vinegar and the mustard? both at the same time?'

I leaned forward on my elbows. 'So come on, convince me.'

'A guy comes to my office' – Harry rummaged around in his pocket, extracted a couple of coins, set them out on the table – 'and tosses these two quarters on my desk. He points and says, "This one's mine. Make it better." So I look at it and maybe' – Harry picked up the coin, turned it this way and that – 'well, it's older than the other and a bit duller. It's got this cute little flaw in it. See?' He laughed again, a happy boy, fresh as a cupcake. 'Every product out there is more alike than different. If I can

13

find one tiny difference – and exploit it just the right way – your product comes out on top.'

'That's it? That's really what it's all about?'

'Isn't it great? I just love it.'

'Oh, I do envy you,' I said then, my shoulders slumping.

Harry's brow knitted and unknitted. He looked down at his plate and fiddled with his chopsticks. Then, eyes still downcast, he said, 'Why not come to Brighton with me?'

'Come where?'

'This English town – their Tourist Board or whatever they call it – wants something like A & R's Philadelphia campaign, and Aldrich chose your own Harry Wheelock for the job. I leave next month.'

'You're making me very jealous. I've never been to England.'

'Why not come along? I mean it. Just for the ride.'

'I only wish – You're not really serious, are you?'

'Absolutely serious.'

'You don't know anything about me. I might murder you in your bed.'

'You can do what you like in my bed as long as you're in it.'

So I went with him.

We'd been living in a flat in Denmark Villas – a pretty, tree-lined avenue back from the Brighton–Hove waterfront – for just under six months before the trip to London and this elegant house in Swiss Cottage. I raised myself up on Nikolas Strakhan's guest bed to study his nephew Harry's beard, which was somehow – but how? – all wrong.

Harry's short, no taller than I am, but aside from that he's your typical American to look at, perfect teeth, perfect nose, perfect forehead. How queer genetic resemblances are, though. He and Nikolas were plainly the same family, but some Disney animator had cleaned up Harry for the children. Only the scar on his cheek separated him from the humdrum.

He's proud of his scar. 'Scar on right cheek,' his passport says. It's a white slash that cuts down from his dimple almost all the way to his mouth – the kind of scar Prussian swordsmen used to sport. 'See?' he said to me, smiling, pointing to it with his chopsticks during that first dinner we had together, 'That's me: scar on right cheek.' Then he added – he has a fetching smile – that he got it when he was seventeen years old, falling down drunk on a wooden bench.

Of course. That was it. His beard hid the scar. How could I have failed to notice such a thing?

I'm afraid I wasn't looking forward to the evening's concert at all. I can't seem to get a grip on music. I like Mozart's Dissonance and Bach's Double Concerto, and there was a piece of Bruckner's that had hunting horns in it (I can't remember its name), but the thought of sitting still for hours in a hot theatre – Oh dear, I'd almost prefer a screenful of error margins.

Nikolas left early for the Queen Elizabeth Hall; Harry, Mickie and I followed in a taxi. As we squeezed through to our seats, the orchestra was making the queer, anarchic sounds that orchestras make when they warm up. I do get a kick out of that: single, pure note over trill over drumbeat, aimless yet haunting, wholly unmemorable in detail yet wholly unforgettable in feel. And what intimacy there is in the prospect of sharing a spectacle in the dark. The audience hummed and buzzed, delightedly self-conscious despite the heat, preening itself now that the moment was almost upon it. I glanced at the programme: Bach's Orchestral Suite in D. Borodin's Symphony No. 2. The Britten Piano Concerto. I'd never heard of any of them.

Mickie leaned over and whispered into my ear, 'See that door?' She gave a sudden giggle that I was certain was not at all like her.

'Which door?' I said.

'There. Just beside the stage.'

'Is that where Nikolas comes in?'

'No. No. After he comes in – right after. That's when to watch.'

If she hadn't nudged me, I'd have missed it. The orchestra fell silent (gust of stillness and last cough). Nikolas entered from the wings.

'See? See?' Mickie hissed.

I glanced at the door. A shadow slithered through it, very thin, all in black with a peaked black hat, and moving fast.

'Is that somebody you know?' I whispered.

'I sure as hell do.'

'Who?'

'Priscilla,' she said.

'Who's Priscilla?'

'Priscilla Carmarth.'

'The name doesn't mean a thing to me. Should it?'

'Welsh timber.'

'I still don't – '

'Ask Harry.'

'Mickie?'

'Hush.'

'Where's the pianist?'

'After the interval.'

Nikolas raised his arms. The opening piece began – the Bach, I guess – and I fell at once into a drowsy, semi-stuporous state. It was very, very hot.

During the interval there was excited talk of the great Sviatoslav Richter over Perrier water in the bar. Mickie told me that he hated people to see his face when he played; and sure enough, after the interval, they dimmed the stage lights as well as the house lights. A behind-the-scenes kerfuffle resulted in a stagehand with an Anglepoise lamp for the piano. After Nikolas came on, there was a tense wait in the semi-dark. Then suddenly this ox of a guy scuttled out, one shoulder up as though to protect himself against the roar of welcome that greeted him.

I'd forgotten how pianists bounce about when they play. Richter bounced so vigorously and sweated so heavily that his iron-rimmed spectacles slipped down his nose and threatened to fall off. Each time a page needed turning, the young page-turner's hand shot out – deft flick of the wrist – and shoved the glasses back into place. It seemed a long, long time and many flicks of that wrist before the audience rose and shouted for encores.

'Enjoyed it, did you?' Mickie said, turning to me with that wry smile of hers. The pace and determination of Richter's exit – bless him – indicated that he'd be half way home by the time the clapping stopped.

'I thought – ' I began, but there wasn't a single thought in my head, so I said, 'Mickie, how come he has a page-turner? Don't people like him memorize for concerts?'

'People like him do what they damn please.'

'Do we go backstage now?'

'Backstage? Us? Why?'

'Don't we want to congratulate Nikolas?'

'I'm not allowed backstage.'

'Not allowed? You can't mean that, can you?'

'Backstage is *her* domain. There should be a taxi for us at the side entrance. Come on, I'll show you the way.'

Back in Swiss Cottage, Mickie made coffee, but we were all tired; talk of Richter, the audience, the acoustics was running thin when Nikolas himself arrived.

'Don't say a word,' he said, taking off his black tails and throwing them down on the floor. He rolled up the sleeves of his ruffled shirt. 'I need a drink. I need several drinks. Drink, Eve? Harry? You've had coffee? Coffee's bad for your liver at this time of night. Whisky's what you need. Soda? You want soda? You don't mean it. Surely not. Nobody wants soda. It

17

ruins the taste. Go get some mineral water, Mickie.' He poured us huge slugs of a malt whisky.

'How do you think it went?' Harry asked him.

'Give me a break, Harry,' he said. 'Don't you think I've had enough for one day? Besides, we went all through that over lunch.'

'No we didn't.'

'Why don't you go shave off that beard?'

Harry gave a short laugh. 'OK, OK. I'll shut up.'

Perhaps all performers react this way. How would I know? I do like whisky, though; and Nikolas's whisky, like the wine at lunch, was the best I'd ever tasted. We drank far more of it than we should have. And while Harry ranted on about Health Service cuts and single mothers, I kept my attention glued to Mickie and talk of her children. Nikolas's gaze, uncomfortable before, was openly embarrassing now.

I wasn't surprised to awaken queasy, parboiled and before dawn the next morning. Harry was awake already – and in the same condition. At least the heat had broken; outside air, the cooler the better, seemed the only hope for either of us. We crept downstairs through the quiet house, shut the front door behind us and followed one street after another until the dark began to lift and the morning star appeared.

Harry stopped short.

'It's beautiful, isn't it?' I said.

'What?'

'The morning star.' He looked at me blankly. 'In the sky. That bright spot. Look up, there's a good boy. Right in front of you. It's Lucifer, Harry, the fallen angel. He shines in the morning.'

'Reviews,' he said.

'Reviews?'

'Reviews. Reviews,' he repeated.

'You mean for Nikolas? Does everybody get reviewed?'

18

'Not everybody gets Richter as a soloist.'

A newsagent sold us all the papers that might cover the concert. A coffee shop near-by was just opening; we sat at a table with cappuccino and opened the *Daily Telegraph*, top of our pile.

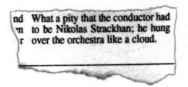

ran the headline on the arts page. Harry and I glanced at each other: such a big headline, such a big picture of the pianist.

The critic could hardly contain himself: Richter's huge effects, his colour, depth, responsibility to the music – oh, and more: the freedom of his expression, his unparalleled integrity. Then came the last sentence of the review:

> nd What a pity that the conductor had
> 'n to be Nikolas Strackhan; he hung
> r   over the orchestra like a cloud.

Harry let out a whoop of glee, much as he had when he'd first seen the announcement of the concert in *The Times*. I stared at him, amazed, astonished. Harry doesn't say bad things about people. He doesn't think bad things about people. He just doesn't.

'Quick, hand me one of the other papers,' he said. 'Come on, come on. Hand me *The Times*. Hey, don't look at me like that. You can't feel altogether friendly about Nikolas yourself. Not with the way he drools over you.'

I shrugged helplessly.

'I don't think – I'm sorry about that, Eve. It's not personal. I'm sure it's not. The day he had his appendix out – as soon as he regained consciousness – he ripped all his stitches grabbing for a nurse.'

The Times review wasn't as big as the *Telegraph*'s, but it too carried a picture of Richter and praise for his performance, although not such wild praise in this case: his playing had 'flattened out in recent years'. And Nikolas? Nothing. Not a word. He might as well not have existed. The *Guardian* dismissed him in a scornful half-sentence for his Bach and Borodin. The *Mirror* didn't cover the concert. The *Financial Times* made a crack about a fat boy – 'a fat boy'; how nasty can you get? – and said Nikolas shouldn't give up his day job.

'Thank goodness I'm not doing his PR,' Harry said then, his glee giving way to pity (carnage on this scale is awesome). There must have been an element of professional judgement in what he said too. He's good at his job. He'd never get himself tied up with a loser.

'It was really that terrible?'

'I just – the sound was kind of aimless, I guess. Plainly the orchestra wasn't happy with him. The programme didn't make much sense either. I suppose Richter chose the Britten. Why did he have to pick the concerto, though? It's so boring. The Yamaha doesn't help.'

'I don't know what that means.'

'Richter won't play on a Steinway any more, and a Yamaha – Who can get feeling out of a thing like that? I know Nikolas is mad about Bach, but – ' Harry broke off. 'At least he's not the suicidal type.'

We finished our coffee in silence, stuffed the newspapers in the café's dustbin and set out walking again, up one street, down another.

'It's after eight,' Harry said. 'We're going to have to go back sometime.'

'Keats lived around here.'

'Did he?'

'We could say we've been out to look for his house. I like Keats. Bored whores and fake orgasms in such pretty, sweet – '

'Eve!'

'What?'

'You say these things just to shock, don't you?'

'Harry, you are an idiot.'

'Well, where is it?'

'Where's what?'

'The house.'

'I don't know. I haven't any idea. We don't have to find it. We only have to look.'

It was nine by the time we got back to the Strakhan house. Mickie was making coffee in the large kitchen. There was a bowl of fruit on the table and a loaf of freshly baked bread – but no Nikolas. Harry and I babbled on to Mickie, half convincing ourselves that our fruitless search for Keats had been in earnest.

Then Harry took courage and said, 'Is Nikolas still asleep?'

'He must be exhausted,' I said.

Mickie shook her head. 'He's never tired. He's been on the telephone since seven.'

'Who can he talk to at that hour?' I asked.

Mickie shrugged. Despite years in America and schooling in England, she is very Gallic. 'The reviews are bad' – her tone was so matter of fact that you'd have thought she was quoting stock prices or train times – 'and Nikolas wants to get a recording company signed up before anybody in the trade figures out just how bad they really are.'

CHAPTER 2

Harry and I had to be on the eleven o'clock out of Victoria that morning; we'd ordered a taxi for a quarter past ten. This was to be his big day – the day of his meeting with Brighton's Tourist Board – the day he presented Aldrich & Rheinholt's plans for the summer season that would start some twenty months from now. When Nikolas didn't appear, Mickie took us up to his study to say goodbye. He was on the telephone, talking animatedly, the morning papers spread out around him; he turned, waved to us, cupped his hand over the mouthpiece and held up the receiver.

'I think I've got one,' he said delightedly. We could hear a man's voice talking on.

'A recording company?' Harry said.

Nikolas nodded. 'Stupid fucker never reads anything but *The Times*, and plainly he doesn't read that very carefully. I'll bet you –' He turned back abruptly. 'Yeah, yeah,' he said into the receiver. 'I thought you'd appreciate a word. The telephone hasn't let up since seven. Bids are coming in from as far away as Tokyo. I'm thrilled – absolutely speechless.'

In moments just before a storm, the light changes. All the

angles, all the shadows, all the emphases look different. Speechless? I was the one who was speechless. I was mute. Stunned. I don't even remember the goodbyes. Not until the taxi drew into Victoria did I manage to cough and say, tentative, half-fascinated, half-repelled. 'I guess I can see why you reacted the way you did this morning – a little bit anyhow.'

Harry winced (he had his own troubles). 'Oh, how I wish I wasn't so awfully hung over. Oh, how I wish I hadn't drunk – '

'How can he do that?'

'Who? Aha, I get it. You caught a glimpse of the real Nikolas, didn't you?'

'Just reading those reviews made me feel sick, and he had them lying open as though they were some kind of triumph.'

'Nikolas is, er, different.'

'I never met anybody like that. I don't believe there *are* people like that – not in real life. You've made him up, haven't you? Or have I?'

'My father calls him Junior.'

I laughed. 'He can't.'

'You ought to hear my father's voice: "Junior, that crook." He says it like it's all one word. Junior-that-crook.'

'Is he a crook too? on top of everything else?'

'I don't think anybody would say he played by the rules.'

Something in Harry's voice caught my attention. 'Why do you look so guilty? What kind of crookedness? Oh, dear, what would Uncle Phineas say? Which side of your family is he on? your father's? your mother's?'

The taxi pulled to a stop just then; Harry paid and collected the bag. 'He's not really my uncle. More like a cousin once removed, I guess. Or maybe I mean a second cousin.'

'If he'd never conducted an orchestra before, how'd he get hold of this one? And who is this Priscilla?'

'Priscilla is Priscilla Carmarth.' Harry turned and smiled at me.

'He's right about the beard, you know.'

'Yeah.'

'It really ought to come off before this afternoon, before you –'

'Yeah.'

'The name Priscilla Carmarth doesn't mean a thing to me, Harry.'

But talk of his beard – and the afternoon to come – had unsettled him. Or at least that's what I thought had unsettled him. 'You ought to read the newspapers,' he said, going a little schoolmarmish on me.

'I hate reading newspapers. Tell me. What's her connection to Nikolas?'

'She's his patron. It's no big deal.' His brow did its knitting and unknitting; some sort of an internal struggle was going on, but I had no idea what. 'She's one of the hundred richest people in the world,' he said then.

'One of the hundred richest – Really? Is this true? Why haven't you told me? What do you mean, it isn't a big deal? *Patron* sounds like something out of a book. Borgias and people like that.'

His eyes slid away. 'Suppose my hands shake,' he said. 'Look at them. They're shaking already. If I try to shave, I'll cut myself. There'll be this raw gash across my – '

'No, there won't. You're going to be fine.'

Harry had been analysing Brighton's tourist industry for nearly six months. Paper littered the flat: drafts of proposals, scribbled-on notepads – he was never without a notepad – and reports from and about hotels, Bed and Breakfasts, the piers, the Lanes, the Pavilion (complicated because of the renovations going on then), various council departments: Marketing & Tourism, Parks & Open Spaces, Public Conveniences. For weeks, he'd worked late into the night, slept hardly at all, glazed over in the middle of conversations.

'Suppose the podium doesn't cover my legs. Suppose the microphone makes that awful noise microphones make, wheee-wheee – What am I supposed to do? Where's it going to be, anyhow? In front of my face? Pinned to my jacket? Suppose – '

'You'll be brilliant. You know you will. And if you don't know that, I do. Tell me about Nikolas instead. It'll take your mind off it.'

He gave me an unhappy glance, strode on a few paces in silence, then said, 'I don't mean to be – Hey, look, it's just that I can't really tell you anything interesting. I don't even know how much of what I know is true and how much is made up. Everybody in the family vies to tell the tallest tale about Junior-that-crook. It's sort of a family game. Except for my father. My father hates him. I wouldn't know where to start.'

'Can't we start at the beginning? What is the beginning anyhow?'

'The very beginning?' His face brightened. 'I guess I can tell you about that.'

'So?'

'Well, in the beginning was the spiderwort.'

CHAPTER 3

The spiderwort gets its name because it cures the bites of all venomous beasts and because, as Gerard says, 'the leaves stand upon the ground with long legs and the knees bowing up like the spider when he creepeth.' The flower is small, blue or purple – it comes in various shades – an airy, eerie thing in clusters that top an erect, succulent stem. Oh, erect, succulent stem: this is where Nikolas's story begins.

John Tradescant the Younger, gardener to Charles I, found a species of spiderwort in the colony of Virginia in far-away America; he brought it back to England in the middle of the seventeenth century. It grew and prospered. A Georgian on a grand tour, a rich Russian Georgian – this is an international story – saw the flower at Kew a century later and took it home with the idea of presenting it as a gift to Catherine the Great. An eminent English botanist told the Georgian that spiderworts are temperamental. In the front garden of the flat Harry and I had in Brighton, they grew easily; we had some in blue-white and some in rich blue-purple. But I've read that the buds tend to rot before they bloom; sometimes the stems wilt. There are special bugs and special diseases. So when the Georgian delivered his gift to his sovereign in St Petersburg, he delivered one of his own specially trained gardeners along with it.

Everybody knows that Georgia produces the most beautiful men in Russia, and Russia assuredly produces the most beautiful men in the world. The gardener was only a boy – fourteen years old – but he had a grace to him as airy and eerie as the flowers he tended; he was almost translucent with underfeeding. Harry's story has it that Catherine the Great saw this boy from the window of her library, where she was studying Diophantine equations. He was on his knees digging in the soil. It was summer. The day was hot. When he got to his feet, he arched his back a little to stretch out the tension under the cloth of his tunic. The year was 1789 and Catherine the Great was sixty-one, a bejewelled hag of a woman – verminous too, if descriptions of aristocratic Russians of the time are to be believed. Vermin itch most in the heat – they feed so hungrily then – and what a lover of men Catherine was even in the winter.

She said to a handmaiden, 'Go to that young man and tell him that if he wishes to sleep, he may come to me.'

The handmaiden did as she was told and returned, trembling, with the message that the boy had declined.

I imagine that Catherine's interest up to this point had been perfunctory; she liked an afternoon's sport with a pretty lad from the guard or the gardens when she felt dull. Injured pride? Never. Catherine was one of the greatest intellects of her time as well as one of its greatest lovers, and a refusal was as unlikely as a shift in the course of the planets. Here was a puzzle – a dash of salt with her afternoon's beef. She commanded that the boy be fetched, whether he liked the idea or not.

She said to him, 'I ask you to come to me. How dare you decline?'

'I wish only to serve Your Highness,' the boy said. As you can see, he was an unusual boy: a serf with the temerity to speak to a queen – and to speak to her with a grace as natural to him as the grace of his body. Furthermore, up close, despite his poor diet, the boy was dazzling; and in his hands he carried a bunch of spiderworts, each atop its erect, succulent stem.

'Then why do you not come?'

The boy frowned. 'I am not sleepy.'

The puzzlement on his face was so deep and the courage he showed so impressive that she roared with laughter. At her glittering dinner table that evening she regaled her company with the story and roared again.

So it was that a peasant boy and his spiderworts tended to the needs of a monarch, and Harry says he tended her every bit as gently as he tended the flowers. For these favours, which went on every afternoon for a month, she made him a Count and gave him a huge tract of land in the Crimea, a house in St Petersburg and the name Strakhan, which she made up for him on that very first meeting because he was so singular that he deserved a name no one had ever heard before. She ordered tutors to teach him to read, to dance and to speak French and German as became his new station in life.

It was an odd beginning for a man of principle, and there is no doubt that the first Count Strakhan was just such a one; as soon as he saw his Crimean land – he was fifteen – he freed the serfs on it. This high moral tone does not instantly bring Nikolas to mind; but in moral matters the Strakhan men yawed like fishing boats in a storm, as male generations so often do, the son forever seeking out an alien quarter of ocean for no other reason than to irritate his father. The first Count Strakhan's high-minded democracy provoked only cynicism and loucheness in his son, whose cynicism and loucheness provoked self-righteousness in the next in line – and so on through the generations.

By the time we get to Nikolas's grandfather, the cycle had produced a revolutionary – Marx, Kropotkin, the proletariat, a better world – who renounced his title and had to leave the country for an exile's life in the south of France. He called his boy Nikolas – I'll call him Nikolas Senior since he's the one who fathered Junior-that-crook – and tutored him so well that he ended up with a perfect command of German, English, French and the most progressive ideas of the day. Nikolas Senior had a smidgen of Russian too – only a smidgen – and a little history; he was fond of the ballet. He was a fascist.

It's with Nikolas Senior, my Nikolas's father, when he was on an extended visit to Paris some ten years before the Second World War broke out, that the upper-crust Middle Western blood of Harry's family enters the Strakhan line. Elizabeth Merchant Milligan was Harry's great-aunt; the first time she saw Nikolas Senior she was having coffee in the Café Régence with her sister Beatrice.

Nikolas Senior sat at a table close to theirs with a woman who had long black hair, loose and waved like a washboard; it trailed on the floor behind her chair, and she combed it in languid, desultory strokes as they talked. They shifted languages over *café filtre* and hard boiled eggs. His English was flawless if brittle-edged, more attractive, though, than the twitter an American ear detects in British plum. Hers laboured hard under Russian gutturals that belonged in a farce. Elizabeth didn't speak enough French to judge them. Fascinating, she thought, studying him in that clear-sighted way she had, not lowering her gaze.

He wore a suit as beautifully cut as any she'd seen before – she was something of a judge in these matters – and a swathe of deep blue silk around his neck. He took out a cigarette, held it in the Russian manner – palm up, cigarette balanced out on the fingers – and looked around idly for a match in the way such people do, assuming that whatever they wish will appear simply because they wish it.

A man from the table next to his – small, dark, goatee beard

– leaped up, bowed, ducking and bobbing, and said, 'You need a match, Monsieur le Comte?'

You see? What the father spits upon, the son reveres and snatches back, even though he has no right to it. Nikolas Senior turned his elegant head. His face hinted at the Tartar – high cheekbones, almond eyes, ferocity barely held in check – as the faces of so many Georgians do. He studied the man a moment, then gave the faintest of nods.

The man was beside himself with joy. 'Let me help, sir. Let me just – Here we are!' He struck a match and held it out, hand trembling (excitement probably, eagerness certainly).

Nikolas Senior studied the flame, the hands, then the man. 'Put the matches on the table,' he said.

The little man bowed, ducking and bobbing as before, shaking out the flame. 'Of course. Of course. Do forgive me. I am so foolish, all in a whirl. It is such a great honour to be in the presence of – I wish only to serve. I assure you of that. I am – What is it? Did you say something?' Nikolas Senior had said nothing. The disdain in his carriage turned to imperial ice. 'I am absurd and tedious,' the little man went on. 'Do forgive me, I am not worthy. I wish – ' With a spasmodic jerk, he reached out and laid the matches on the table. Then he backed away, ducking and bobbing still. Only then did Nikolas Senior pick up the matches and light his cigarette.

Elizabeth was dazzled. She was an impetuous woman, rash as brilliant people so often are; her sister Beatrice used to tell her that she had no sense when it came to danger: afraid when she needn't be, courageous when she shouldn't be.

'Pardon me, sir,' Elizabeth said.

'Elizabeth!' Beatrice reached out and put her hand over her sister's mouth, the way she used to when they were little girls together in Illinois.

Nikolas Senior turned his head much as he'd turned it to view the little man. 'I, Mademoiselle?' he said.

'May I ask you a question?'

When he focused on her, there was a flicker of something else at the corners of his mouth, which curled. A well-tended American voice is warm, intimate, full of promises; he'd never heard one so pleasing. Besides, Elizabeth was a celebrated beauty in her own right – and plainly a rich one.

'I am at your disposal, Mademoiselle.'

'Why didn't you take the light from his hand?' she said.

Nikolas Senior looked down at her a moment, then said, 'I take nothing from the hand of a Jew.'

What a delicious pleasure shock is, especially in the uneasy suspense of an uneasy time – financial collapse on one side of the Atlantic, Nazism rising on the other – especially for people like Elizabeth, fresh from Midwestern aristocracy, where the sanctimony of republican ideals lived cheek by jowl with the exclusion of Jews from the country club. Her sister's horror only added to her delight; she insisted that they go together to the Café Régence for coffee the next day – and the next. Nikolas Senior was there both times; and Elizabeth could tell that he was aware of her, although no more words were spoken, and he was always accompanied by the woman with the long, loose hair.

Music entered the Strakhan line along with its American blood. Beatrice Merchant played the violin and adored it, but she could never rid herself of the faulty grip on the bow she'd acquired as a little girl. Elizabeth Merchant was luckier, better taught; she had serious ambitions – concert pianist no less – and when she was old enough her father arranged an audition for her at the Juilliard School of Music in New York City.

But Elizabeth never got as far as the school, much less the audition. Why? Let he who is without fear amongst you cast the first stone. Auditions are awesome things. There sit the black-capped judges. There sit the prisoners in the dock, called up to plead their cases one by one. Judgement is immediate, sentence carried out at once. Down swings the guillotine again and again, razor-sharp and bloodied. Whop! A head in the basket. Whop! Another head.

Then the polite smiles turn toward you. 'Next?' they say.

Elizabeth knew about this. She'd heard all kinds of stories; on the train ride east her muddled sense of danger flew off at a tangent. She didn't know what was happening to her. Why did she tremble at the Indiana border? Why nausea throughout Ohio? Why this retching on the approach to Pennsylvania Station? By the time she reached the taxi rank on Thirty-fourth Street her terror was so abject that she could barely walk. She stumbled, fell, broke her wrist – and so saved herself from the ordeal.

Back home at the University of Illinois in Carbondale she mourned by day and wept by night. She hated herself for failing and accused herself of mediocrity. She couldn't bear to touch a piano any more. She couldn't even look at one. This romantic gloom attracted many young men; one of them was Courtney Milligan, son of the biggest sausage manufacturer in Chicago. Courtney had a red Stutz Bearcat; he drove her out to the cornfields one night. In the dark, on the damp ground – she couldn't think how it began – he ended up pumping her as energetically as his father's factory pumped sausage into sausage skins.

He pumped on through engagement and wedding day, through honeymoon and early married life. No babies came of it. Everybody blamed Elizabeth. Courtney had no doubt that she was at fault – God knows, he'd done his duty and more – and she felt guilty. By the time she'd been married ten years, she slept in a separate bedroom and resented everything he did and everything he stood for. She began playing again for no other reason than to spite him.

Almost at once, though, her old exuberance returned. She began to glow again, to laugh, to sparkle as she'd sparkled before her ill-fated trip to New York. Courtney had never known her like this. He frowned at the piano. He tut-tutted. Then suddenly – Well, sure, he'd fancied misery at twenty-one. Who doesn't? Thirty-one is different and he fell in love with her all over again. Everything about her inflamed him, even her resistance. One afternoon, ripping open his flies with one hand – grappling beneath her skirt with the other as she sat on the piano stool – he saw more than resistance in her face. He saw contempt. He reeled back from her and ran, purple lollipop sticking out flip-flap and bobble, to fetch an axe.

He hacked her piano into firewood.

So it was that music played a decisive role not only in Elizabeth's marriage but also in the extraordinarily advantageous negotiations that ended it. Her father, who was an eminent Illinois lawyer, secured for her the highest divorce settlement of the day; she was worth two million dollars in triple A Swiss franc bonds. He sent her to Paris with her sister, where she could catch up on the training she'd missed all those years ago in New York. This time she applied to the Paris Conservatoire. This time she went through with the audition.

'Was she really talented?' I said to Harry. We were on the train, half-way back to Brighton. 'Talent's such an odd thing. It needs a spur doesn't it? What do you think? Was she for real?'

'There were hundreds of applicants, and only a couple of places for foreign students,' he said. 'She was one of the few who got through.'

'But was it talent? Or was it just because she was rich and pretty? Where'd Nikolas get that – what is it? I don't know what to call it – is it a manipulative streak? or just a thick skin? You've got a good streak of it yourself, haven't you?'

'You can't mean that.' Harry looked hurt, a little alarmed too.

'Of course not, Harry. You're a fine, upstanding citizen and a champion of the downtrodden.'

'Just because you don't have opinions about anything.'

'I know, I know,' I said, relenting. 'I'm only teasing.'

Harry stared out the window a moment. 'Nikolas says she had talent. He should know. Besides, where'd he get his own talent from if not from her? He couldn't have got it from the Strakhans.'

'If those reviews are anything to go by, he didn't get quite enough from anybody.'

Elizabeth certainly worked hard. She practised all day and went to concerts every night. The only thing she did for fun was play for ballet classes in the Studios Wacker, which doesn't sound like much fun to me. And Harry insists that if she hadn't taken on this one frivolous pleasure, she could have become a professional pianist – on one level or another.

The ground floor of the Studios Wacker sold pianos. Elizabeth had heard the tinkle of accompanists while she was buying a grand for her Paris flat, and the sound so charmed her that she went around to take a closer look. At the back door of the shop a circular staircase climbed past a café, where theatrical queens of the old school in crushed velvet and multi-coloured turbans lisped at each other over cups of coffee. She caught her breath, felt wonderfully daring, dashed up another twist of the stairs to a pair of huge rooms with mirrored walls. In each of these a pianist played, one for a ballerina with her legs wrapped around a half-naked faun, another for Josephine Baker in a sequinned tuxedo, feathers in her hair (she was opening that night at Le Casino de Paris on the rue de Clichy). Two twists further, the stairs now rickety and narrow, revealed an ancient hag – rouged, mascara'd, fat, gypsy-shawled – shouting insults in Russian at a ballet class of little girls. There was a piano here but no pianist.

'*Qu'est ce que vous voulez?*' the hag screamed, swinging around to face Elizabeth.

34

Elizabeth went over to the piano and sat down.

'*Vous jouez?*' demanded the hag. Elizabeth nodded. The old woman hobbled over to the piano and pounded out a rhythm on its cover: '*Adeen, dva, tree, chiteery. Vous jouez ça?*'

Elizabeth nodded again and began to play. Thereafter she played at the Studios Wacker whenever she had a free hour, even though the hag never paid her a single centime.

Coming down these same stairs six weeks after her sister Beatrice left for home – it was November, unseasonably cold – Elizabeth ran into the woman who'd sat with Nikolas Senior in the Café Régence. The woman stopped short and stared into Elizabeth's eyes. Elizabeth stared back and thought of starving dogs on an Arctic ice floe.

'I do not murder husband,' the woman said at last.

'Well, that's got to be good news,' said Elizabeth, amused, intrigued.

'In prison, only cabbage soup. Bad for bowels. Terrible. I eat nothing. Nothing.'

'You work in this place?'

The kohl around the woman's eyes was as thick as the white pancake that cracked at the corners of her mouth; black hair spread out over her shoulders and hung in a veil to well below her knees. She spat out the words: 'I titch Spanish dancing.'

'It can't pay you much,' Elizabeth said. She took out her purse. 'Will you take something from me?'

'I am Carmen Santandela.'

'But you're Russian, right?' Carmen shrugged. 'How about ten francs? Will that do you any good?' Carmen shrugged. Elizabeth smiled delightedly. 'Here,' she said. 'Here's two hundred. Go find yourself something to eat.'

Carmen held the notes up to the light. She squinted at them, snapped them between expert fingers, then pushed them into the folds of her flowing scarves. 'You come.'

'Me?'

'We eat together.'

'I don't want anything.'

The starving dog's eyes narrowed. 'You spit on me.'

'No, no,' Elizabeth laughed. 'How'd you get that idea? I'm just – '

'First spit, then laugh. This is how to treat Carmen Santandela?'

'Look' – Elizabeth forced her face into an expression of earnest concern – 'all I had in mind was giving you a good meal. I don't want to offend anybody.'

'Then why you not eat?'

They went to the Café Régence. Of course they did. Carmen called over the waiter, whose name was Prosper; she ordered the *menu gastronomique* for two.

'I can't eat that much,' Elizabeth protested.

'You eat.' Carmen said.

'But I – '

'You are guest. You eat.'

Elizabeth did as she was told. She ate things she'd never eaten before: frogs' legs, quail, brains in black butter. She drank a fine white from the Loire. She drank a burgundy.

'Eat! Eat!' Carmen said whenever she flagged.

'Tell me about this friend of yours, the Count,' Elizabeth said when they reached – somewhat dizzily – the relative calm of coffee.

'In Georgia, you have two sheep, you are Prince.' Carmen set down her coffee cup and stared into Elizabeth's eyes again, and again – despite all the food – Elizabeth thought of starving dogs. 'You play for Agrafena Ignatyevna at Studios Wacker? Yes? She is his lover. She give him money. You want?'

'Whose lover? Count Strakhan's or his father's? You can't mean Count Strakhan. She's way too old for him.'

'I see your face. I look you how you are. I watch. You not see, but I watch. Once: very beautiful, Ignatyevna. Now: very old.

You can have if you want. You want?'

Elizabeth realized suddenly that they were both very drunk. 'Are you offering this guy to me?' she said, incredulous, delighted all over again. 'As if he's a glass of cognac?'

Carmen shrugged much as she had on the stairs. 'Why not?'

'He just might have a thought or two of his own on the subject.'

'Count Strakhan? He have no thought.' Carmen sipped her coffee. 'Cognac you say? Yes. Now we have cognac. You give me *menu gastronomique* with cognac: I give you Count Strakhan. I do this for you. Is fair exchange.'

The idea was so outrageous and the brandy so delicious that Elizabeth shook hands on the joke without another thought. As her sister said, she had no sense when it came to danger. Carmen called Prosper over and set up a *tête-à-tête* for lunch the next day.

Later that evening, when Elizabeth had sobered up, it was too late. Only Prosper knew how to reach Carmen Santandela or the Count, and Prosper worked only the lunchtime shift. It froze that night. Paris isn't often as cold as this in late autumn.

Elizabeth went to the café through a downpour of sleet. Nikolas Senior rose from his chair to greet her. 'Mademoiselle,' he said. He took her hand, bent over it, straightened. 'You are well?' The Tartar cheekbones were as elegant as she'd remembered.

'Hang up my coat, will you?' she said, taking it off her shoulders, shaking the wet from it and handing it to him. 'It's soaking.'

Annoyance flickered across his brow. 'We will call the waiter to deal with this matter.'

'Too big a job for you, is it?' Elizabeth said.

There was a slight pause. 'You Americans are very special. You say such extraordinary things.'

'Yeah? Like what?'

37

He smiled then, and his face changed. Elizabeth would never have expected something both sweet and bawdy in the smile of such a man; she was so intrigued she couldn't quite look away. And why hadn't she noticed the dissonance in his voice? It was ebony-keyed, vibrant.

'You puncture my vanity with such offhand ease,' he said, bowing again, this time with an element of self-mockery. 'Will you have champagne? You are beautiful, American, as well as extraordinary. I think you are the most beautiful woman in Paris. Will you drink champagne with me?'

Prosper brought glasses and a bucket of ice. He hung up Elizabeth's coat. Nikolas Senior toasted her with an ebullience as surprising as his smile; he toasted her beauty and the cornfields of Illinois that had made her so.

'I play for Madame Ignatyevna,' she said, uneasy with so rich a flow of compliments and casting about for something to deflect it. 'Did Carmen tell you? She says you've been friends for ages.'

To Elizabeth's amazement his cheeks flushed and then went pale. 'What a woman you are. I hardly know how to answer you. First you strike down my public defences and then, at once, my private moral worth. You have a very penetrating glance. You are perhaps not aware that such acuity is frightening to people who do not have it themselves.'

'So now I frighten you, huh?'

'Ah, you Americans. I begin to wonder if I will survive this lunch at all. Carmen tells me you are a fine musician. While I have no talent myself, I am a great judge of it, and I can see that she has told me the truth. Nobody without such a gift could know so soon that I am bad and not good.'

He gazed at Elizabeth with such intensity that she touched the corners of her mouth to check for errant dribbles of champagne. Why did these Russians stare so? Why were they so easily affronted? Elizabeth already had the feeling that she was losing hold somewhere – and she'd been with this man just a few minutes.

Keeping his gaze on her, he lowered his voice almost to a whisper (she had to lean close to hear):

> 'Toward good and evil shamefully impassive,
> In mid-career we fade without a fight . . .'

The only man who had ever recited to her was her beloved father. 'Do you know any more?' She cupped her chin in her hands. 'Say some more.'

Nikolas Senior smiled and spoke even lower (she had to lean even closer):

> '. . .With every autumn that comes I bloom again;
> Desire seethes up – '

He stopped short. 'This perhaps is a little intimate,' he said. He picked up the menu and eyed her mischievously over the top of it. 'I think perhaps we have had enough of poetry. I must be careful not to provoke another attack on my affectations. Shall we eat snails instead? I am very fond of snails. Cold weather needs butter and garlic more than it needs verse.' Then without any transition: 'Agrafena Ignatyevna was the greatest ballerina of her time.'

He sighed, frowned, signalled to Prosper, ordered the snails. 'When I was fourteen,' he went on, 'my father sent me to spend the winter with my grandmother in St Petersburg. She took me to the ballet, to the Maryinski, and the moment Agrafena Ignatyevna stepped on stage, my soul was no longer my own. For weeks I haunted the theatre. I ached for a picture of her, a scarf, anything that had been hers once and could be mine. On the night she danced *Raymonda* I was allowed to harness myself to her troika.

'After the performance, three of us drew it over frozen streets to her house. It was a canary yellow troika, ormolu and gold — very, very beautiful.' His expression changed yet again. Elizabeth (more than half transfixed by this time) could almost feel the skid and crackle of Russian ice beneath her own feet. 'You see how abject I am? How guilt-ridden? All that fourteen-year-old boy asked was a token but — God forgive me for my sins — he had more than a token in exchange for his soul that night.'

He reached out, took Elizabeth's hand in his, turned it palm down, studied it, turned it palm up. Head bowed over it, he hummed a few bars of music.

'*Raymonda*,' she said.

'*Raymonda*,' he said.

Now I ask you, *this* to a woman fresh from Chicago sausage machines?

What people these were, these Russian exiles in Paris: princes who drove taxis, duchesses who roamed the Left Bank hawking fried veal cutlets from wicker baskets — and counts who lived off ancient ballet dancers. There was a pine-tree scent to them, a smell of winter ferocity brought inside, hung with tinsel and baubles, tamed for this night only. Is it any wonder that by the time lunch was over Elizabeth had forgotten music, piano, ambition, past, future? everything but this day and this man?

Is it any wonder that she married him on Christmas morning?

She was pregnant at once — which tells you something about Courtney's fecundity, if not his sausage machine. They moved to Geneva where Russian expatriots had more money than in Paris, where his title made him welcome, however tenuous its provenance, where his Nazism was more popular than anybody cared to admit — and where her triple A bonds were safe from his politics as well as the rest of the world's. Soirées, nocturnes and delicate interludes in the Jardin des Plantes, talk of racial purity and flower arranging, dinner parties with lace tablecloths, glittering chandeliers and titled ladies encrusted with jewels.

Countess Elizabeth Strakhan's first child was a girl, born on the day the Nazis secured a majority in the Reichstag. Brown shirts? Hitler? What did she know of such people? What difference could they make to the sight of Nikolas Senior's thighs when he woke from sleep? Her second child, born scarcely a year later, was also a girl. Nikolas Senior toasted the birth and Hitler's chancellorship with the same glass of Veuve Clicquot. Nikolas Junior was Elizabeth's third child in under two years. This time the pregnancy was not easy. The delivery went awry; she almost died, and her health was never the same afterwards.

Nikolas Senior was not at her side either. He'd passed out in a whore's bed in far-away Berlin, filled with triumph and schnapps because the year was 1934, and Hitler was at last the head of state.

For five years after this Elizabeth lay on a chaise longue in the music room, eating poached white fish while Nikolas Senior and his guests in the dining room talked animatedly of the German war machine, of Pushkin, of the price of Fabergé eggs. She wasn't unhappy – not exactly. But there were so many things she didn't understand. Why didn't she ache with love any more? Why didn't she weep because she couldn't play the harpsichord that her ever-constant father had given her in celebration of her marriage to the ever-changing Nikolas Senior? The keyboard was closed and locked. She hadn't touched it since Nikolas Junior was born.

She'd just assumed that Nikolas Senior and the harpsichord were alike. She'd assumed his Tartar cheekbones, heated *élan* and prickly dignity were like its inlaid wood – such a beautiful instrument – finely tooled, elegantly wrought. She'd assumed his exterior only hinted at the promise that lay beneath it. And yet – She couldn't put her finger on it, but something was

41

missing. Late in August 1939, listening to shouts of delight from the dining room (the Russians and the Nazis had at last joined hands) she thought of Carmen Santandela, who'd swapped Nikolas Senior for a *menu gastronomique* with cognac.

Elizabeth felt an abrupt surge of resentment – and saw the truth. The Café Régence had had a very good chef in those days. *Menu gastronomique*? Count Strakhan wasn't worth a *menu gastronomique* – with or without cognac. He wasn't like the harpsichord. Of course he wasn't. There were no strings, no quills, no locked-away keyboard. There was no evil (despite his politics), no culture (despite poetry and the ballet), no ferocity (despite his Russian turbulence), no human warmth (despite the Strakhan spiderwort).

Just an empty shell.

This realization so jolted her that her illness receded a little; in its wake, it left a yearning for long, straight rows of corn and hot nights that extend well into September. She booked passage; she packed suitcases. She left Nikolas Senior in charge of her daughters and set out for Illinois with Nikolas Junior.

I was born in Illinois myself. My parents died when I was tiny, and I was sent to California to live with my Uncle Phineas and my Aunt Peggy. Sometimes I dream of cornfields, but I was taken aback when Harry asked me to go home with him and meet some of the same people whom Elizabeth had taken little Nikolas to meet all those years before.

'I don't know, Harry,' I said. 'I can't see why I'd want to go there.'

'Hey, come on, it's a great idea.'

'I'd be entirely dependent on you. That bothers me enough living here, but in Illinois – Oh, Harry, I'd hate it. Besides, your mother and father haven't seen you in months. I'd only make everybody uncomfortable.'

'They want to meet you. They said so.'

It was the evening after he'd presented his advertising campaign to the Brighton Tourist Board. Not one of the projected terrors had come to pass. He'd shaved off his beard without scratching himself. If his hands shook while he gave his presentation, I didn't notice it. The podium covered his legs. The microphone behaved. And plainly the Tourist Board had been impressed. Harry really is good at what he does; there'd been cheers, congratulations and toasts to the future.

Back at the flat, we opened a bottle of champagne and toasted the future again.

Then Harry turned moody. 'Marry me,' he said.

'What?'

'Let's get married.'

'What's the matter, Harry? You can't really be upset, can you? I'm told there's always a let down after a performance – except for somebody like Nikolas, that is.'

'I'm never let down.'

'You certainly have no reason to be. I bet you could sell Bibles to the devil himself.'

He stared into his glass. 'Remember how you used to talk about going to New York?' I nodded. 'After Illinois, I've got eight days in New York and a cabin on the QE II back to Southampton.' His brow knitted and unknitted. 'I've told my parents I'm going to marry you.'

'What did you do that for? You shouldn't frighten them that way.'

'I don't think mother will insist on a church wedding or anything. What about your aunt and uncle?'

I looked at him in alarm. 'Harry – '

'Captains still marry people don't they? Hey, wouldn't the QE II be great?'

I studied the lamp beside him. It reminded me of the embroidered lady's-panty thing that my Aunt Peggy hangs in her closet to keep the moths away. Every lamp in the flat had a shade like it. 'I don't know what to say.'

'You don't have to say anything. I'll arrange – '

'Harry, you're a paragon of a friend, the best friend I've ever had. You know I'm never going to be any good at housewifery and babies.'

'Who said anything about housewifery and babies?'

'I'd end up washing socks like Aunt Peggy.'

'That's all that worries you? I'll wash every sock that enters our household. I promise. Hey, don't shake your head like that. Scout's honour. Any sock, all socks.'

I took in my breath. 'It isn't . . .' I trailed off unhappily, then added, 'I have other things I want to do.'

'You've never said so. Like what?'

Like what? How could I explain to him? How could I tell him about wild elephants? about explosions? about the excitement I'd sensed before my depressing months at Edison Laboratories? All I knew by now was that I wanted – needed, craved – something fresh and raw, something. . . Well, something like I'd had before. I just didn't have the push in me to go out and find it again, not yet. I just couldn't find the spur – the faith in myself, I guess.

I turned away. 'Nobody gets married any more.'

He balanced his champagne with deliberation (if with something of a wobble) on top of the frilly-shaded lamp. 'What's *housewifery* anyhow? Where'd you find a word like that? I don't care what other people do. Besides, all kinds of other people *do* get married. I thought all girls wanted to get married.'

'I thought you didn't care what other people did.'

'You're quibbling.'

'We're both quibbling, but we made a deal. You said – '

'Can't you shut up about that?' he shouted.

Harry's father bullied his mother. He'd told me so. I suppose it's only natural that he try his father's tactics out on me. But I hate shouting. I hate being shouted at. My Uncle Phineas says that if you lose your temper you lose your shield. Back then – back in Brighton – I was still as dutiful a student in this as in other matters; I'd never lost my temper. Never once in all my life had I thrown a tantrum or boiled with rage or seethed or smouldered. I went cold instead. Endothermic Eve.

'Make up your mind,' I said, and I could see that the ice in me shocked him. We'd never had a fight before. 'Either you want to talk about this or you don't. We can't do both at once.'

'Talk. Talk now.'

'We had an agreement. You agreed. I agreed. I was just coming along for the ride. We shook hands on it.'

'What a bitch you are.'

'Is that what stating the terms of an agreement makes me?'

He grabbed his glass off the lamp, swallowed back what remained in it – then sagged into his chair. One of Harry's charms turns out to be that he can never stay angry for long. 'You've found out about me,' he said, as wretched now as he had been angry only seconds before. 'Nikolas told you, didn't he? When? How'd he get you off by yourself?'

Aunt Peggy keeps telling me that I must learn to read between the lines. I do try, but Harry? A secret of some sort? What could be secret about such a person?

'Don't do this to me, Eve. What I've done I sincerely regret, but I was so – ' He took in an uneven breath. 'Come to Illinois.' He looked away. He looked down. Were there tears in his eyes? 'Come with me. Just that much. As a personal favour. We've had a good time, haven't we? You've already said so. Maybe in Illinois – Please come. Say you will. Please.'

Could it really be? a whisper of intrigue in the soul of an advertising man? not slick all the way through? So I agreed to go – and with a tingle of anticipation at that.

PART II

The Second Week in September

CHAPTER 4

There are a surprising number of similarities between my trip to Illinois and the trip Elizabeth took nearly half a century before me. We'd both been away a long time. We both started from the eastern side of the Atlantic in September. We both flew to Chicago and headed out of it along Interstate 55 – she with little Nikolas, I with Harry. We both branched off on to the long, straight secondary road that – at regular intervals and perfect right angles – cuts across roads that are indistinguishable from itself.

This is the richest farmland in the world. On a hot day with the car windows open, there's a regal sense of quiet, as though the land itself knows its worth. Nobody's on the road in front of you. Nobody behind. No living thing anywhere to be seen. But if the corn is high you've got every chance of hearing a meadowlark. You won't see one – at least I never have. They make a clear, liquid, many-noted sound that floats above the fields – that you find yourself thinking about years later and hundreds of miles away in places and climates where a meadow-lark couldn't possibly survive.

Then you approach a city, and the charm of the place snaps

shut. Midwestern cities are as fortified as medieval boroughs. First comes a moat of shopping complexes surrounded by fields of macadam as vast as the cornfields you've just left. After that come mile upon mile of motels, gas stations, industrial sites, ramshackle tenements, abandoned lots, half-demolished buildings: a desolation as terrifying in its way as the chopped-off heads that once decorated town walls. Inside, on tree-lined streets, crouch the houses – bland, expressionless, naked to the world, no hedge, no fence – structures that give away only financial status, nothing else, not even taste or lack of it. Here live a people who hide their secrets very deep.

Both Elizabeth and I headed towards the same street in this same town and to the same house on it. For as long as anybody can remember, the same family has lived in this house; it's the biggest property on Rifferman Avenue. Harry's father, Canfield Wheelock owns it now. When Elizabeth and little Nikolas arrived here all those years ago, Canfield was only ten years old, a bright-eyed, dark-haired, very American small boy, whose only real sadness in life was that he hadn't been named Fred or Harry, which is why he gave these names to his two sons. He grew up into one of those tall, hard-to-know Americans, much taller than either of his children; he has the wide-set eyes, too, that seem to be a family trademark – except in Harry's older brother Fred.

We sat together – Harry's family and I – on the patio at the back of the house, drinks in hand, ice bucket sweating on the mosaic of the table. It was sticky and hot, not yet dark. Heat in the Middle West makes London heat seem refreshing. This house was one of the first in town to be air-conditioned, but Canfield doesn't like air-conditioning; so we rich people sweated as heavily and as uncomfortably as the poor in their ramshackle tenements on the other side of town. A row of grizzled old beech trees separated the end of the garden from the house beyond.

Harry's mother is a nervous woman, skittish almost, old before her time, but forthcoming, friendly – making a special effort because Canfield wasn't making any effort at all. Harry says his father is the stuffiest man in Overton. It's easy to see why. Canfield lounged in his chair, hands knitted atop his belly, eyebrows sticking out in a shelf over an irritable face. When we fell silent – and we fell silent often in that first hour – he hummed. Hum-de-hum-de-de-de-hum-hum-de. It's hard enough to make conversation without this sort of thing.

As to Harry's older brother Fred, I didn't know what to make of him. He didn't look like his mother or his father. He was tiny – not a dwarf exactly, but as close to that as a he could get without falling into some kind of classification – little round nose, too, and cheeks permanently flushed. He sat upright in a straight-backed chair, ankles together, and studied us all with raw distaste. At first I thought of Munchkins. Then I thought, no: it's Rumpelstiltskin.

'Maybe we need another drink, dear,' Harry's mother said. She'd told me to call her Violette. 'The meat won't be ready for twenty minutes.'

Canfield said, 'You've already had your two ounces, Violette.'

'The young people might like a sweetener.'

'They can ask if they do.'

Hum-de-hum.

'We went to your cousin's concert in London,' I said brightly.

People are so fickle. Despite my probing of only a week or so ago on the trip between London and Brighton – despite my fascination with Nikolas then – I'd half forgotten him. Perhaps there'd just been too many other things: Harry's shift of the ground rules between us and my mixed feelings about this trip. But even as I spoke I was aware of a queer sense of disorder, and I knew it had come to me first in Swiss Cottage: a widening gap in the logic I'd trusted, an instability at the core of things. And yet if it hadn't been for Canfield's hum, I still think Nikolas might never have crossed my mind again.

'What cousin is that?' Canfield said.

'Eve doesn't really – ' Harry began.

'Nikolas Strakhan,' I interrupted. Had that been alarm in Harry's voice?

'The less said about Junior the better,' Canfield said.

'Junior?' I laughed. 'Oh, I remember now. Harry told me. Junior-that-crook. But *Junior*. It's all wrong applied to him.'

'That's what we called him.'

'It isn't really apt though, is it? It's so American. I mean – After all, he's Russian. Shouldn't he be Nikolas Nikolai-something? And his father would be different, wouldn't he? I don't know. Nikolas Petrovich maybe?'

'We called him Junior.'

Hum-de-de-hum.

How could Violette bear this? How could anybody? 'Did you know he'd become a conductor?'

'Nope.'

'The night we saw him he conducted one of the most famous pianists in the world. I wish I weren't so awful at names. What's his name, Harry?' Harry looked down at his shoes and mumbled something that I knew was supposed to warn me off, but I'd gone too far to stop. 'What'd you say?' I said.

'Richter.'

I nodded vigorously. 'Mickie said Richter hardly plays for anybody any more. Yet here he was playing for Nikolas. He didn't wear tails though. He wore a plain jacket.'

'You don't say,' said Canfield.

Hum-hum-de.

'The reviews were terrible,' I blurted out.

Oh God, this time I could actually see Violette wince (and I could hear my Aunt Peggy whispering in my ear), 'Why do you *say* these things, Eve?'

But to everybody's surprise Canfield perked up. 'Reviews?' he said. 'Bad were they? Like what?'

Violette managed a tremulous smile, and Harry looked up from his feet. 'Can you remember them, Eve? She can't remember names at all, but she's great with poems and things.'

Even so, I may have exaggerated a little (only a little). It was hard not to; as I spoke, Canfield expanded as prettily as one of those Chinese paper flowers that bloom in water. He grew merry. He laughed out loud. He got up of his own accord, made another pitcher of Martinis and poured one for all of us, even Violette. I figured if I went on this way we might even be allowed air-conditioning during dinner.

'What was Nikolas like when he was a little boy?' I said to this changed person, this new Canfield.

He snorted. 'Had a nanny to pamper him.'

'This was when he came with his mother? They took a nanny along too?'

'Forty-ton truck of a woman. Brown habit like a nun. You know: peaked wimple and starched white collar.' He gave another snort. 'All I could think was, "How am I going to explain this to Dutch Hashman and Johnny Shaw?" '

'Tough kids?'

He nodded. 'Junior had on a velvet suit. Stupid brat looked like a sprig of parsley. Plus fours and a little jacket – moron, weakling – lace collar. Patent leather shoes that buttoned up.'

Canfield and this awful apparition stared at each other, as unblinking as street-corner dogs.

'Say hello to Junior,' Canfield's mother said.

Canfield croaked out a wretched, 'Hello.'

And did this velvet-suited boy say hello to his cousin? No, he did not. Did he hold out a hand to be shaken? No, he did not. Did he hide behind his nanny? show the slightest awareness of how grotesque he was? No, he did not.

Nikolas Strakhan clicked his heels and bowed from the waist.

Canfield burst into tears.

Harry's grandmother lives right next door on Rifferman Avenue. Harry took me to meet her the morning after our arrival in Illinois, down the garden path, across the lawn, past the line of trees.

Old Mrs Wheelock is as tiny as Fred. She's thin and bent. The hair on her head belongs to a Soviet realist statue from the Forties, cast-iron curls in an opaque grey; her neck bows under the weight.

'So this is Eve at last,' she said, taking my hands in hers, which were gnarled with rheumatoid arthritis.

'Now I see where Harry and Fred get their height,' I said. 'Harry talks about you all the time, Mrs Wheelock.'

The surprise on her face told me that my Aunt Peggy's despair was on course as usual. What was it I'd said this time? The boys' height? Harry's talk?

'Oh my,' she said, recovering. 'Do call me Beatrice. I know I'm fearfully old, but I rather like the name Beatrice, and I've always hated being called Mrs Wheelock. There's something so – I don't know – so final about it. How lovely she is, Harry. No wonder you've hidden her from us. Bring the coffee like a good boy. It's laid out on a tray in the kitchen. Come through to the living room, Eve.' She walked ahead of me with troubled steps, her spine not just bowed but telescoped beneath that enormous weight of hair. 'I want to hear all about you. Harry tells me you have a scientific mind. You have no idea how much I admire you for that. How do you put up with him? He's a Luddite these days. People change so, don't they? Sit here. It's comfortable here.'

'Has he really changed? What was he like before?'

'He's altogether different. I like it when people change. Certainty terrifies me.'

'Wasn't he always interested in advertising?'

'Why, only a few years ago – .'

She broke off as Harry brought in the coffee and set the tray down on a large, low table. He poured – her hands were too painful to manage the pot – and we chatted. After half an hour, in the middle of a sentence, Harry got up. I got up too.

'No, no,' he said, backing towards the door. 'You stay here and entertain Beatrice. I've got to meet dad in town.'

'You don't want me to come? Are you sure?'

He shook his head.

'Please stay, dear,' Beatrice said. 'I don't often get the chance to talk to young people.'

But with Harry out of the room, we didn't seem to have much to say – or rather I had the feeling that she had something to say but couldn't quite bring herself to it. We went over again what I thought of England. We discussed the weather and the garden outside, even though we'd discussed both before. There were no silences and certainly none of Canfield's humming, but the conversation was getting harder – certainly for me, but also, I thought, for her.

'This room – ' I said suddenly, looking around me.

There were few furnishings here, nothing of the frou-frou I'd expected to find in such an old woman's house. It was spare, moneyed design – unsettling somehow and very familiar – leather chairs, a handsome wood floor, uncarpeted, no pictures, a mirror wall. How things link, one to the next. Canfield's humming and Beatrice's living room.

'I can never figure out families,' I went on. 'Is he your nephew? Nikolas Strakhan?'

'You're as smart as Harry says, aren't you, dear? Nikolas designed this house from start to finish.'

'Is he an architect too? I thought he was just a musician. Oh Lord, I don't mean "just a musician" – that sounds awful – I mean, well, houses are so much easier than music.'

'Are they?'

'He's awfully good at this sort of thing.'

She nodded that mighty head of hair. 'Did Harry tell you that the first piano Nikolas played was the upright in the front room of the big house? You could even say his musical career was my idea.' She sighed. 'How difficult children are in summer.'

Elizabeth's September in Illinois – the very September that the Second World War began – was a typical Midwestern summer. At night she and Beatrice wrapped their fractious little boys in damp sheets and laid them down just inside an open front door to catch whatever breeze might stir. During the days, the air was gelatinous with heat. Ten-year-old Canfield escaped as early as he could from the house and the embarrassment of his cousin. Nikolas stayed behind with his nanny, who read to him, played games with him, splashed cool water over him. But he had a rash; he was bored; he whined. His nanny gave up, and Elizabeth tried to comfort him. The whine became a howl. He threw himself on the floor; he kicked and screamed.

In desperation – anything to stop the racket – Beatrice suggested a tune on the piano.

It can't have been an easy moment for Elizabeth, who sat down at the upright – a delicate, feminine thing, more a piece of furniture than a musical instrument – ran her fingers over the keys, then picked out that long-ago phrase from *Raymonda*, the one Nikolas Senior had sung to her at the Café Régence.

The howl stopped at once. 'More,' demanded Nikolas.

'More music?'

'More! More!'

He struggled up from the floor, face still streaming with tears, and ran across the room to stand beside her, sniffling and snuffling. She played the first line of 'Twinkle, Twinkle, Little Star'.

His face was alight.

'Now Nikolas,' he said and scrambled on to her lap. He banged the keys for a moment, then twisted around to her with a puzzled expression. She wiped his face, blew his nose, placed his hands on the keyboard and pressed his fingers on the notes, one by one.

By evening Beatrice was begging her to teach him something else. Anything else. A day more and her hatred for 'Twinkle, Twinkle, Little Star' was exceeded only by her hatred of 'Three Blind Mice' and 'Row, Row, Row Your Boat'. News of the declaration of war against Germany came in the very next afternoon; Beatrice blessed it, hating herself, because she knew by then that nothing less than war in Europe would restore peace to the Wheelock household on Rifferman Avenue. Travel restrictions were expected any minute; Elizabeth had to leave at once.

War in Geneva was as remote as war in Illinois. While nations collapsed and millions died, Nikolas's piano lessons became the focus of Elizabeth's life, even though her health began to fail again. His progress was so swift and so sure – he rarely hit a wrong note; no metronome was more regular – that when he was six, the Grand Duchess Drubetskovna asked Elizabeth if he could play at one of her musical evenings. Even Nikolas Senior was impressed. The Grand Duchess had been lady-in-waiting to the Tsarina; court circles had known her as Tatiana Andreyevna because she was not only a Grand Duchess in her own right but the wife of Prince Yuri Andreyev.

Two grand pianos faced each other at the end of her illustrious salon. At one sat a tuxedo'd pianist. The audience bristled with jewels and fanned themselves while tiny Nikolas and his nanny walked hand in hand to the other piano. She wore her wimpled habit and carried a huge carpet bag; he wore a parsley-green suit like the one he'd worn in the Midwest. She lifted him on to the stool. It was too low. She lifted him off it, opened her bag, pulled out a copy of the Geneva telephone directory, placed it on the stool. Still too low. Out came a second directory.

The Grand Duchess herself, haughty in diamonds, presented the grown-up pianist with a composition she'd pieced together that very afternoon. The pianist played it through. Nikolas listened, then played it unseen – this fleck of parsley caught in the grand piano's vast jaws – with never an error, never even a moment's hesitation.

The audience applauded in delight. Nikolas's nanny picked him off the stool, turned him upside down and dandled him by his ankles above the keyboard. He played the composition again, and the guests shouted 'Bravo!' One of them said he was Geneva's Josef Hofmann. Another said that one day he would be a Busoni or a Rachmaninov. Nikolas clicked his heels, bowed from the waist and was mightily pleased with himself.

Throughout the Second World War, Elizabeth devoted herself to her son's talent. After the war ended – Nikolas was eleven years old – she decided the time had come for a new teacher and a fresh approach. Through friends of friends she hired a Spaniard by the name of Teresa Lopez-Vega to take over from her. Music draws huge audiences in war; newly declared peace produces not only armies of veterans but armies of displaced musicians too, all of them penniless, some of them very gifted. Señora Lopez-Vega was such a one – a big woman in her early thirties, as big as Nikolas's nanny, with black eyes and a pointed nose.

At their first lesson, Nikolas played Bach's Gigue from the Partita No. 1 in B flat; it's a darling of a piece, so Beatrice told me, a show-off piece, with the left hand constantly crossing over the right. When he'd finished, Señora Lopez-Vega asked him to repeat it.

'Why?' he demanded.

'Because I want you to.'

'Why should I? *I* don't want to.'

'Play and I'll tell you.'

He played, but he was seriously displeased. Elizabeth never

made him repeat. By what right did this new person – this interloper who was not his mother – take such liberties with the Josef Hofmann of Geneva? He hadn't made an error. He never made errors.

When he'd finished, Señora Lopez-Vega only said, 'And once more.'

'You're silly.'

'You might learn something.'

'How would you know?'

Señora Lopez-Vega took in her breath and let it out again. She needed the money. 'When you have actually played the Gigue *once* – actually *played* it – we will have achieved something. I don't deny that you hit the right keys in the right order. But what is that? A little music box can do that or a carousel pump organ or a hack playing in a hotel lobby. That's not music. It's wallpaper.'

Nikolas gasped in shock. He went dizzy with rage. He hurled himself on the floor, kicking and screaming.

She surveyed his tantrum calmly. When it showed no signs of abating, she sat down at the piano and began to play Bach's little piece herself.

There are explosions in everybody's life. Some are public, some private. Private ones have special dangers all their own. Nobody bothers with a countdown: '. . . five, four, three . . .' The best you can hope for is a quiet warning – something like 'Firing now' – which doesn't give a frenzied boy time to yank his dignity clear. And yet the smash and the fireball are as fierce and as terrifying as any bomb dropped by any bombardier over Europe in the war that had just ended.

Nikolas had never heard the full depth and range of his mother's Hamburg Steinway; he'd caught hints of its power, sonority, subtlety, colour, but he'd never before realized that a piano actually could sing.

Only once again in his life would light boil up inside him as it boiled up when he heard Teresa Lopez-Vega play that afternoon. Only once more would the earth quake like that beneath his feet.

Beatrice had told the story so charmingly and with such pleasure that when she stopped – and stopped so abruptly – I cried out in alarm: 'Are you all right?'

'Yes, yes.' Her eyes peeped out at me from under their crêpe marquees. (How terrible to be old.) 'Do forgive me, Eve. The past is such a bafflement. Most of the time I think in terms of anecdote. Then a pattern appears without any warning – and it takes my breath away.'

'I've tired you, haven't I? Harry says I never know when to leave.'

'Does he? Why would he say a thing like that? I'm not at all tired. What could he mean?'

'You should hear my Aunt Peggy on the subject. "Oh, Eve," she says, "if you don't learn a little tact you're not going to have a friend left in the world." I really haven't tired you?'

Beatrice shook her head.

'You're sure?'

'Not a bit.'

'I've never heard a *real* story like this – not a real, live story. What was it that took your breath away?'

'What I'm really supposed to tell you – '

'What did it mean? This explosion in Nikolas's life?'

She smiled, picked up her coffee cup, took a sip. 'Nikolas is – I hardly know what word to use – implacable, I guess. Once he gets an idea in his mind, nothing can stop him. He seemed prepared – If only I could remember his precise words. How could I have missed his meaning for so long?' She took another sip. 'I can see it now: at that very moment he decided to steal Señora Lopez-Vega's talent from her.'

Well, why not? When Nikolas wanted his sisters' toys, he took them – or figured out how to take them. When he wanted his mother's attention or his nanny's love or the cook's fresh-made *borscht*, he took it. Why should talent be any different?

He surveyed Señora Lopez-Vega's strengths. He studied her character. When she set him exercises – Czerny or Clementi – he refused to master them. When she gave up prodding him, he worked hour after hour. When she asked him to play slowly and think the notes through one by one, he burst into tears. When she tried to placate him with chocolates and tin soldiers, he threw them across the room.

Then one day she bought him a chess set, and she said to him, 'As long as I checkmate you, you must do everything I say. If you checkmate me, I'll give you anything you ask for.'

What devil could have offered more alluring terms?

I'm no good at chess. I did play once when I was about twelve – about the age Nikolas was when Señora Lopez-Vega gave him his set. One Sunday morning when I was bored, my Uncle Phineas said he would show me the moves and play a game with me after dinner. From the look on his face I could see he was already getting a kick out of what seemed to him an inevitable result. Nobody would call my Uncle Phineas soppy about children. In a desperate attempt to stave off defeat I spent the morning with *The Children's Encyclopaedia*. It worked too. I checkmated Uncle Phineas twice in a row with the same four classic moves I'd just learned from the entry on chess.

'That doesn't make any sense, Eve,' said Harry. 'He just let you win.'

It isn't so. I know it. Perhaps Uncle Phineas didn't have any feel for the basics of the game. How would I know? I never played again. As for Harry, he calls himself a patzer, but he can and does play. He tells me that Nikolas became an aggressive player, a winning player if not an elegant one. That was later. At first he only dreamed of winning, and what's the good of that?

As the months wore on, he came to hate losing so much – and he lost with such ill grace – that beating him became a modest pleasure for Señora Lopez-Vega even though he played so badly that there was no challenge in it.

Little by little – I'm sure he wasn't aware of it himself – his concentration shifted from the complexities of music and checkmate to the simplicities of revenge.

A year passed. The crucial shift took place one afternoon when he was thirteen; he went with his mother, his father and his two sisters to take their monthly ritual of tea with the Grand Duchess Drubetskovna, in whose salon he'd performed when he was only six.

The Grand Duchess sat alone at a small table in splendid isolation from her guests. As always, a rococo samovar with handles and a spigot stood in front of her. On her shoulder perched a parrot called Luluc. Behind her loomed an aviary so vast that one filigree cage of the many cages in it served as a hospital for ailing song birds (she tended them with expertise and homoeopathic medicines); dozens of canaries, thrushes, sparrows cheeped and warbled without let up, chitta-chick, chitta-chit, twitter-tweet.

As always, Nikolas's duty was to ferry hot China tea in glasses across the room from the Grand Duchess to his mother and father (reclining in easy chairs), to the Prince (a fine, gaunt figure in spats) and to the Countess Meliukova, who had lost everything to the Bolsheviks. His sisters passed plates of many-layered little cakes, some chocolate, some with pink icing.

As always, when Nikolas had finished his duties, he prowled the room, tea and cake in hand. Russians are indulgent with children. He fingered the ranks of photographs that stood at attention on almost every polished surface; he peered under the Tsar and Tsarina in their diamond-encrusted frame. He studied the gold icons on the mantelpiece and the Fabergé eggs and ruby snuffboxes in the marquetry display case. He sat down at the Prince's desk, opened the drawers, closed them, squirmed with the tedium of adult company and, squirming, noticed for the very first time the titles of the books displayed in the malachite bookstand.

One of these was *My Best Games of Chess* by Alexander Alekhine. Nikolas's heart began to beat a little faster. He'd never played with anybody but Señora Lopez-Vega; it hadn't occurred to him that there'd be books on the subject. He drew the Alekhine toward him, stared down at the pages of strange symbols and knew – he knew – he'd stumbled on the weapon he needed. He opened a second book: *To Play the Game*. The title of Chapter One was 'Chess on the Page'.

Harry says chess books are to chess players as maths texts are to mathematicians: no books, no player. This shouldn't have come as such a surprise to me; my own small experience with the game was pure book learning. With the very next game Señora Lopez-Vega would have realized that Nikolas had new allies. Perhaps she even knew Alekhine was amongst them. She smiled and said, 'So? Well, well. And now what?'

She must have been a little taken aback by the raw foretaste of victory in those wide-spread eyes. She'd also have seen – and what a shock *that* must have been – in just what form he planned to claim his spoils. How dare the brat? He had the unfinished look that pubescent boys have, bread dough mixed but not yet risen, nowhere near ready for the oven. How *dare* he?

Piano lessons took on a new ferocity. Nikolas tossed his envies aside. He forgot his resentments and his disappointments. He was a boy possessed. He thought only of the plunder that was to be his – that was almost his already. When he wasn't at the piano, he was poring over classic chess treatises; he concentrated on annotations; he memorized opening, mid-game, end-game. Chess magazines arrived in Geneva from three continents. His pockets overflowed with clippings and sheets of music. Wherever he went he left a Hansel-and-Gretel trail of Alekhine, Capablanca, Nimzovich – and of Bach, Chopin, Mozart.

All he had to do was beat her once. Just once.

But the better he got, the better she got. He raised his game. She raised hers. He improved and improved – and lost and lost. She set him more and longer tasks at the piano. His work improved. He grew a few inches. His hands developed strength and reach. Sometimes Señora Lopez-Vega thought, hearing him play – only half-aware as teachers sometimes are, that she was hearing not him but herself reflected through him – that his talent might flower yet.

Six weeks before he turned fifteen – the month was June, confirmation petits fours and ice cream only a few days before – he sat down with Señora Lopez-Vega for the game he was at long last to win.

They played in the music room on a marble chess table in front of French windows that opened on to the garden beyond, a large, lovely garden with a stone patio and a stretch of lawn. It was afternoon. The day was warm, sunny, fresh.

Harry says that there's a deep internal logic to chess – deviate from it and you're lost – but that there are many kinds of logic. Señora Lopez-Vega played chess much as she played the piano, with a clear-eyed passion – Capablanca rather than Steinitz. Nikolas knew he would never beat her if he played the same way. His game was as rough and ready, as brash and brutal as a Soviet hospital. But he was slow where she was quick. Sometimes she kept a book to read while he pondered his moves; this day she had a detective novel with her. They tossed a coin for white. She lost, leaned back and opened her book while he mused over his opening.

For some thirty moves the game progressed more or less as their games usually did. The warm sunshine from the open windows fell over the table between them. Nikolas sat with his back to the light. She always gave him this advantage – he always took it – even though so much light disturbed her.

Some sort of crisis occurred: he offered her his queen.

She put down her book and studied the board. Harry tells me that there are queen traps in the opening game but that all players over the age of six know them; offering a queen in real-life chess is so rare that when it happens the game isn't just a game any more; it's one for the books, for posterity. A man with victory in sight – a boy with victory in sight – is sometimes inspired beyond his natural abilities.

'A little careless of me, wasn't it?' she said.

'Yes.'

'I can't quite see how I let – '

'Move.'

She studied his glowing face, lifted her hand to the board, paused. 'If I take the queen, you have a mating net.'

Nikolas said nothing.

'If I don't, I lose both queenside pawns.' His eyes swept from her forehead to the buttons of her blouse and back again; she frowned angrily. 'Don't look at me like that.'

'Why not? I've won.'

'The sun's in my eyes.'

'You want to call it off for now? finish later?'

'Yes,' she said, rising from the table.

'Is this cowardice, Señora Lopez-Vega? from you? from my teacher?'

'Don't be ridiculous. Why should it be?'

'If the sun really bothers you let's move the table. What's a little sun in the eyes? Your end-game's hopeless. Is this the way it's to be? Am I never to win? Even when I've won already?'

She sat down again to study the board, but there was a tremor in her fingers. The queen? She didn't take it. He captured both pawns.

Almost too easy.

All this I heard sitting in Beatrice's handsome living room decorated by Nikolas but − now I come to think of it − decorated with an uncluttered intensity that must have been the essence of Señora Lopez–Vega's game.

'Did she pay up?' I asked Beatrice.

'I asked him that myself. He said to me, "Señora Lopez–Vega was a woman of honour." ' Beatrice bowed her head. 'I'm far fonder of Nikolas than I should be, but there are times − '

'Why did he tell you about it? It's a funny sort of thing to tell your aunt. I'd never tell my Aunt Peggy anything like that. She'd have a heart attack.'

Beatrice shrugged one of those little shrugs of complicity. 'I told him I didn't think he'd been very fair. He laughed and said, "If she'd been playing fair she'd have told me about books in the first place." '

Besides, the dough of this boy was rising fast. Hot in the oven: a hard crust and a steaming interior. No wonder they call it the staff of life. He led Señora Lopez–Vega out into the countryside. He'd scouted for precisely the right place and found it in a moss–lined cranny near the lake where cherry trees and wild flowers bloomed.

And he knew with all his heart and in the innermost reaches of his soul that her music would bloom inside him just as he himself was set to bloom inside her − just as the cherry trees bloomed around them both − now that the source of blooming lay absolutely in his power.

CHAPTER 5

Undressing after supper that night, Nikolas glowed with triumph. His naked body was again the naked body of a great artist-to-be, just as it had been before that first lesson with Señora Lopez-Vega, when he was still the Josef Hofmann of Geneva, a future Rachmaninov, a future Busoni. He'd been in a kind of limbo ever since. The texture of this skin, isn't it fine? The colour of the belly, isn't it roseate? Even the ripples of warm water in the bath paid their respects with eddy and flow, slippery soap and froth of suds. He succumbed to sleep with a smile.

The smile was still on his lips when he woke. He ran down-stairs to the kitchen where Cook was taking the morning's bread out of the oven, her sleeves rolled above the elbows of her strong arms. He grabbed a whole loaf, sank his teeth into it, took a bite where nobody had bitten before – where nobody was allowed to bite.

'Fool,' said Cook, as he spat out the scalding piece and ran to the sink, hand to mouth, for water.

From the kitchen he ran to the music room. He sat down at the piano, spread his hands out over the keys and began to play the Gigue that Señora Lopez-Vega had played at their very first lesson together.

The piano sang for him. It did. Just as it had sung for her. Laughter welled up in his throat. He'd won. He'd –

But if a boy soars too high too quick, he'll fall into the sea like Icarus. Sometimes even the best tricks just don't work. Hear that? The last phrase? Nikolas stopped, frowned, took in his breath, played it again. Hear it? Was that the hotel lobby pianist? Could it be? The very sound Señora Lopez-Vega's first fateful lesson had taught him to despise?

He tried the phrase again. He played on a little. June is such a lovely month, so full of promises, so full of bloomings and thrustings in mossy crevices beside lakes. And yet the sound was unmistakable, absolutely unmistakable. The hotel lobby hack was still in place: a wallpaper of notes, a little music box, a carousel pump organ. How could three years of unrelenting drive come to this?

Several hours later a parlour maid came to fetch him for lunch. He didn't respond. She came again. He said something – he didn't know what – and forgot her as soon as she left him. Sometime during the afternoon, Elizabeth (leaning on Cook's arm) made her way downstairs; she laid her painfully thin hand on his shoulder. A tear trickled down his cheek.

Vary your parameters, increase your magnification of detail and the mathematical border between calm and catastrophe becomes more and more random until suddenly – without warning and from deep within the heart of disorder – a form as familiar as your own face appears, every pore, every nuance of shape, every freckle in place: a young life takes many shifts forward and back before it settles into anything recognizable like this. That night the body that had delighted Nikolas only twenty-four hours ago was so loathsome a thing that he could barely bring himself to touch it. By the end of the week, when Señora Lopez-Vega arrived for his lesson, he was sick with despair.

'Good afternoon, Nikolas,' she said, a greeting as formal as her greeting of last week and the week before – as formal as all her greetings over the years. 'Shall we begin?' God knows what he'd expected from her or even what he sought. Absolution maybe. Maybe something as simple as forgiveness. He took in a ragged breath and played a few bars of whatever it was that they were working on.

'What's the matter with you?' she said. 'You're not usually *this* bad.'

'My hands hurt,' he said. Why did he say that? Why should such a thought have come to him?

'Where?' she asked.

'Around the joints.'

'Let me see.' She took his hands in hers; she squeezed the joints one by one between her middle finger and thumb.

'Help me, Teresa.'

'Teresa? Who is this Teresa? You take too many familiarities. There's nothing wrong with your hands. Feign an illness, and you'll end up suffering from it.'

'Is that true? I never heard that before.'

'Don't you know about curses?'

He swept his eyes across her face and down over her shoulders. 'I'm learning fast.'

'Then you will learn about this one.'

'Come with me to the lake.'

She sighed irritably. If he mistook the colour in her cheeks for a blush, her voice disabused him at once. 'I don't remember losing another game,' she said.

'Do you have to lose again?'

'Most assuredly I do.'

'Let's set up the table.'

'Not today.'

'What do you mean, not today?'

'I mean not today.'

'I challenge you.'

'Nikolas, I said no. I meant no.' She gave a short laugh. 'But if you will not play music for me, I will play for you. Come, come, get up off that seat. It's my turn.'

She settled herself and played the little Gigue that meant so much to him. He realized at once – why hadn't he noticed it before? – that for all the years of lessons she'd modulated her work to bring it within his emotional range.

She broke off. She glanced up at him from the keyboard. 'Do you see?' she said.

'Yes,' he said.

'Now listen carefully.'

She turned back and began again – and there was the hotel lobby pianist. There was the wallpaper of notes.

She glanced up at him again. 'Did you think I can't hear it when you play?'

Nikolas stared at her.

She closed the piano, packed up her music, walked over to him. 'Goodbye, Nikolas,' she said.

'That's all?'

'What more could there be?'

'What about the curse?'

'Curse?'

The question wasn't as idle as it sounds. While she was playing, the tips of his fingers had begun to tingle, a queer kind of a tingle, rather like a funny bone that's been tapped. 'My hands,' he said.

'Oh, poor little Nikolas. You look quite green. Have I frightened you?'

'You didn't tell me if it was true or not.'

'Sometimes you are very stupid.'

'Teresa, please – '

'My Christian name again? Even though I've told you not to use it?' She studied him with regal disdain. 'Perhaps you deserve a curse. After all, I can give it to you of my own free will – unlike some other things I've given you.' Nikolas looked down at his hands. He turned them palm up. 'Never mind, little Nikolas. You're a pretty boy with an undoubted flair for what goes on under a cherry tree in spring. This is a compliment. A compliment and a curse: what more does a man need for a full life?'

He hardly heard her. The tingling had reached his thumbs.

'Every good boy deserves favours,' she said, patting his cheek.

Two days later she was dead.

Precisely what happened to bring about her death is more than a little murky. Suicide? Possibly. Even probably. But why would she kill herself? Anyhow, the coroner brought in a verdict of accidental death. Beatrice, telling me the story, stopped again – again uncertain.

When I was little, my Uncle Phineas took me to see the bird skeletons in the natural history museum; I remember thin, frail structures afloat above claws as gnarled as Beatrice's hands. For days afterwards I felt uneasy. I don't mean that there was anything frightening about Beatrice. But the pity of those hands, especially as she spoke of Nikolas's hands, gave me the same sense of unease – of injustice too, I think. In his way Nikolas sounded startlingly innocent. Imagine believing you can control the world around you.

I said, 'You think he had something to do with it, don't you? Could he have killed her? Oh, why is my family so stodgy? No pianists. No chess players. Not one of us even throws tantrums.'

Beatrice sighed. 'I don't have the energy for tantrums any more.'

'Don't you? I've never had one. I've been carefully trained to turn to ice instead. Everything slows down: you can make sense of what's going on.'

'If you keep at that, there'll be an explosion one day.'

'Oh, I don't really think so.' I laughed. 'The margin of error is way too large.'

'I'm not sure you know yourself as well as you think, dear. You get carried away so easily. I did not say Nikolas was in any way responsible for – '

'You think so, though, don't you? I do want him to have murdered her. It's so much more fun if – Oh Lord, why do I say these things? I'm so sorry. You were a musician too – the violin, wasn't it? Harry told me.'

'I was one of the vast majority who just weren't good enough.' She peered at me with her bird eyes. 'You mustn't look so sad. I was lucky. I could blame my failure on a technical flaw. Not like Nikolas. Nikolas was very fluent even when he was a small boy, but he couldn't – It's hard to describe. Elizabeth said he just couldn't bring the music to life. She said he'd sell his soul for the gift. She said – '

'What comes next?' I said happily. 'It's the devil, isn't it? Go on, go on. I can't wait. Tell me. Stories never really take off until the devil arrives.'

Think of the crowds of humanity, all begging, pleading, wailing to sell boot, baggage, soul, sinew – anything and everything – for the tiniest snippet of a talent that will set them apart. Somebody's got to oversee the triage. Who better than the Lord of the Morning? After all, think of the paradox. Human warmth saps your strength. Other people's troubles distract you at the critical moment; you trip, fall, lose hold of the devil's gift, just as Elizabeth had fallen in Pennsylvania Station and again in the Café Régence. Only when you're ice at the core – only when nothing and nobody can deflect you – do you have a chance of surviving long enough to warm an audience.

Well, if this boy Nikolas is willing to carry out murder just to catch the impresario's eye – Surely such a one rates a test of his mettle.

On the day of Señora Lopez-Vega's funeral, Nikolas lost all

sensation in his hands. He couldn't get out of bed either. He could no longer taste or smell the food that Cook prepared for him. Doctors were summoned. They stuck pins in his fingers. He felt nothing. They poked and prodded, listened and thumped.

'Neurasthenia,' one of them said.

'Depression,' said another.

'Hysterical obsession,' said a third.

Elizabeth decided to take him to the mountains, although for nearly a year she hadn't managed anything more arduous than a trip from her bed to her bathroom. Her plans took ten days to complete; each day Nikolas sank deeper into a stuporous state. By the time the two of them left – with a bevy of servants and Nikolas's devoted nanny – he was almost comatose. They travelled by ambulance to Bern, by hospital train to Lucerne, then by ambulance again through the valley beyond the lake and up into the Bernese Oberland.

By the pricking of my thumbs: Nikolas's recovery started with a tingle of sensation in his fingers. Not long afterwards he smelled the bread as it baked. Then he sat up in bed. He stood. He began to move around the house. The numbness left his hands. One morning he woke early, went to the window and watched dawn break. The house was a wooden structure on a slope across from the Reichenbach Falls, where Sherlock Holmes fought his epic battle with Professor Moriarty. It's a long vista, cold, pure, savage, majestic – not at all a landscape that suggests cuckoo clocks, gingerbread houses, gnomes and dirty money.

Nikolas stared out at the beauty that houses such kitsch and corruption and said to himself, 'I will be what I am and I will never regret what I do. I will never feel guilty for any act or thought or feeling.'

He dressed. He went to Elizabeth. 'I want a piano,' he said to her.

By afternoon a piano stood in the living room of the chalet.

Nikolas sat down to it. He was weak. No doubt about that. He was out of practice. No doubt about that either. But a sound came from that instrument. A real sound. Not Señora Lopez-Vega's passion. Not Josef Hofmann's chaste elegance or Rachmaninov's virile sonority. But a sound – oh, the daring of it – that flirted with the gingerbread, the dirty money and the cuckoo clock in that Alpen snow outdoors. A sound that got so breathtakingly close to the hotel lobby without ever touching it that Elizabeth, hearing him play from the room beyond, couldn't restrain a smile.

Señora Lopez-Vega herself would have approved this sound for its irony and for the risks it took, if not for its profundity. This Nikolas himself realized at once.

In the autumn he auditioned for the Geneva Conservatoire and gained a place. Two years passed. He won a local prize. He won a regional prize. The summer he was eighteen was to be his first summer on the European circuit. The way seemed clear. But in March Elizabeth died; and despite the ice at his heart he wept and was bereft.

At the dinner table he sat across from his sisters, the one blonde, the other dark, and hated them with all his old intensities. How dare they be alive and eating Cook's *zakuski* when Elizabeth was dead? They were aimless dilettantes – easy, facile, empty, vain. Nikolas Senior himself, past sixty now, sat at the head of the table, as facile and vain as his daughters, his hair streaked white, a forkful of pastry half-way to his mouth.

'I have matters of importance to discuss with you, my children,' he was saying in the voice that had enchanted Elizabeth all those years ago at the Café Régence. 'I have pondered these matters in the light of my background as a Russian and an aristocrat, and I have come to a decision that I believe my ancestors would approve as correct and prudent.

'Finance does not amuse me. I have no penchant for trivia. However, it is clear to me that when you have left me, the taxes on my fortune will be so great as to cast me out into the street. No, no, do not protest. Allow me to finish what I have to say. You, Ekaterina, are soon to be married.' Ekaterina was the fair one, tall, engaged to a banker whose advice Nikolas Senior had not sought on this matter or any other. 'I have given my consent and my blessing. I would not dream of going back on either. I sacrifice myself for you willingly, gladly, as is a father's duty – and his privilege.' He turned to his second daughter, the dark one, who was about to be engaged to a town councillor. 'You, Natalie, have my consent and my blessing as well. I do no less for you than for your sister.'

A fire burned in the dining room fireplace; Nikolas Senior's buffed fingernails shone in the light from it as he put another bite in his mouth, chewed, swallowed. His clean-shaven Adam's apple bobbed, and he patted the corners of his mouth with a fine linen napkin. 'Now my only son. Now Nikolas. You will soon be starting out on a career as an artist, which was Countess Strakhan's wish. Because it was her wish, it is mine. I would cut off my feet rather than stand in your way. You need give your poor father no thought at all on this point.

'My children, Countess Strakhan's accountants inform me that the investments your grandfather made for her – he was clever in these matters if a philistine in all others – fall into three parts. They do not, however, fall into three equal parts. To remedy this inequality would reduce the whole of the capital to not much more than the largest third. Therefore – now listen carefully – the third and largest share of my total assets I will bestow at once, as soon as my legal advisers can draw up the papers, on whichever one of you promises to care for me in my advancing years as though it were a sacred duty.'

'Like King Lear?' Young Nikolas said, looking up, smiling for perhaps the first time since his mother's death. 'Is that what you're getting at? What happens to the rest of the money? Are you going to give us all of it? Every penny?'

Nikolas Senior motioned the butler to refill his wineglass. 'That is my intention.'

'It's the stupidest idea I've ever heard,' young Nikolas said.

'Nikolas!' Ekaterina cried.

'Nikolas!' cried Natalie.

Nikolas Senior turned his elegant head to view his son much as all those years ago he'd turned his head to view the man who offered a match for his cigarette. 'Do you have something serious to say, my son? Or are you just behaving in an unconscionable fashion for the pleasure of it? I speak to you of my heart. It does not become either of us for you to mock. I have no objection to pleasures, however bizarre, but you owe me a son's consideration on this grave and difficult question.'

'All right,' said Nikolas. 'What do *you* get out of it?'

The silence this time was sepulchral. The great clock in the hallway gonged. 'I beg your pardon?' said Nikolas Senior.

'What does *taking care* of you entail?'

'That must be obvious.'

'Not to me.'

'If you are going to partake of my fortune it would pay you to mind your manners.'

The fire crackled. 'The question is,' said young Nikolas, 'will minding my manners be to my advantage? I rather doubt it. I imagine you've worked out a fiddle that will pay you and strip us. Do you know – it amazes me to say so – but I don't think I'd do that. Maybe I'm wrong. Certainly Ekaterina and Natalie would and, after all, you're my father as well. I don't understand taxes. I wish I did. It would be a help, wouldn't it? Let me see, do we pay your taxes out of our own pockets? So you keep all the income at no expense to yourself? Something like that?' Young Nikolas laughed. 'You'd better watch yourself, old man, because I'm going to play Cordelia – '

'Enough!' Nikolas Senior interrupted, averting his eyes in distaste.

' – and you're going to get burned, just like Lear.'

'Nikolas!'

Young Nikolas laughed again. 'What a pity to shut me up now. I was just beginning to enjoy myself.'

'Plainly your grief has affected your wits,' said his father. 'This is very disagreeable. I see that I must wait a little longer despite my own suffering. The matter is closed for the present.'

That night young Nikolas dreamed about the Grand Duchess Drubetskovna's escape from Russia in 1917. Elizabeth used to tell him the story. As soon as everybody knew the profligate days of the aristocracy were gone for ever – that the Bolsheviks had won the Revolution – the Grand Duchess and her Prince sat down in the marble ballroom of their St Petersburg palace to spend a day plying needles and strong cotton thread. They sewed her jewels, boxes full of them, into her petticoats; they sewed Fabergé eggs into his trousers and ruby snuffboxes into their jackets; they sewed gold icons into their overcoats – even that diamond-encrusted photograph of the Tsar and Tsarina, heavy cotton stitches looping over priceless stones. Then they dressed themselves in these clothes, fled to Odessa or Sevastopol or some such southern port and clanked aboard a British destroyer bound for Calais and a new life in the West.

Nikolas awoke in buoyant mood. All the next day he reconnoitred and evaluated. This set of gold forks? That cloisonné box? At night, very late, he packed what he'd chosen as his inheritance into two large leather bags. Then he put on his coat, shut the door behind him and – not a backward glance as he walked away – hoisted his suitcases aboard a bus to Geneva airport and set off towards a new life, just as the Grand Duchess and the Prince had done before him.

CHAPTER 6

On Sunday at two o'clock in the afternoon, the Wheelock clan gathered at Beatrice's house for midday dinner in my honour; an assortment of aunts and uncles came too, as well as tiny Fred with his little round nose and his furious face. There was chatter about townspeople interspersed with Canfield's humming and an aggressively plain-spoken meal of fried chicken, mashed potatoes, ice water and apple pie. Beatrice's cook did the kitchen work. Violette dished up. Harry and Fred passed the plates, and the occasion was pleasant enough, I guess, if obedient – and as fiercely respectable as anything my own uncle and aunt could produce.

As the cook cleared away, Beatrice delegated Fred to show me the neighbourhood. He was not pleased at the prospect. Nor was I. I'm fairly tall – as tall as Harry – and I towered over Fred. Looking down on him, my height almost made me dizzy. I didn't know what to say either. Or how to say it. Should I bend down? Would he hear if I didn't? Did it matter? He bristled with anger, porcupine-like, at my side.

After we'd walked a couple of blocks in silence I said to him, 'Is Fred short for Frederick?'

'Fred is short only for Fred, who is very, very short indeed, isn't he?' (Oh God, how could I have used the word *short*?) 'Here I stand. I can do no other: Canfield's childhood fancy brought to life, product of his mad passion to be called Fred himself – and if not Fred, then Harry. Can you imagine Canfield in the grip of a mad passion?'

'Suppose he'd had daughters?' I said, treading as gently as I knew how.

'I'm adopted. Surely you know that – or can guess it.'

'No,' I said. 'Harry didn't say.'

He ground his teeth with rage. 'I'm the shame of the Wheelocks. The marital womb refused to deliver up an heir despite six long years of prayer and a tax-deductible donation to Memorial Hospital. Canfield had to pick up the yellow pages and play Dial-a-Baby like some member of the lower orders. Even so, the poor schmuck took six months to realize his nursery held only the spawn of a teenage whore's night out in a flea-infested jalopy – a primal ooze made up of acne, bubble-gum and a split condom. By this time it was too late. The mutation already bore the most blessed of all names: Fred. When *I* was little, all I wanted was to be called Canfield. *Fred*. Listen to it. *Fred*. It's the dullest sound on earth.'

'Doesn't being so angry all the time tire you? It must take an awful lot of energy.'

He laughed abruptly. 'I'm never tired.'

'If your name were Canfield, you'd be Junior – like Nikolas.'

'Nikolas?'

'Nikolas Strakhan.'

'I can think of worse fates. Junior-that-crook. Rather lively, don't you think? Certainly better than Fred-the-dead. If we turn down this street, I can show you the park Harry used to play in.'

'Didn't you play there too?'

'Sometimes.'

79

We walked towards an outcrop of trees. A slight breeze stirred beneath them, almost enough to dry the sweat that rolled down my back under my shirt. We sat down on a bench beside a path, along which people jogged despite the heat. Plod, plod, plod. Each time they passed us, their pace juddered a little. Plod, plod, hiccup, plod. What a family this was. Nikolas. Canfield with his humming. And Fred, whose fury unnerved even strangers who'd never laid eyes on him before.

'He ran away to London when he was about nineteen, didn't he?' I said. 'Beatrice told me.'

Fred shook his head. 'He was younger than that.'

'Really? Beatrice was so certain.'

'She's getting old.'

'She was very clear about his childhood in Geneva.'

There was a pause. 'We're talking at cross-purposes.'

'Are we?'

'I thought it was the sainted Harry you had in mind.'

'Harry? Harry wouldn't do a thing like that.' It was only later, mulling it over, that I decided I'd missed something in this exchange. 'No, no. I meant Nikolas.'

'I see. Hum. Nikolas interests you.'

'He's unusual.'

'Like me?'

I laughed. 'You certainly are not usual.'

'Are you avoiding me?'

'I'm trying not to.'

'How come you're playing hide-and-seek with a dope like Harry?'

'I want – ' I broke off.

'What?'

'Why can't I have a whole new pattern? Something beautiful and rare? Unalloyed? Unadulterated? Why does everything have to be so tame?'

'Hardly a description of our Harry. I suggest applying to your local fairy godmother with wand and filmy dress.'

'I don't have to go that far, do I? What about a single malt or – let me think – caviar, maybe? I love caviar. What's more pure than caviar? or more real? or wilder, for that matter? I love elvers, *foie gras* – all those rich things – Roman tesserae, Tiffany glass. I'd really like to own a Dürer some day, an original, not just a print or anything, and a couple of – '

'Wand and filmy dress. Definitely. Or rob a bank.'

I laughed again. 'I've never liked filmy dresses.'

We sat in silence for a few minutes, then Fred said, 'What joy we Wheelocks get out of ripping Junior to shreds. Carve up the body. Swig down the blood. Nobody knows any more how much is Canfield's jealous sanctimony and how much is Beatrice's tactical evasion.'

'Is she evasive? Really? She told some amazing stories about Nikolas in Switzerland.'

'He ran away to London.'

'Oh, lucky London! To be first on Nikolas Strakhan's list.'

But, as Fred went on to tell me, Nikolas hadn't chosen London. The airport had chosen it for him. He'd booked a seat on the first plane out of Geneva, any old plane. Who cared where it was going? He landed at Heathrow and entered Britain on a three-month tourist visa.

The time was the early Fifties, and London was just crawling out from under wartime rations. Fenced-off bomb-sites interrupted street after street. The food was terrible. Good liquor was scarce. Women were drab. But a young man on the loose hasn't changed much since biblical times. Eat it, drink it, screw it – whatever it is, as long as it doesn't run away (or run away too vigorously) – fighting, gambling, art, music, theatre: fall asleep exhausted in his tracks, wake up a few hours later ravenous again. Exuberance like this takes money, and Nikolas was the most exuberant of young men.

He sold his Geneva trinkets for a fraction of what they were worth and woke up one morning in the most elegant whore-house in London – right in the heart of Mayfair – hung-over and stone-cold broke. He didn't have a single shilling to put towards his bill.

The windows near the bed he lay in were beautifully proportioned, tall and narrow, not unlike the woman beside him. The room was large, the carpet deep, the mattress wide. He went into the bathroom, sat at the dressing table and studied the matched set of silver dildos – marvels of a bygone age, large and small, plain and fluted. He laid them out according to size and elaboration. He hefted each in his hand; they sparkled in the morning sunlight the way well-polished silver does.

The whore in his bed was even more hung-over than he. She slept on while he dressed and packed the silver in his pockets. Then a chambermaid (who'd taken an hour off from her cleaning duties to share his pleasures of the night before) sneaked him down the service stairs and took him home with her.

The next year in his life calls for, well, a little delicacy. After all, a man must live. With the help of the chambermaid and her family, Nikolas became one of the first of those noble entrepreneurs to exploit the Welfare State in Britain – to spot the flaws in the regulatory system and expose the greed and gullibility of low-ranking civil servants.

He signed on in Westminster and found a large, airy flat; he decorated it himself with the profits from the Mayfair dildos and the beginnings of the clean-lined taste that showed itself to such advantage in Beatrice's house. He placed a discreet notice in the personal columns of the *International Herald Tribune*: 'Count Nikolas Strakhan's Westminster flat' was available to tourists by the week. Meantime, he signed on in Hackney under another name and lived in cheaper rooms there.

In a Hackney pub he met a mercenary in between jobs (much the sort of profession and position he considered himself to be in at the time). The two of them got to talking about the black markets of the world; they weighed each other up, parried a bit, then shook hands on a partnership. The next morning they set out to find Nikolas a passport that wasn't stamped with an out-of-date tourist visa.

The building trade always attracts foreign labour, but no Irishman on the bomb-sites under reconstruction was willing to sell an Irish passport. The mercenary couldn't talk his way past the gates of a Jewish cemetery to look for names of boys who had died as babies. Nikolas tried a hospital for mental defectives with the same aim; he was too distressed by what he saw to take on the identity of any of the inmates. In the end, a singer in an Indian restaurant sold him a Norwegian passport for £20, and a pawnbroker sold him a Lebanese passport for £5.

Nikolas and the mercenary flew to Turkey. They bought fake American jeans there and sold them in Bulgaria. In Bulgaria they bought hashish; they sold it to Swedish dealers. They bought ballbearings in Sweden and sold them in Spain. Spain's aspirin and sulphonamides went to India. And India's religious artefacts took them back to London, where Nikolas married the chambermaid who'd helped him, renounced the Lebanese citizenship that one of his illegal passports conferred on him and became a British citizen (as well as a Swiss one and a Norwegian).

For almost seven years he lived this way, shifting goods from one continent to another, sometimes with the mercenary's help, sometimes without it. But the life, as Fred described it, lacked elegance. It wasn't conducive to the making of music either, and Nikolas, despite his love of money and pleasure, never let go of the thought that he was first and foremost a musician.

CHAPTER 7

Nikolas's sense of vocation was so strong that when he thought of his childhood back in Switzerland, which wasn't often, he thought mainly of Teresa Lopez-Vega. Not that he felt guilt about her. Why should he? He'd conquered her, and a victor who regrets his victory is a fool. In his own way, though, he communed with her. Sometimes, just to twit her ghost, he took on a job playing the piano in a restaurant. To his annoyance he couldn't bring himself to play in hotel lobbies; so from time to time he hired himself out to a small, very exclusive establishment in Knightsbridge called Bressingham's.

The food at Bressingham's was English nursery food at its worst, as awful as the food in the House of Lords; and it catered to so elevated a clientèle that its manager, whose name was Thomas Englewood-Bone, received a knighthood for services to the crown. His taste in decor was legendary. Every detail of the room complimented every other detail, the cut glass, the linen, the china, the flowers on the tables – even the pianist. All were of a piece. Now imagine a palate as exquisite as this: whenever Nikolas was to play, Sir Thomas ordered spiderworts to decorate the tables, and yet Nikolas had not said a single word to him about the Strakhan heritage.

Bressingham's was spacious, the ceilings high, the floor a Roman mosaic. Large windows along one side looked out into a private park. One spring lunchtime, as soon as the crystal flutes on the tables held their fresh spiderworts – early, maybe twelve o'clock – the *maître d'hôtel* showed two women to a table. The younger of the two was very young, eighteen maybe, nineteen at the most. Nikolas couldn't have said why he noticed her. There wasn't anything to notice.

She was tall, slender, as drab as any – indistinguishable from many other well-bred English girls – nose a little large, legs a little thin, chest a little flat. She conducted herself with a finishing school's cold obedience; but her shoulders sagged somewhat, which touched him (although again he could not have said why), and she only picked at the plate in front of her. Whatever else she was or wasn't, she was plainly bored out of her wits.

He woke the next morning remembering her ears, which were small and delicately shaped, and thinking how rare it is to find really nice ears. Most are too large or too convoluted or too flared. But why should such thoughts make him uneasy? Why should they plague him throughout the day? There was a queer ebb tide in his chest, a weighted-down feeling – compression or stricture, odd, unpleasant – a little worrying. Toward evening he went to the chemist for a bottle of aspirin. He swallowed a tablet, then another. They did no good. For the whole of the next week the girl occupied his mind so relentlessly that when he saw her coming out of Harrods, at first he assumed she was only a figment of his imagination.

Knightsbridge was wet. The forecast was gloomy. The sun's appearance at just that moment was unexpected, a fluke, unlikely to last. He charged after her, so frantic to reach her that he almost knocked her over. She staggered a little and dropped her packages.

'Oh God, I'm so – ' He stopped short, retrieved the packages and began again, covered in confusion (which was very unlike him). 'Are you all right? Tell me you're all right. I can't bear it if you aren't. I hate people who are clumsy.'

'Of course I'm all right,' she said. He could see that she didn't recognize him. She reached for her packages. He clasped them tighter. It wasn't provocation. It wasn't teasing. He just couldn't bear to let her go. 'You *are* going to steal from me, aren't you?' She squinted to get him into focus the way near-sighted people do. 'What a bore.'

Nikolas was not extraordinary in repose. He didn't have the translucent beauty that Catherine the Great saw in his ancestor, the garden serf she turned into a count. He didn't have the Merchants' American beauty either, despite his wide-spread eyes. But a woman sees in a man what she wants to see (and vice-versa, of course). Besides, repose is nothing. It's movement that counts. He struggled with the feelings that had dogged him all week – that threatened to overwhelm him now – and, oh dear, what a spectacle laid itself before this girl.

Was it insolence she saw? Was it hilarity? Was it both? Nikolas had one of those faces where clowns cavort and acrobats fly, where the action is in thrall to animal enchantments – to dancing bears and prancing stallions, to lions and tigers that growl in cages – a lusty, insouciant, dangerous face that promised secret pleasures never imagined before. But hang on a minute. What's this? Is it – could it be? – a streak of pain? some inexplicable lapse in the gaiety? No, no, ladies and gentlemen. We have true theatre here. What entertainment really works – what magic is complete – without a few drops of the beast's blood?

The girl laughed in delight. 'You do appeal to me,' she said.

'I know,' said Nikolas happily. 'I appeal to everybody. Except – you know, it's the funniest thing – my cousin Canfield doesn't like me. Or rather he didn't, but that was long ago. He must have changed his mind by now. Don't you agree?'

'You're American.'

'Kind of.'

She wore a tweed skirt and a string of pearls. The Sixties hadn't properly begun; the pall of the late Fifties endured. The 'Quiet Generation'. That's what they called it in America. A lot of fear, not much spirit, many shrugged shoulders – oh, why bother? – an edgy, depressing time with the world's powers in a monumental stand-off. Good girls still dressed like that.

'What does "kind of " mean?' she said.

His smile shifted with every flicker in her face. 'It's kind of complicated.'

'Mysterious?'

'Very mysterious.'

'A Cold War agent? CIA? Something exciting?'

'Cold War? What's that? Is there a war on?'

She laughed again. 'Don't you ever say what's expected of you?'

'Why are you questioning me about wars? I don't want to talk about wars.' His very eagerness to please her made him sound testy, and yet he did show the most unexpected blind spots. Or was he pretending again? Just trying to throw her off balance? How could a black marketeer of the time not know about the Cold War? How could *anybody* not know?

'Oh, don't turn away,' he went on. 'I'm not going to steal from you – at least not yet. I'll talk about anything you want. Is there some particular war I ought to be doing something about?'

But the delight was gone from her face; the boredom had settled back into it – how crucial this girl's boredom was to Nikolas's life – and her voice took on an arrogant whip. 'It's asinine to pretend you don't know what's going on in the world. Now, if you don't mind, I need to get home.'

'You're irritated because I don't know about some war?' He refused to believe he could lose her like this. He'd just found her. How could he lose her? 'I'll talk about any war you like. I'll learn everything there is to learn about it. I'll sign up to fight in it. No, I won't. But I'll talk about it – I promise – or about anything else you want. I'll be a CIA agent if that's what pleases you. I could manage that. In fact, I think I'd make quite a good CIA agent. It's just – How can you look at me like that?'

She reached again for her packages. Again he held them back. 'I never read newspapers,' he went on. 'They're so dull. Don't frown. Please don't. I can't – ' Nikolas never tripped over words, and here he was, breaking up sentence after sentence, scrambling on half out of breath. 'What kind of war is a cold war anyhow?'

'I don't understand the intricacies of politics.'

'You sound as though you do. You certainly know more than I do. You sound as though you have a lot of opinions too. Can't you express one?'

'No.'

'No?'

'I've been expensively trained to have no opinions. I thought you said you weren't going to steal from me.'

'I didn't promise, did I? If stealing's what you want, I'll do it at once. What have you got here? Anything I might use?'

'Knickers and scent. You could get a refund on them. The bills of sale are inside.'

The sky clouded as abruptly as it had cleared only moments before; a smattering of rain struck the package wrappers even here, even well beneath the awning. The street was very crowded. People jostled, fought each other for taxis, pushed empty-handed past Nikolas and the girl into Harrods, staggered out of Harrods loaded down. 'I saw you a week ago,' he said. 'I haven't been able to think about anything else since. I can't understand why. You're not very pretty.'

'I don't have to be pretty. I'm rich. Look here, will you please give me back – '

'Couldn't we have coffee together? Why not? I mean, there

can't be any harm in a cup of coffee. You'd feel safe in Harrods, wouldn't you? Even with me? Or Harvey Nichols? We can wait out the rain together. Maybe I can figure out why – '

'Are you trying to pick me up?'

'I guess that's what it amounts to,' he said helplessly. She smiled an abrupt smile. She wasn't a person who smiled much, and the very rarity of the expression gave her face a spring freshness much like the rain that swept in under the awning to spatter her packages again.

'Is this how one is usually picked up?'

'No.'

'You're something of an expert?'

'Yes.'

She cocked her head to one side. 'I've never liked Harrods much. Or Harvey Nichols. Isn't that odd? All I do with my time in London is shop and go out to lunch. I don't actually like shopping either. There's a place in Basil Street that claims it has the best French coffee in London.'

They ran together, he with her packages, she with her raincoat flying. Taxis screeched to a halt as they crossed to Basil Street; ladies with jostled boxes stared indignantly (and also perhaps indulgently) after them. They found a staircase down into a restaurant – small, tight, with dark walls, candles in wine bottles and a smell of garlic. They sat at a corner table, stowed the packages beside them; Nikolas ordered two coffees in his flawless French, offered her a cigarette (which she refused), lit one himself.

'Americans don't speak French,' she said.

'I grew up in Switzerland. Would you like something to eat?'

She shook her head. 'What are you doing in London?'

'I'm a musician.'

'I'm not very musical.' On the street, she'd been so surprised by the movement in his face that she hadn't really noticed his eyes. Strakhan eyes are blue, but they shift to purple if you look into them long enough. (These are the Tradescant colours, you see.) There's a wash of clarity followed by opalescence. Perhaps it was just a trick of the light, she thought. Candles flicker so. The smoke from Nikolas's cigarette wafted, feathered, curled, swirled in the light from this one. The girl was sensitive to smells; if you've never smoked, there's a special sweetness to tobacco. Here, in this place, it caught something else, reminded her of something. She leaned closer to him to see if she could identify it – and felt suddenly short of breath.

That was when she looked down to check her watch; she'd often thought (not without reason either) that her control over herself was close to absolute.

'You don't have to go so soon, do you?' he said. 'Please don't say you have to go. We've just got here.'

'No.'

'No what?'

'I don't have to go.'

But she kept her head bowed. All he could see of her was the tip of her nose and the parting in her hair: a sharp parting, fine hair, light in colour, curled in a pageboy the way girls curled it then, not distinguished in any way he could think of, and yet – He reached out to touch her hand, but withdrew before he reached her.

She shook her head wretchedly.

'Something's the matter, isn't it?' he said.

'I don't know what to do.'

'We could have lunch. If there's no harm in coffee, there couldn't be much harm in lunch. The board over there says they make bread themselves – did you see it? – and the fish sounds good.'

'I'm not talking about food.'

'I know.'

'Nobody's ever tried to pick me up before.'

'They're mad.'

'But you said yourself – '

'I deny everything.'

She studied his eyes again – and winced.

Nikolas was quite taken aback. People didn't wince at him. They just didn't. 'What's the matter?' he said. 'Do you see something you don't like?'

She didn't answer at once. She couldn't. She bowed her head again, took in her breath, then said, 'I quite like being picked up.'

'But you wince at the first guy who does it.'

'Sorry.'

'There's nothing to be sorry for. You're not going to make a habit of it, are you?'

'Wincing?'

'Getting yourself picked up.'

'It's too early to say.'

A waiter brought coffee cups, filter pot, spoons, napkins. The girl watched him, but she didn't see him. He set down a small plate of chocolates in multi-coloured wrappers – red, green, silver, gold – but she plainly didn't see these either. Nikolas studied this queer, attentive inattention as eagerly as he'd studied the chessboard when Teresa Lopez-Vega had first brought it to him. He nudged the girl's coffee cup a little closer to her.

'When I was little,' he said, trying (and failing) to catch her eye. 'I used to think that if I felt a chocolate in a wrapper, if I really, really concentrated, I could touch the taste – know what it was – before I took off the foil.' He held up one of the chocolates. 'What do you think? Sweet and bitter both. That's my guess. Maybe a tang of orange.' She glanced at him quickly, glanced away. 'Sugar?' he said.

'Sugar?'

'In your coffee.'

'Coffee?'

'That's the wet stuff in the cup in front of you.'

'Oh, of course. Sorry.'

'What for this time?'

'I'm no longer – ' She broke off.

'Please tell me.'

'I don't know how to start.'

'The direct approach sometimes works.'

'I'm in love.'

The pain he felt was so sudden, so unexpected, that he dropped his cup. Coffee splashed everywhere, on the table, on the floor, on his clothes, on hers. The candle crashed to the floor in its bottle. He leaped to his feet. Two waiters came running.

'I might not see you again. If I don't tell you now, I'll probably never have the chance,' the girl said, still seated, uninterested in the fuss around her, her brow furrowed, concentrating, a little wan and yet a little wry.

Nikolas was too hurt – too shocked by his own intensity – to catch her meaning. 'What's that got to do with anything?' he said.

'Oh, do sit down.'

'Why should I?'

'I've never been in love before. If you leave now, I won't even know how to start looking for you.'

He caught his breath. 'You mean me?' he said. She looked up at him. 'Are you sure you mean me? You've just met me. I've got coffee all down my shirt.'

She studied him as she had before, and this time the flinch that followed was visceral. 'It's not a particularly pleasant sensation, is it?'

'What? A wet shirt?'

'Love.'

'Do you talk like this to lots of guys? Don't answer that. I don't want to know. When did this happen?'

She tore her gaze from him – and checked her watch. 'Just under five minutes ago.'

'As long as that?'

She'd known as soon as she caught the scent of azaleas: that heady mixture of musk and jasmine – not the red azaleas or the pink ones, but the yellow ones, the wild ones, the ones that hint at the dark side of spring, at the power it carries alongside its freshness. She'd noticed the smell first – remarked it in her diary first – when she was only ten years old. She'd waited for it each year since, not aware she was waiting for it until it came to her. This time it had come right through a swirl of tobacco smoke at a restaurant table, not an azalea in sight. She'd known at once.

Of course, what she saw in him was only what she wanted to see. Maybe it was there. Maybe it wasn't. (All lovers are the same.) She was so bored, poor Priscilla. She'd been bored every day of her life – until this day.

'Suppose you fall out of love just as abruptly,' he said. 'If you've never done it before, how can you know? No, no, don't look at your watch again. Please don't. There's no sign of a change yet, is there?'

'I think it's getting worse.'

'We must eat,' Nikolas said. 'I'll order for two. Whatever you don't eat, I will.'

One of the waiters got off the floor, tucked his wet cloth under his arm, took out his order book. Nikolas ordered everything. The whole menu. Fish, meat, vegetables, salad, cheese, a bottle of Pouilly Fumé, a bottle of claret.

'I'm not going to like you fat,' the girl said. This may not sound like a prophetic comment, but it was to have serious – critical, crucial – repercussions for Nikolas in years to come.

'Why not?' he said. 'Think of it: there'd be more of me.'

'Butchers' wives are fat.'

'Shame on you. Snobbery is such a public vice.'

'Is that what it is? just snobbery?'

'You can always get yourself a dog,' said Nikolas.

'A dog?'

'You can feed it what you want.'

93

'Sorry,' she said. 'I didn't mean – '

'Why do you keep saying you're sorry? That's the third time so far. You British are the least sorry of any people I know. I'll bet you've never felt sorry for anybody in your life.' The waiter appeared with the bottle of white wine and poured a little for Nikolas, who motioned him to fill both glasses.

'Do you really think that?' she said.

'What?'

'That I've never felt sorry for anybody?'

'I don't know your name,' he said then.

'Priscilla.'

'Priscilla what?'

'Priscilla Carmarth.'

'Welsh?'

'More than that actually.' She glanced down shyly, glanced up again. 'You're American. You wouldn't understand. I'm a Countess in my own right.'

He smiled. 'Well, well, well. We're quite something, aren't we? Butchers' wives and Countesses. How about that?'

'I thought a title might impress you.'

'Not unless it means money. I like money.'

'I've already told you I'm rich.'

'Suppose that's all I want?'

'I enjoy buying my own luxuries. How do you feel about marriage?'

He laughed, enchanted with her, enchanted with himself. 'This is to be an outright purchase?'

'Yes.'

'Maybe I'm not for sale.'

'All men are for sale.'

'You shouldn't say things like that to strangers. I'm going to tell your mother on you. I bet she doesn't know what wicked thoughts you think. Besides, I just might up my price. Where does this fortune of yours come from?'

'Timber.'

'It's all yours? the timber?'

'It will be.'

'"It will be"? What good is a Countess in her own right if she doesn't own her own timber? There must be guardians and trusts to protect people like you from people like me. I don't know that I can sell myself on such an unpromising promissory note. This is an important point, you understand. I'll have to consult my accountant.'

The waiter brought plates of seafood – prawns, sole, crab. The restaurant filled with customers and noise. 'What kind of musician uses an accountant?' she said.

Nikolas tipped his glass at her, looked at her over its rim. 'I'm a businessman.'

'I see,' she said.

Priscilla had always thought of herself as a simple person. She was wrong of course – something she was soon to find out – but it's what she thought at the time. Make a request, and she would try to fulfil it. After all, if this boy asks something, it's because he needs to know. Why else would he ask? Why should she deny a need if there is no reason to? What is the point in subterfuge?

'My father broke his neck when I was a baby,' she said. 'He lay in a bath chair for five years. One day he wasn't there any more. It was several years after that before I realized where he'd got to and several more before I thought to ask why solicitors addressed me as Lady Carmarth. Because I was so young when he died . . .'

The mouth: he liked her mouth particularly. The skin was fine too; English skin so often is. But as he watched her, he decided she'd bought that calm of hers – and that deceptive simplicity – at a very high price. Knowing how much he'd already upset it gave him the strangest amalgam of sensations. Pride of capture, a child's delight in a new toy, raw lust – all those things – but something else too. Could it be? just the faintest salt of foreboding?

'I take control of everything when I come of age in two years time,' she was saying. 'Are you a gigolo as well?'

'As well as what?'

'As well as a musician and a businessman.'

'Would you be horrified if I were?'

'No.'

'You don't even know my name,' he said.

'No.'

'Aren't you interested?'

'Not particularly, but I suppose it's best if you tell me. What is it?'

'Nikolas Strakhan.'

She turned her head aside. In profile her nose had the elegance of a saint on one of his father's icons. He reached out and touched the pink of her cheek. She turned back in alarm. He dropped his fingers to her neck and gently traced its curve. She was holding herself rigid.

'I've never known anybody called Strakhan,' she said.

'What's your mother going to say about all this?'

'She'll fight me. She's one of my guardians unfortunately. But my grandfather presents no problem, and Mr Braithwaite – '

'Mr Braithwaite?'

'The family solicitor. He's quite clever enough to understand that the future lies with me – not my mother.'

'Any other family members to worry about?'

'The only person who matters is my grandfather, and he never objects to what I do.'

The waiter carried away their fish plates and brought plates of rare beef; Nikolas spooned out vegetables for them both, cabbage, carrots, beans. 'Eat, Countess of Carmarth,' he said, his mouth full. He stopped mid-chew, scanned her shoulders, her cardigan, the girlish strand of pearls that overlay it, the discreet chest that it covered – and reached out a forkful of beef to her. 'Come on. Eat.'

'I don't like rare beef.'

'Then you've got to learn to like it quickly. You're going to need it.'

'What for?'

'Fucking takes energy.'

This time the alarm drained the colour from her face. 'Is that what comes next? So soon? Is this why I feel the way I do? I feel very odd. I've never felt anything like it before. I've never been to bed with anybody.'

'It's about time you began,' he said. 'How old did you say you were?'

'Nineteen.'

'Nineteen is very old.'

'Is it? I thought – '

'There's not a moment to lose. Give me your hand.'

'Now?'

'Now.'

'Here?'

'Here.'

'You're still eating.'

'I'd always be eating if I could manage it. Come on, come on. I want the hand. I need it. Give it to me.'

'What for?'

'It's all I can take on of your body until I finish my lunch.'

She picked up a bite of the cabbage he'd served her, let it dangle limply on her fork, shook it angrily for no reason she could think of and put it back on the plate. 'I'm afraid to touch you,' she said.

He set down his knife and fork, put out the candle with his fingers – their corner of the restaurant darkened so much she could hardly see the plate in front of her – and leaned back in his chair. 'Touch me anywhere,' he said softly.

97

'I can't.'

'Why?'

'I don't know.'

But as Señora Lopez-Vega had noted, Nikolas was gifted at what goes on under cherry trees in spring. He took Priscilla home to his flat near Hackney Downs to enjoy her as he'd enjoyed the chocolate in the café, a caress of the shape – every nook and cranny – to guess the taste before he took it, both bitter and sweet before he ate. Even so, how could she (who knew so little) have guessed that it was her snippet of cabbage that told the truth? that tells the truth for practically every beginner? Who can forget that helpless flopping about on the prong of an angry fork? Priscilla had rather thought, not thinking much, that people just lay together, a nice, quiet communion of some sort. This was, after all, as much the end of the Fifties as the beginning of the Sixties – still a prudish age (not like us). Where had all the thrashing come from? How could you get the rhythm of it even if you could put up with the pain? What twisted mind could have decided that love consisted of shoving one hank of raw meat into another?

Once she was initiated, though, in the days that followed her first experience – once she learned to keep up with the moves of this fascinating new appetite – she found herself as greedy for Nikolas's flesh as he was for hers, as they both were for lunchtime's prawns and sole and rare beef that gave them the strength to repeat the trick in bedrooms of hotels when they couldn't wait to reach his flat and in parks when they couldn't wait to reach a hotel.

It was Nikolas who encountered complications. He needed no introduction to screwing for pleasure (or for profit either), but his heart was virgin territory. Nobody outside his mother and his nanny had ever touched it, much less invaded it. This is to say that the passion he felt for Priscilla, for the shock of her direct response to things as well as for her slender body and the

exhilaration that underlay its calm and its profound boredom —
This passion was no less of an explosion inside him than that
first explosion had been, the one that had come when he was
eleven years old, when he'd first heard Señora Lopez-Vega play.
Here with Priscilla was the same boil up of emotion, the same
fierce light — and he knew again with her, as he'd known before
with Señora Lopez-Vega, that what had been real to him before,
ceased to be real for him now.

What had been meaningful before, now lost its meaning.

However adept at secrets men and women become later on in
life, it's hard to hide a first real happiness from the world. See
that roseate glow in Priscilla's cheeks? See that swing to her
walk as she rounds the side table, heading for kidneys and eggs
at breakfast? See the way she moves her shoulders as she reaches
for her plate? As though her own skin feels good to her? Here
was a girl who only ten days ago was sunk so deep in boredom
that nobody had a qualm about her sense of duty. Now look at
her. That smile — Good God, could it be? Our Priscilla? A saucy
smile? Her mother watched her with a grim eye.

Priscilla Griffiths, Countess of Carmarth, was so eminent a
personage that when she was a pale little girl of twelve she'd
attended the Queen's coronation as Hereditary Lord High
Constable of Wales. I kid you not. You can look it up for
yourself in *Debrett's*. She wore ceremonial robes and a coronet;
she carried a spike-headed mace and took precedence over
dukes and every other hereditary honour after the blood royal.
For a young woman in Priscilla's position, the pool of eligible
young men is small.

Her mother knew each and every one of these eligible young
men; she knew their parents and their backgrounds. Priscilla was
already engaged to one of them — something she'd neglected to
tell Nikolas — and this one was back in Wales. The wedding was
planned for the following year to coincide with her twentieth

birthday; her fiancé's land marched alongside hers, as they say in such circles. They'd known each other since they were children, and his water rights married to her timber would make them one of the richest and most powerful couples in the United Kingdom.

But the rifts Nikolas had caused in Priscilla's façade were so transparent that her mother had contacted a private detective less than a week after the affair began; an hour's investigation had uncovered Nikolas, no longer at the piano of Bressingham's (he rarely played more than a few days at a time), but haggling over a shipment of raw opium from Laos in some low London dockyard. Another three days and the detective knew Nikolas's background. Priscilla's mother never acted rashly. She had a straight back and the haughty nose that Priscilla had inherited from her. Her name was Eugenia – this Dowager Countess – and she waited while her daughter filled her plate with kidneys and eggs.

The estates of the Earl of Carmarth, Priscilla's dead father, were in such a remote, inaccessible area of Wales, and their produce was so important to the export markets of the United Kingdom, that two world wars had only enriched the family. At a time when most aristocrats were forced to exercise a measure of the resilience that always characterizes the poor of a nation – and its criminal classes – the Griffiths family of Carmarth remained feudally rich. The Earl himself had been a weak man, charming in a boyish sort of way, perhaps a little stupid. But he'd more than compensated for these shortcomings by marrying Eugenia – who had a cool, clear mind for finance – and by managing to die before the punitive postwar estate duties came into effect. Carmarth House in Hamilton Place was one of the few grand London houses left that kept a fully occupied servants' quarters and an Edwardian breakfast steaming every morning on a massively ugly sideboard.

'Your appetite has improved, Priscilla,' Eugenia said.

'Mm,' said Priscilla.

'You've always hated kidneys.'

'Have I?'

'A month ago you told me you hated eggs.'

'Really?'

'We must talk.'

'Mmm.' Another of those smiles had skittered across Priscilla's mouth.

'Aren't you curious?' her mother said.

'Curious?'

'Don't you want to know what I have to say to you?'

'Do you want to talk? Is that what you're saying?'

'Precisely.'

'Sorry. I'm somewhat preoccupied. What do you want to talk about?' She unfurled her napkin with a snap that made her mother cringe.

Eugenia's grim face grew grimmer. 'Come to me after breakfast. We'll talk in the library.'

'I have an engagement this morning.'

'Cancel it.'

'What?'

'I said, cancel it.'

'Oh, I'd rather not. It's quite important. It's with, er, the dentist.'

'Nonsense. You're going to see Nikolas Strakhan, aren't you?'

'Oh,' said Priscilla.

'Just so,' said her mother.

They ate their breakfast in silence. Half an hour later, Priscilla paced while her mother watched, sitting at a huge desk. The library is where Eugenia kept the books for the estate. It was a dark, forbidding room despite large windows overlooking the trees of Park Lane and Hyde Park beyond. Ancient books on property law lined one wall; dark panelling on the other walls had grown darker with age and darker still with generations of varnish. Dour, gilt-framed paintings added to the gloom.

'I love him,' Priscilla said.

'That is immaterial.'

'I'll always love him.'

'How tiresome you are. How much has he taken you for?'

'That, I believe, is my business.'

'You are nineteen years old, and you have a position to think of. What you do is my business as well as yours. It's your family's business. It's your country's business. What about Edward?' Edward Waltham was Priscilla's fiancé.

'He knows all about Eddie. I've told him everything.'

'I don't mean Nikolas Strakhan, you silly girl. I mean Edward. Have you said anything to Edward?'

Priscilla was so amazed at herself that she missed the question. She'd just lied to her mother: she hadn't told Nikolas about Eddie. She hadn't dared. Suppose Nikolas didn't give a damn? How could she bear it? Which is to say that she'd lied to Nikolas too. And yet she never lied. Not to anybody. Why bother? Life was so boring. How could one work up enough interest in anything to lie about it? Yet here were two lies. Both at once. On the same subject. What could it mean? She felt a sudden zest, an abrupt power as though she'd taken on a lungful of pure oxygen. Was this freedom? Is that what it was? No wonder people fought for it.

'Answer me, Priscilla,' said her mother.

'What?'

'I asked you if you'd talked to Edward, and I would very much like an answer.'

'Eddie? How could I? I haven't seen him in weeks.'

'No letters?'

'Why would I write to Eddie?'

'Well, thank God for that.'

'I'm going to marry Nikolas. It's all settled.'

'You know he stole from his father? Sit *down*, Priscilla.'

'Nikolas did?' Priscilla said in delight, and the pink in her cheeks grew pinker. She continued to pace. 'Really? I know he's capable of almost anything, but he didn't tell me that.'

'He doesn't have very much money.'

'Is that what your reports say?'

'You know how he earns what he does earn?'

'He's a musician.'

'A musician. Is he indeed? He plays in Bressingham's.'

Priscilla paused, leaned her head against the window frame and stared out at the gardens beyond. 'He rather enjoys that.'

'He deals – let me put this at its least offensive – in black market items.'

'He must be quite good at smuggling,' Priscilla said dreamily. 'It's the sort of thing he'd do well. I wouldn't be surprised if he has more money than he lets on, especially if your detective only tracked down recorded earnings. I'd imagine the black market has ups and downs like any other business. Don't you think? A lot of money one day. None the next.'

The trees along Park Lane and in Hyde Park were already in full leaf. The library was very cold even so; because it was officially summer, the single bar electric fire in the elaborate marble fireplace remained resolutely switched off.

'You must realize that the affair has got to stop,' Eugenia said.

'He'll be a great pianist one day.'

'How would you know? You're practically tone deaf.'

'Well, then, one day he'll be the greatest villain in London. I don't care what he does. It can be everything or nothing – as long as he's with me.'

'He's foreign,' said Eugenia, trotting out this silliest of arguments, regretting it at once too – Priscilla only shrugged – knowing that now she had no choice but to use the heavy artillery.

Beyond the window, the leaves of the trees swayed in that glorious wave motion that communicates itself – who knows how? – from leaf to leaf, so that when one frond of leaves is in, another is out, in and out, in and out: a gentle insistence that seemed to Priscilla to go to the heart of the plant, to the trunk, to the very sap inside. Nikolas was waiting for her in his flat right now. Right this minute.

'You need my consent to marry,' Eugenia said. 'I do not give it.'

Priscilla glanced at her mother, glanced away, began to pace again, said nothing.

Eugenia said, 'A misalliance of this order will kill your grandfather. Have you thought about him? Have you thought about anybody but yourself? Do sit down, Priscilla. Please. I can see there's no point in protecting you any longer. Your grandfather is dying. I will not have his last days ruined by some irresponsible whim of yours.'

Priscilla stopped her pacing to study her mother. They were too alike to get on easily. What this meant in practice is that there was very little depth in their relationship. They negotiated rather than talked, mediated rather than discussed. They were good at these techniques too, both of them, although Eugenia was more practised; also, she'd prepared her case this morning: Priscilla adored her grandfather. He was one of those irascible, self-centred, self-indulgent, Englishmen – Welshmen, I guess, although I can't see the difference myself – now so stooped that his belt came up to just beneath his chin when he sat.

'I don't know whether to believe you or not,' Priscilla said.

'Cancer of the prostate. It was diagnosed six months ago. He won't go on long.'

Priscilla sat down slowly. 'Is this true?'

'I'm afraid it is.'

'Who says so?'

'Who do you think, Priscilla? His doctors, of course.'

'Dr Tuttle?'

'Yes, yes. And Mr Northcote too.'

'Mr Northcote?'

'The consultant. We've had several consultants in. They all agree. There is no doubt whatever.'

'Why didn't you tell me?'

'He didn't want me to. He's ashamed.'

Priscilla looked out at the tree again. Its leaves were still now. 'I don't know what a prostate is.'

'Some part of the male equipment.'

'I see.'

'If I had other children – or he had other grandchildren – their presence might mitigate your selfishness. As it is, I simply cannot allow you to destroy what little pleasure is left to him.'

'He doesn't like Edward very much.'

'He wants you settled. You have to give up this young man. It's as simple as that. You're not only causing pain to somebody who's already in pain, you're doing so by making a complete fool of yourself and your family. I can't allow it.'

In a properly ordered society, somebody like Priscilla would have been preparing for a university career, history perhaps or chemistry – she'd been good at chemistry for the short period she'd been allowed to study it. Or maybe finance like her mother; she had her mother's cool, clear mind. Why a brain like hers had to be tossed away on an idiot like Eddie Waltham is one of the mysteries of the age. Another mystery is why, until this very moment, she hadn't resented it.

On the trip to Nikolas's flat, she sat on the edge of her seat, hands twisted in her lap, and railed against the strictures that held her. As soon as the taxi stopped, she threw open the door and ran into the building, which was squashed between a cheap dress shop and a hairdresser's not far from Hackney Downs. She scrambled up the narrow staircase, so preoccupied that she tripped twice and skinned her knee, so preoccupied that she failed to experience even the faintest of flutters at going into this most deliciously low of places.

'Bed at once,' she said, burying herself in Nikolas's arms as soon as he opened the door.

But things were not as they had been.

This flat was as light as her mother's library was dark, only one room, not small, but noisy from the street below. White walls, raw wood floor, skylight, mirrors – black grand piano, to be sure, but shiny black and with a light-coloured shawl thrown over it. White duvet on the bed, legacy of a childhood in Switzerland. Oh, bed of beds, that had seen such afternoons as any girl would dream of.

But Nikolas did not rush her there as he usually did, tearing at her clothes while she tore at his. He stood still and held her to him, just stood, the front door open beyond them. She could feel him tremble.

'What is it, Nikolas? What's the matter?'

'Don't speak.'

'But – '

'Hush.'

'You're hurting me,' she said in surprise.

'I know.'

Hurting her? Of course he was hurting her. Who isn't half-mad when the trap is absolute? Wolves gnaw off their own legs to escape. Wildebeest run until their hearts burst. Priscilla was so slender, so small-boned in his arms that he could crush the life out of her if he wanted to. All he had to do was tighten his grasp until her breath stopped and then, maybe then –

'I don't – ' he began. But there seemed to be something in the way of his own breathing – a cough, a sob, something.

'You're bruising my ribs,' she said.

'Good.'

But he released her a little so he could stroke her back (he could feel the knobbles of her spine) – so he could hold her out from him and shake her gently, his hands enclosing her shoulders.

'No,' he said. 'No.'

'What are you talking about?'

'No bed.'

'Nikolas, I need – '

'No.'

'Why?'

'You've got to go home. Now.'

And yet he didn't release her. He couldn't. Nor could she shake herself loose from his eyes. She stared into them as though the answer to it all lay there. The dark ring around the iris that intensified the blue – or was it purple? – the way kohl intensifies a woman's eye: what secret was not to be found there? She could see the window behind her reflected in his pupils. She could see the buildings in the street beyond the window – even the sky above it.

'I agree with your mother,' he said.

'Mother?'

'This has got to stop.'

'She talked to you? How dare she? She didn't tell – '

He shook her again, as gently as before. 'It's not just her. It's me too.'

'Why are there tears in your eyes then? Those are tears, aren't they? You can't mean it. I know you don't. Why are you crying?'

'Hay fever.'

'Hay fever?'

'Don't you follow the ragweed counts in the newspapers?'

But the pain in his face, playing out some elaborate tug-of-war with the ragweed count in newspapers (that he so often insisted he never read): this turmoil so moved her that she couldn't speak. He pushed back a stray lock of her hair, touched her cheek, her neck, then pushed back the lock of hair again even though it showed not the slightest hint of rebellion.

'I thought you were for sale,' she said. 'I thought I'd done the buying.'

'I haven't noticed any money changing hands.'

'Nothing on credit? Not even for valued customers?'

'Handing out credit is no way to run a business.'

'Business after.'

'You've got it wrong. Business before.'

She wrenched her gaze from his, sat down on the bed, opened her purse, took out a chequebook, scribbled, handed him a cheque.

He glanced at it. 'Not enough.'

'Enough for what?'

'To get to Italy.'

Priscilla, already drowning in love, sank at once to one of love's abyssal plains, where no light penetrates and the oxygen is rare. She studied his face for clues, but this time she found none. Was it anxiety she saw? doubt? Was it contempt? certainty? shame? pity? Was it all of these?

'Don't say that,' she said.

'What do you want me to say? You want me to lie to you?'

'What I don't understand is why you *aren't* lying to me.'

'Maybe I am.'

'You don't lie this badly.'

'I can find what I want in Italy.'

'Nikolas, this cheque will get you anywhere you want to go. You can go to Australia. You can go to Japan or the Philippines or Guam. Why do you need more?' What else was she to say? to do? She figured – he was so contrary – that money to go abroad would keep him in London. And yet –

'Well, well, so we come to a mean streak, do we? You want an accounting? penny by penny? I'm going to have to stay somewhere. I'm going to have to eat. Not everybody can rely on Daddy's Welsh timber.'

'You're determined to hurt me one way or the other, aren't you?'

'Nothing personal. Make out the cheque to "Cash".'

'No.'

'No?'

'For cash I must sample the product in advance.'

And then? Sweaty heave? Smack of meat? Oh, dear, how dreary it sounds. So let me tell you what it feels like instead: sprinkle iron filings on a piece of paper. There's random scatter. Now bring a magnet up from the underside. Whoosh: the filings swoop into a pattern. It's like a flock of swifts caught in an updraught, beating their wings as they go; it's a shoal of fish that scent a predator. There's a shock sunburst that arcs from north magnetic pole to south, ties positive to negative, links together what cannot be united by any force known to physics. Sex is the very stuff of life. This is what it's all about. The rest is cobwebs, apple sauce, marking time.

Later, lying tangled in the duvet with him, drowsing, she said, 'Why don't you use your title?'

'I don't have a title.'

'My mother – The detective told her. It would be easier to get money from people if you used your title.'

'It's too easy already.' He turned his head away from her.

'Nikolas?' she said. He said nothing. 'Nikolas?' she said again, and when again he did not respond, she rose on her elbow and leaned over him. 'Speak to me.'

'Even I have my principles.'

'I don't believe it.' When he said no more, she reached out and turned his face towards her, held it there in both her hands. 'Is this really true? Are you a communist or an anarchist or something? It doesn't sound like you.'

'How would you know?'

'I have ownership rights.'

He shook her hands from his face and turned his head away from her again. 'What I am is none of your business.'

'You're actually quite annoyed with me, aren't you? Why? What have I done?'

He sighed angrily but said nothing.

'I think I have a right to know how I've affronted you,' she said.

He sat up abruptly then, his naked back to her, the muscles in it taut, sinuous, as angry as his sigh had been.

'Nikolas?' she persisted. 'It's not like you to be as unfair as this.'

'You fail to understand what matters to me.'

'I thought what mattered to you was money.'

He said nothing.

'There's more than money?' she pressed. Still he said nothing. 'What could it be?'

'*I am a musician.*' He swung around to face her, and the strength of his feeling – the ferocious upset in it – glowed in his cheeks, brightened the whites of his eyes, chased itself this way and that across his face.

'Of course, you're a musician. You're the most gifted person I know.'

'What do you know about talent?'

'I mean it, Nikolas. I do.'

'What *could* you know? Look at the self-obsessed, attenuated, decadent people you come from. You're bored to death, the lot of you. Whatever's trivial, you value. Whatever has value, you trivialize. How dare you judge me by such standards?'

'Won't you tell me why you're angry with me?'

But he couldn't. He simply couldn't. He was caught in one of the tantrums that he'd once used to such effect on other people. Only this time he was the victim of it himself – just as he was the victim of his own inexplicable passion for this girl – seething with it, helpless on the boil of it, and helpless too when he caught sight of a delicate line that ran from her knee up under her thigh – where had it come from? why hadn't he noticed it before? – a line he grabbed for, a sanctuary he sought like some medieval flagellant in search of his God, a place where he could purge himself and a rage that was meaningless, directionless, without hope.

Some time later, drowsing again, snuggling comfortably down in the bedclothes, she said, 'You don't suffer from hay fever, do you? You don't sneeze or sniffle. Why do you tell me such lies?'

'I like lies.'

'I'm not very good at them yet. I'm trying, but I haven't really got the technique worked out. I must try harder. I'm certainly beginning to understand their appeal. You're not getting up already, are you? Ten minutes more, don't you think? Couldn't we – '

But he yanked the warm duvet off her. Playfully, she grabbed it back. He tore it out of her hands. Not playful either. Not at all. She let him. Of course she did: the draught she felt was more from sudden fear than from the cool air of this unexpectedly cool June. Nikolas's face, always expressive, was as expressionless as a death mask, not a flicker on it.

'Do you plan to leave me nothing of my own?' he said, in a voice as expressionless as his face. 'Not even lies?'

'Nikolas, I'm cold.'

But he wasn't listening. 'I don't understand. I just don't – ' He ran his fingers along the sanctuary of that delicate line. 'Oh, God,' he said, more to himself than to her. 'I can't bear this.'

'What can't you bear? What is it? Speak to me.'

He shook his head and lowered it to the sanctuary. 'Why can't I get enough of you?'

'Nikolas? What are you going to do? I'm afraid.'

He glanced up at her then and – Well, it's entirely true that he didn't understand. He didn't understand any of this. She did, though, and all at once. Sometimes it comes to us in a flood of exhilaration. After all, what lover hasn't wished it? craved it? dreamed of it? to inhabit the beloved's soul? to be on the inside looking out? to conquer the territory so absolutely – if only for one fleeting moment – that every defining characteristic is

111

gone? that the beloved's face has become your own face, the face you might see in the morning mirror, expressionless because you alone are the one who views it?

'Let's get married today,' she cried. 'This afternoon. There's no need to wait. If it's done, nobody can undo it. It might even give my grandfather some pleasure. What are you doing down there, Nikolas? It tickles. Haven't we had enough bed for one day? We can go to Italy together. Nikolas, you must . . . Stop that. Oh, wait . . . You can be a musician and I can dream up new ways to spend money on you. Oh, I see. Oh!'

Afterwards, she slept. When she woke, it was evening and he was gone.

CHAPTER 8

Fred had talked on and on telling me this story, face flushed (mine too probably). I'd forgotten the heat of the day. I'd forgotten the ugliness of Overton. I'd forgotten everything. But at just this point, mid-swing in a sentence, he gave me a startled glance, turned on his heel and ran off without another word.

'Wait!' I cried after him. 'What happens next? He couldn't really have left her, could he? Come back. Where did he go?' But Fred had already dashed up a nearby slope of lawn and disappeared through some trees.

I had no idea where I was. I hate waking up from dreams at the best of times, but at least I usually wake up in a bed I know. Well-to-do American streets are all alike. No hedges. Swathes of coarse grass. Paths to front porches where push bells go ding-dong. There were no people about to give me directions, no telephone booth, no shop or filling station. It isn't wise to knock on the door of a strange American house even in a neigh-bourhood where the money is on show; a lone young woman on foot just plain smells of trouble. I didn't know what to do; but it was only late afternoon – there was a lot of daylight left – so I wandered up this avenue and down that, each a minor

113

variation on the one that preceded it, never precisely the same but never different enough for me to be certain I hadn't walked along it before. At the end of one street I turned back to glance at what I'd passed – and there stood the Merchant house.

How can such things happen? There was no doubt. None at all. Number 4669. I didn't even have to check that I was on Rifferman Avenue. Who could forget a number like 4669? Divide it by a thousand and you have Feigenbaum's number, a magic number, a fantasy, the number that signals order on its way to turbulence. There's serious excitement here, real power. Which, now I came to think of it, touches something of the elusive spirit of Nikolas himself. An odd thing: that a number should hint at the essence of a man. Perhaps it was the sense of borderline to him, of the known and the frightening unknown, of a not-unfamiliar type of person on the verge of a Grimms' fairy tale.

And, like Nikolas, no part of Number 4669 Rifferman Avenue was what it seemed. Harry had told me its history. It began life as a mud prairie hut and started to grow as houses around it got bigger. Bedrooms sprouted out of its top. A fine staircase appeared across the front, a kitchen and dining room out to one side, a porch out to the other, a huge living room on the back – marble fireplace, wood-panelled walls. Wheelocks screeded all this over; nobody could guess from looking at it that at its heart lay a secret so much at variance with its smooth exterior.

The wood-panelled living room is where today's Wheelocks convened for Martinis in the evening. Not Fred though. I waited impatiently for him to appear. He didn't. Violette explained to me in a whisper that when he locked himself in his room like this, he wasn't to be seen for weeks. I was so disappointed that I hardly noticed Canfield's humming.

The next morning, as early as I dared, I tapped on Beatrice's front door.

'Fred told me half a story yesterday,' I said to her, 'and then locked himself in his room.'

'Did he? A story? What about? Oh my. Nikolas. I see. Do you really want to know, dear? Are you sure?'

'I wish – ' I began.

But I wasn't sure what I wished. While Fred had talked, I'd found myself straining so hard to see the young Nikolas that I began to lose track of the man I met over lunch in Swiss Cottage. The more I struggled to restore the division between the fat man and his younger self, the more absolutely I lost the battle. The queerest of certainties settled in on me. I knew – I *knew* – that if I caught the angle of light just so – just exactly right – I'd see Nikolas as he was then, a quarter of a century ago in London with Priscilla, a young and sinewy Nikolas with danger in his face.

'It's driving me mad,' I said to Beatrice as we sat over a tray of coffee and cookies. 'Most people – Well, most of the time, I can get a sense of them. It doesn't matter that I don't know what goes on inside. But Nikolas? I can't see it. It was so stupid to leave her. She was a con man's dream come true. She'd have given him everything he wanted.'

'Mostly a person doesn't want everything he wants.'

'That's no answer.' Beatrice looked startled, and I went on in a rush, 'Oh, I'm so sorry. I don't mean to be rude, really I don't.'

She laughed. 'You'll find out. We all do.'

'When?'

'There are some things that do become clearer as you get older. Yourself, for one. You begin to see – '

'Oh, no! Oh, please, Beatrice. Don't make me wait until I'm old. What use will it be then? I need to know now. Today. Where did he go? Why?'

CHAPTER 9

Nikolas raced – stumbling, shaking, feverish with anxiety – straight from his bed and Priscilla to Heathrow to book himself a seat out of London, just as he'd raced to book himself on a plane out of Geneva to escape his family. Which is doubly absurd because only the night before, he'd laughed at a detective Priscilla's mother had hired to buy him off.

The guy had offered him fifty quid. Fifty quid! The cut-rate Countess! How Nikolas had relished the thought of telling Priscilla her cash value. He took the money, though. Of course he did. He planned a feast of caviar with it and with her. It was too early in the season for fresh Beluga, but in 1960, £50 would buy a whole pound of malossol. They'd eat it with spoons. What other way is there to eat the best caviar? Yet he couldn't sleep after the detective left. He didn't know why. And he'd ended up telling her nothing. He didn't know the why of that either. He simply didn't.

In a daze he handed over the detective's cash for a ticket more or less in the direction he'd figured on.

The night on the plane was worse than its predecessor. The journey seemed endless. How could a trip take so long? any trip? How could a night last so long? He checked his watch again and again and wondered in a vague sort of way why it seemed as adrift as he did. His muscles quivered beneath his skin, and his skin felt scalded, flayed. He recoiled when the stewardess shook his shoulder

'I'm sorry, sir,' she said, recoiling too. 'Are you all right?' He nodded. 'Your landing card, sir.'

He took it from her and studied it. 'Come back here,' he called after her then. 'What's the meaning of this? I booked a flight to Italy.'

'You did what?'

'Are you deaf?'

'This is a charter flight,' she said, smiling the bright smile her job required of her. 'You embarked at – '

'Nobody asked you where I embarked. This plane is supposed to be going to Syracuse.'

'It *is* going to Syracuse. We land at Syracuse/Hancock International Airport in an hour.'

He sighed. 'So there's a Syracuse in the United States, is there? How tiresome. What'll they think of next? Never mind. One country's as good as another. Is this new Syracuse on the west coast? east? Don't go away, damn you. Don't you know where the town is either?'

'North-east.' The tension in him – and the exhaustion – made her own nerves tingle. 'Near the Great Lakes. How could you get on a flight to the wrong place?' He shrugged wearily. The passport he'd been travelling on for the past few months – one of those half-lucky, half-malevolent quirks of chance – said he was J. Stamford Harlingby of Little Rock, Arkansas. The stewardess's voice softened. 'Did you really mistake the plane?' He shrugged again. 'I can radio Airport Services. They'll reroute you, but you'll have to go via Boston or New York.'

'What do you care where I go? Just tell me how much time I've lost getting to this benighted country of yours. Five hours?

Six? You don't have to be so nasty about it. Are all Americans as sour as you are?'

The plane landed at the deadest hour of night. There was no car rental office open at the airport, no banking facility, not even a restaurant. Nikolas could have ordered a taxi to take him to a motel room, but he was too restless. He set out on foot, reached the darkened streets of the city an hour or so later and prowled them until morning. As soon as the banks opened, he rented a vast car with fins that belonged on a land rocket. But when he set out, he was still in such a dislocated state that he forgot to ask the way to Illinois and his cousin Canfield.

He didn't know where else to go. New York? For the music? For his career as a pianist? Ah, yes. But there's a piece missing here – something he hadn't told Priscilla, something he hardly dared think of himself, something that makes his running away from her all the more difficult to understand.

I'll get to it.

There wasn't any mention of Illinois on the road signs as he left Syracuse. But if Syracuse was somewhere near Boston and New York, as the stewardess had said, then Illinois had to be south and west. On that first lap of the drive he felt a surge of energy – a brand new country, all laid out in front of him – but within an hour he hit Buffalo where traffic clotted, stuck, oozed. Free again, fighting to stay awake now, he wheeled in and out to pass with such abandon that brakes squealed all around him. Horns howled. Why he wasn't stopped is just one of those stupid miracles. Landscape? What landscape? Until Lake Erie appeared, he saw only the macadam of the road. He couldn't avoid Erie. It's an inland sea, a weird, opaque green-blue in those days because it was dying; it so oppressed him that he took the first left turn that came up, just to get away from it.

The country road he found himself on twisted into a forest. He upped his speed; he waltzed the car from side to side, screeched around a hairpin bend, two wheels off the pavement, the acceleration lifting him out of his seat –

And saw Priscilla right in front of him.

They say the devil protects his own. It must be true because by all rights Nikolas was a dead man. The car skewed sideways. At upwards of a hundred miles an hour, it sheered off a route that was tree-lined in either direction – except along this one stretch, just over the line into Pennsylvania, where a field of carrots grew right up to the edge of the road. The car flew into the field; it leaped, jumped, bumped, shuddered, skewed again and ploughed its way back to the verge.

There's an extraordinary sense of calm after an accident. Everything seems so leaden. Nikolas knew he hadn't really seen Priscilla. He knew he would never see her again (although he was wrong on this score). Besides, what a stupid name Priscilla was. How could anybody have a name like that? Why couldn't she be called Rosalie? or anna? or Margaret? He liked the name Rosalie. His hands were shaking. So was the rest of him. Cautiously he stretched his arms and legs. No apparent damage. He checked his face in the mirror. Not even a graze. Only then did he remember that he hadn't eaten for a day and a half.

He started up the car again – no damage to it either – and found a grocery store a mile further down the road. Neon stars flickered around its sign:

HERMAN'S SUPERMARKET

The door creaked on its hinges. The smell inside was of raw wood and apple cider. Nikolas stood a moment and gazed around him.

'They're over there,' a voice said.

'Where?' said Nikolas, swinging around.

A clerk – thin, spectacled, sparse-haired, po-faced – stood

119

behind a wood-topped counter. He cocked his head in the direction of a wedged-up row of metal baby buggies.

'What are they for?' said Nikolas. Nobody in Europe had shopping trolleys yet.

'You take one,' said the clerk.

'Take one? Me?'

'Yep.'

Nikolas pulled out a buggy. 'Now what?' he said.

'Push it around and put what you want in it.'

'Anything I want?'

A faint smile touched the corners of the clerk's mouth. 'Anything you can find on the shelves anyhow.'

Nikolas had never seen a summer squash before. He picked up a sample, turned it this way and that, sniffed it, put it into his buggy. He'd never seen a lima bean before either. The grapefruit were huge. The cherries were black. The sliced bread in cellophane squashed so abruptly in his hands that he dropped it, shivered in disgust, put it back on the shelf – then paused and added it to his buggy. Rows of boxes stood side by side; he studied their snappy names. Toward the back of the store he found cheeses wrapped in shiny paper and chose one with 'Coon cheese' written on the label. There were pickles in a barrel, rye bread, mustard, wines from California and New York.

'You got quite a selection here,' said the clerk.

'I have, haven't I?' said Nikolas, surveying it. 'Can I get as far as Illinois today?' He pronounced the word Ill-in-*oeil* with that queer muddle of vowels that sometimes overcomes people brought up to speak several languages.

'Say what?'

'Ill-in-*oeil*,' Nikolas repeated crossly, as though this cornbelt state were some ophthalmic disaster area.

'Never heard of it.'

'It's a state of the United States of America. Everybody knows that.'

'Not me.' The clerk began checking Nikolas's items through the till. 'Hey,' he said then, weighing the squash, 'you don't mean *Illinois* by any chance, do you? Chicago's state?'

'Whatever else might I mean?'

'Well, now, I don't rightly – '

'How far is it?'

The clerk suppressed a smile. 'I think you'd better plan to stay closer to Manhassat.'

'Where's that?'

'You're in it.'

Nikolas's irritation flared again. 'I want to go to Illinois today. Why do you refuse to tell me how far away it is?'

The clerk pulled out a paper bag, opened it with a shake, sighed. 'A thousand miles west, give or take a couple of hundred. Somewhat south too, I reckon.'

'Oh.' Then (his irritation abruptly forgotten), Nikolas said, 'What are you doing with that paper bag?'

The clerk sighed again. 'I'm going to put your stuff in it so you can carry it away with you to Illinois today. What else would a dope like me be doing with a paper bag?'

Nikolas scanned the man's face. 'I'm sorry,' he said. 'I'm new here.'

'No kidding?'

'I can't get that far today – or maybe ever. You're quite right. Of course you are. I'm not even sure I want to go there any more. Does anybody in, er, Manhassat take lodgers?'

'Rent rooms, you mean? Depends on what you want, I guess. There's a motel down the road about fifteen miles.'

'No private families?'

'There's Mrs Johnson. She's foreign too. She pronounces her name Yonson, like in the song. Funny way to pronounce a name. The husband was Swedish. So she says anyhow.'

'What song? I didn't say I was foreign. I said I was new.'

'Suit yourself.' The clerk handed Nikolas a card with a

121

number on it and pointed him to a pay telephone not far from the counter. Nikolas studied the black box that hung there. He bent forward to read the instructions on the little metal plate, lifted the receiver off the hook, listened, then peered at the instructions again.

'You need a nickel,' the clerk called over to him.

'Nickel?'

The clerk came out from his counter. He selected a coin from the change Nikolas held out to him, turned to the telephone himself, inserted the coin in its slot and dialled a number.

'Hey there, Mellie,' he said into the receiver, his voice going soft, 'I got a foreign kid here wants a room.' There was a pause. Nikolas could hear a woman's voice at the other end. 'I don't know,' the clerk said. 'Didn't ask him.' He put his hand over the receiver and turned to Nikolas. 'How old are you, kid?'

'Twenty-six.'

'He says he's twenty-six,' the clerk said into the telephone. 'Come on, honey,' he went on, 'you know me better than that. I wouldn't give him your name unless I liked the look of him – even if he is a bit of a smartass.' He gave Nikolas an amused glance. 'You want to talk to him?'

Nikolas took the receiver the clerk handed him. The clerk nodded reassurance. 'Hello,' Nikolas said.

'Why do you come to Manhassat, young man?' The voice was the rasp of a heavy smoker; the accent was inescapable.

'My God, you're Russian,' Nikolas cried. 'What's a Russian doing with a name like Johnson?'

She let out a gasp of delight. '*Vie gavaritie porusski*?'

'No, no – only the tiniest amount, and I speak that very badly. I was brought up in Geneva.'

'It isn't so! Geneva? God bless America. I live many years in Monte Carlo. There are Russians from Geneva there. Your mama and papa are Russian, yes? Ah, your papa only. You know Monte Carlo?'

'My father took me there' – he laughed – 'and taught me a thing or two.'

Mrs Johnson told Nikolas to come to her at once. She ordered it. Plainly he needed feeding. Russians always think people need feeding – and quite right, too, in this case. Her tiny clapboard house was only two blocks from the Supermarket; she opened the door as he reached out to knock on it.

He bowed a formal bow. 'Nikolai Nikolaievich Strakhan,' he said.

'Amelia Semyonovna Johnson.'

And – oh – the memories she brought back.

Nikolas Senior, my Nikolas's father, used to say that Russian whores were the greatest of Monaco's many glories. What a noble history they had. The rich men of Russia – the shrewd ones – had made their stately exodus well before the tumult of the Revolution; they'd spared no luxury either. They'd packed up whole trains with splendour. They'd travelled with cars, horses, personal staff, household staff, garden staff, assorted hangers on. Whores, too. And the whores had pleasured and plundered the entire entourage like seagulls in the wake of a garbage scow; then they'd settled in the craggy, warm cliffs of Monte Carlo to pleasure and plunder some more.

On that trip with his father, Nikolas had been about nine years old. One morning – his nanny dismissed for the day – his father took him on a visit to a special friend, who wore a chartreuse dressing gown with acres of pink ruffles and purple lace; she lived in an apartment overlooking the sea. Nikolas kissed a cheek that sagged (just a little) under its weight of rouge and studied a mouth that was a maraschino chirrup on its icing of pancake. This merry creature gave him sweetmeats and wine; she sang to him, taught him to puff her cigarette, dropped pearls down her cleavage for him to ferret out. He fell asleep in a chair and wakened to a hilarious escalation of grunts – to say nothing of a dazzling lesson in life – from the canopied bed in the room beyond.

Mrs Johnson's dressing gown may have lacked the opulence of pink ruffles and purple lace, but she was – oh, most definitely – a Monte Carlo whore of the old school; she even smelled of tobacco and wine. She threw her arms around Nikolas. They kissed each other three times, right cheek, left cheek, right cheek. They held each other out at arms' length, ogled each other up and down and embraced again.

'Where do you get this name Strakhan?' said Amelia Semyonovna Johnson, holding him still, patting him on the back, smoothing his lapel, patting his back again.

'Where'd you get the name Johnson?'

'Aha, I tell you. I marry big, blond boy of Utah because he says to me, "I want to give you Bible." ' Nikolas was too tired to disentangle himself from her embrace; he hung there, stuporous, as she talked.

' "Bible?" I say. "From Mormons," he says. I do not know Mormons. What is Mormons? But to give me Bible: this is new. I like. Also, he is very nice, very polite' – she released Nikolas with a final pat – 'and very, very energetic.'

She hung Nikolas's overcoat on a curlicued coat stand that stood beside the door. 'But he is dead, my young Buddy. And his family? They are not so happy with me. They give me money to go as far away from Utah as this great country will allow. I go until the money is finished – and this is Manhassat. Now I must know everything about you. Why are you here? What do you plan? Come to meet my daughter and my mama. Who are your people that they give you such a name? You put valise down there. Yes? Then you know where to find it.'

The small room she led him to overflowed with ugly furniture and lace antimacassars. A platoon of icons stood three deep on a mantelpiece facing a battalion of photographs on a mahogany table; dark pictures hung askew over dark, wall-papered walls. A single shaft of sunlight cut through the midden and lit up the most beautiful girl Nikolas had ever seen.

'I present you my Svetlana Buddyovna,' said Amelia. 'Say hello, Sveta. This is Nikolai Nikolaievich.'

There was a lushness to the girl, salty fresh and cream at the same time. Despite himself, all Nikolas could think of was caviar to be eaten with a spoon, the very feast he'd planned for Priscilla to celebrate her family's meagre estimate of her price. But as he bent over Svetlana's hand he had to fight back a wave of nausea. His eyes watered with it.

Svetlana watched him, her prettily plucked eyebrows raised, her chewing gum as silent in her cheek as the giggle that quivered at the corners of her mouth. When he didn't straighten as soon as she expected, she burst into a guffaw so raucous that the walls of the clapboard house rattled.

'My daughter is sixteen years old and uncultured like a sheep,' Amelia said, but there was only indulgence in her voice. 'She is pure America. All Americans are like this. But you must not think these are ordinary sheeps. No, no, no. I tell you. Signs – big signs – on streets say: "Buy paper to wipe your ass." Paper! What people are so fierce they use paper for such delicate matters? I cannot do this. Mamochka cannot. But Sveta, to her it is right. It is proper. It is hygienic. You see? Sheeps that are fierce? This is very interesting.'

'She's too beautiful to need culture,' Nikolas said.

'You ain't so bad yourself,' said Svetlana, recovering from her guffaw, chewing her gum with abrupt vigour. 'Leastways, your clothes ain't. What's the shirt made of?'

'The shirt?'

'The cloth, dude. The cloth. What cloth is it?'

'I don't know. Shirt cloth. What cloth should it be?'

'Come here. Come on, come on. Lemme see.' Nikolas took a step toward her (there wasn't room for more than a step). 'Open your jacket some.' He opened his jacket, and her lovely mouth stopped its chewing. 'It's silk,' she said. 'Geest, I never seen one of them before. You got a silk shirt on, know that? Can

125

I – ?' She reached out, then pulled back. 'Hey, wait a minute here. What's a guy in a silk shirt doing in a dump like this? We gotta – '

'And this is my mama,' said Amelia, interrupting with a theatrical flourish of her dressing gown, turning her back on her daughter – not an easy feat amidst such closely packed furniture. 'Mamochka, this is Nikolai Nikolaievich Strakhan of Geneva.'

The ancient toad in the chair opposite Svetlana squinted up at Nikolas. She was round, squat, toothless, leathery, kerchiefed – somewhere between evil and eternal – a laundry bag of a woman with a scanty Chinese beard beneath her chin and fat, chapped fingers stitching coloured threads into a piece of crewelwork.

'Umph,' she said, as Nikolas bowed to her.

'Now here we are together,' Amelia said, clapping her hands. 'God bless America. Is it not marvellous? Sveta, get up. Up, up, Pretty Mouse. What will you eat, Nikolai Nikolaievich? You sit in Sveta's chair. I feed you at once. I bring cheese. I bring bread. I bring cake. You like a glass of – '

'Hey, I mean it,' Svetlana said. She made no move to give up her chair. 'What in fucking hell is a dude like this doing here? Think about it, Mama.'

'Do you think I've come to rob you?' Nikolas said.

'Guys in silk shirts don't come to our house. Whaddya want here?' Her lovely face turned sour. 'Come on, tell me. Whaddya doing here?'

'Doing here?'

'Yeah. Yeah. Whaddya doing here?'

He looked at her in amazement. 'You know, I haven't the faintest idea,' he said.

At once a deep fatigue overwhelmed him. He swayed. He reached out to steady himself on the mahogany table and heard photographs fall to the floor.

'You are sick, Nikolai Nikolaievich,' Amelia said. 'Get out of chair, Sveta.' This time the command in her voice was absolute. 'Get out. Now. Go. Sit, Nikolai Nikolaievich. I can get you brandy. This will help. You need doctor?'

But Nikolas sank into Svetlana's chair, sliding past her as she vacated it, and fell asleep at once – just as he had when he was a little boy full of sweetmeats and wine in a Russian whore's apartment overlooking the Monte Carlo bay.

As Nikolas slept, Amelia, Svetlana and Mamochka sat watching. They measured his intake of breath and the rise and fall of his silk shirt. They surveyed his tie, his jacket and his trousers, which revealed, as my Aunt Peggy says, 'a fine masculine presence'.

Amelia raised an eyebrow, but Svetlana only said, 'It's a good weave to them pants, ain't it?'

'Oumph,' said Mamochka.

'Fifteen to twenty threads per centimetre,' said Amelia.

They kept their voices low, and they spoke English because from the time Svetlana was very little she'd refused to speak anything else. It was likely – the thought saddened Amelia even while it made her proud of her very American daughter – that Svetlana could no longer speak more than a word or two of Russian.

After an hour – Nikolas had barely moved – an exchange of glances and a shrug of shoulders, Amelia and Svetlana tiptoed to the kitchen to put the lunch together. Mamochka went too; voluminous as she was when she was on her feet, she moved as quietly as any laundry bag in its route from clothes basket to washing machine. But space here was tighter even than in the sitting room; the door would not shut with the three of them on the far side of it. Lunchtime preparation – clatter of pot and potatoes, whoosh of water, chink-chink of plates and glasses – would have wakened practically anybody. Not Nikolas, though. He slept on, sprawled in Svetlana's chair.

When the meal was ready, Svetlana put up a card table in the living room where the squash of furniture forced one side of the table against Nikolas's chest. She unfolded a cloth, spread it out (tucking it neatly around him), laid four places and carried in four plates of food, one for each of them, one for their sleeping guest. Over knives and forks – over cold meat, carrot salad and potatoes – the women continued their surveillance.

'You check him out?' Svetlana whispered.

'Only while I say hello,' her mother whispered back. 'Only pockets.'

'All the pockets?'

'Sure all pockets. What you take me for?'

'So?'

'Forty dollars, some change, passport, also foreign money. Passport is American. J. Stamford Harlingby. Huh: not Strakhan. He has Russian background. All Russians know of Strakhan. Why he say to us Strakhan? This is foolish. He knows I know. They are big like Trubetskoy.'

'Yeah?'

Svetlana reached out and skewered a chunk of potato from the plate in front of Nikolas; she put it to his lips. 'Hey, you, wake up. I ain't gonna whisper at you no more. Wake up!' He didn't stir. She frowned, stuck the chunk of potato in her own mouth and munched it pensively. 'OK. If the guy's got nothing to say for hisself, what about his suitcase? Don't you think it's about time he showed us what he got in there?'

'It is good horsehide.' Amelia cocked her head toward the hallway, where Nikolas's bag rested against the wall. 'French perhaps.'

Svetlana fetched it and set it down in the middle of the table, pushing plates and glasses aside to make room. She forced the lock with an expert flick of her fork, peered inside and drew out a piece of intimate male clothing, which she handed to Amelia.

'Ooof, he has not washed it, filthy beast,' Amelia said. She studied the seams. 'I have not had my hands on underwear like this for many years. Silk underwear and silk shirts. This is interesting. These pyjamas: silk as well.' She sniffed them. 'Also not washed. Where do you come by such finery, young man?' Amelia went on, smiling at a jacket in grey and then at the prostrate Nikolas. 'Look here, Lambkin. Here is stitching I have tried to tell you. It brings tears to my eyes to see such craft. And what is in here?' Her knife zipped through a seam in the suitcase.

'I certainly seen that stitch,' said Svetlana contemptuously, studying the suitcase's insides. 'He ain't exactly a hot shot with a needle, is he?'

'Always check your gentleman's lining, Rabbit. Ah, hah! See here. You are naughty boy, are you not, Nikolich? We have three, four, five – *Eight* passports. Yugoslav, Irish, Norwegian – All pictures of our young man, and all names different. God bless America, Swiss passport say – Aha. Look. Look. This is very, very interesting. English passport say Strakhan. Swiss passport say Strakhan. I do not – And what is this?' She pulled out an envelope, turned it this way, that, slit it open. 'Now this is very, *very* interesting, eh, Nikolasha?'

What did she find? I'm embarrassed to tell you. Really I am. Not embarrassed for Nikolas. For myself. Why didn't I guess at once?

'God Bless America, it is one more British passport. British money. See, Cricket? More Swiss things. Swiss chequebook: Crédit Union Suisse. Oh, how very interesting.' Amelia flipped the pages of the chequebook and giggled; she unfolded a heavy piece of paper tucked into it – it had a wax seal – and laughed merrily. 'I see. I see. Our gentleman, he is very deep. He also uses special name: Countess of Carmarth. He is a girl sometimes, I think.'

See what I mean? Not only had Nikolas run away from Priscilla, he'd stolen from her. He'd opened her pocketbook while she slept in his bed and cleaned her out, down to a pair of diamond earrings due at the jeweller's for repair.

He'd broken the earrings himself. They'd been walking along the Serpentine – a sunny day, warm. Or had it been raining? He'd pulled her to him so fiercely that one earring had caught in his jacket. They hadn't noticed until later. Then they'd laughed in delight, seeing it there, one diamond earring in her ear, one on his lapel, emblems that identified them to each other as the only members of the only secret society either one wanted to join.

But he stole them from her (the very earrings Amelia is fishing out of the envelope right now and dangling at her own ears). He sewed them into his suitcase with her other valuables and walked out of his flat near Hackney Downs, leaving her behind without even enough cash for the long taxi ride home.

'Our dude here don't exactly got the makings of a girl,' said Svetlana. She picked the passport off the table and turned idly to the photograph of Priscilla. 'Naw, this ain't him. Ah, geest, will you look at her, though? Now ain't it a crying shame to go through life looking like that? Why don't he wake up and tell us where he lifted this junk?' she went on irritably. 'It ain't polite to sleep at lunch. Wake up! You think you can sleep in that chair for ever?' She shook his shoulder. He slumped; his arm slid off the chair, and his hand dangled to the floor. 'Hey, he ain't really sick or something, is he? Suppose he dies on us.'

Amelia shrugged. 'If he dies, we bury him in root cellar. I think is only Herman' – she pronounced the name *Gairman* – 'knows he is here. And Gairman? He will not say against us.'

American schoolchildren like Svetlana are already on summer holiday in June. She was a surprisingly good student – an effortless gift for figures, textiles and geometry – but she preferred her summer shift at Herman's till. American money is so pretty. Her wage wasn't bad either, and she could always pick up the odd tip or two as well as a proportion of the takings, if

130

she treated Herman with what her mother referred to as 'respect'. God knows, the three women needed all the extras they could find. That's why they took in lodgers. The scope of Amelia's trade, given her age, was limited in a small New England town.

Amelia and Svetlana set out for work together after lunch, leaving Nikolas asleep under Mamochka's watchful eye. He was still sleeping when they got home for supper, and he slept, comatose, while they ate again around the card table. It was only afterwards, after they'd cleared the dishes and turned on the television, that Svetlana noticed a house spider on Nikolas's shirt.

My Uncle Phineas told me once that a cultivated silkworm eats from white mulberry trees; he said it spins a thread hundreds of yards long to make a cocoon that will protect it while it grows up. Such an unhappy irony. Don't protect yourself, and you grow up safely because nobody cares whether you live or not. Protect yourself, and you die because somebody like Nikolas buys your protection for his shirt. Yet here he lies asleep in it – entirely at a girl's mercy.

This girl's mercies weren't likely to be particularly tender either. She resembled her mother just as Priscilla resembled hers, and she had a clarity of mind not unlike Priscilla's. But she wasn't bored like Priscilla. Nor had she ever shown a soft spot for any man, old or young, as Priscilla had for her grandfather, for numerous pop stars – and then for Nikolas. Svetlana collected no movie magazines. No James Dean poster adorned her bedroom wall. She mooned over no boy at school, waited impatiently for no telephone calls, wore no signet ring around her neck. She didn't even fancy her English teacher, who had sideburns and a rare old 1933 Packard. Money? OK, screw the guy if he's got it. No money? Tell him to get lost. A rough girl. A tough girl. But she brushed that house spider off Nikolas's beautiful shirt – and suddenly felt troubled in her mind.

131

Warm silk, silk warmed by the body of a man, has a feel all its own. This warmth so fascinated her that when her Friday night date arrived clutching the requisite $25, she sent him away at once. She spent the evening ironing Nikolas's clothes, which Mamochka had washed and hung out to dry during the afternoon. She noted that silk warmed by an iron was not the same as silk warmed by a man, an interesting point in the purest of scientific terms.

Why she didn't experiment more I can't say. She ached to. There was nothing she wanted more. But for some inexplicable reason she dreaded the experiment even while she yearned to perform it. Not until bedtime did she gather the courage to touch the spot where the spider had crawled. To her astonishment, her heart turned over in her chest. This is a painful pleasure, a purely physical thing that echoes elsewhere in the body.

The next morning, Nikolas lay in the chair as before. He slept through breakfast. He slept through lunch. At supper, Amelia said, 'This boy begins to annoy me. Five meals we set before him. He does not wake. He does not eat. He does not die. He does nothing at all.'

'Hush!' said Svetlana.

'What for?' said Amelia.

'Be quiet, Mama. He's sleeping.'

Mamochka turned her usually impassive face on Svetlana, then on Amelia, and a small crinkle of smile crept into her Chinese beard.

On this second night of Nikolas's sleep, Svetlana insisted – she absolutely insisted – that they leave the dishes unwashed in the little kitchen for fear that the sound of washing them might wake him before he was ready to wake, even though no noise so far had had the slightest effect on him.

And in fact, it was the sound of dishes being washed that woke

132

Svetlana the following morning. She threw on a dressing gown and ran down the narrow stairs to the kitchen. The refrigerator in this kitchen was a thumping, chuff-chuffing presence of rounded curves from a bygone age; it almost blocked the door. The sink beyond was a washtub wearing a flowered curtain to hide the pudenda of its pipes; at it stood Nikolas, awake, alert, alive – even shaved – dishcloth over his shoulder and his shoulder garbed in one of the shirts she'd ironed for him.

She saw at once how wrong she'd been. This wasn't silk reeled in from the *Bombyx mori* of the mulberry tree. Not this boy – not cultivated silk at all, despite his shirt. No, no. Here was wild silk from the tussa worm of India and China that feeds on oak – roughcast, rough-hewn yet still silken and luxurious – both at the same time – and colour doesn't boil out with the gum. Just the thought of it makes your skin tingle all over.

A pot of coffee bubbled on the cooker. He swung around to greet her. 'Good morning,' he said. 'I've already been to market. That's not at all a bad market, you know – open all night, so the clerk tells me. He says his name is Herman. Do you always sleep this late?'

'You slept two whole nights and most of two whole days,' Svetlana said. She pulled her dressing gown tighter around her, shy somehow, a reaction as alien to her as all the others he'd provoked.

'No wonder I was so hungry. Do you mean to tell me it's Sunday? Are all shops here open on Sunday? That's a very ugly dressing gown, Svetlana.'

'I thought you were dead.'

'Thank you for being so patient with me.' He spoke gravely. 'Where does this pot go?'

'Under the oven.'

'Do you think that's the best place for it?' Nikolas squatted down and peered into the metal drawer under the cooker. 'It's hard to get at pots when they're under an oven, don't you think?'

133

Amelia emerged from the hallway just then and stood in the door to the kitchen with an unopened packet of cigarettes in her hand. Without her make-up, she was a fine, dissolute figure of a woman, deep, hooded eyes, delicate arch of lip, generous body on the loose beneath a dressing gown not drawn perhaps as tightly around her as the hour demanded.

'Good morning, Nikolai Nikolaievich,' she said.

'Amelia Semyonovna,' Nikolas said, eyeing her with approval and the requisite hint of proposition. 'How can I ever repay you for your gracious hospitality?'

Amelia snorted. 'You marry with Svetlana. I am happy to tell you that she consents.'

Nikolas laughed.

But how perplexing it is when you laugh, and nobody laughs with you. He turned to look at Svetlana. Her ears were pierced; she wore gold hoops in them. Her hair was black. Her answering smile was bemused and a little lopsided; it made her more beautiful than ever.

Behind him, Amelia ripped the cellophane off the packet in her hand, crinkled it, put a cigarette in her mouth, tapped him on the shoulder, indicating that he was to light her cigarette, which he did with a kitchen match. Then he accepted a cigarette for himself and a light from the burning tip of hers.

'So?' she said, picking a fleck of tobacco off her tongue.

He made a helpless, self-deprecating gesture with his hands.

'Come, Nikolai Nikolaievich, what do you say to proposition? It is good idea, yes?'

'Well, I – ' he said. He shook his head. 'I seemed to have missed something.'

'You do not wish to marry?'

'I can't say it, er, was the foremost thing in my mind this morning.'

'Now I say it, how do you think?'

'About marriage?'

'About marrying with Sveta.'

'Sveta?'

'I think you nod in your chair still, Nikolasha. Your head is not awake.'

'This is all very, er, flattering,' he said.

'We do not flatter, Nikolai Nikolaievich. I make you proposition – very serious. My daughter likes silk very much, ever since she is little girl.'

Nikolas looked from Amelia to Svetlana and back again. 'Am I being particularly dim-witted?'

'Mamochka gave her swatch – only little swatch – when she was six years old. She keeps under her pillow. It is there now, and ten years have passed. Ten years is long time. This is how I speak of silk shirts and of marrying with Sveta.'

'Marriage and silk shirts.'

'Yes, Nikolai Nikolaievich.'

'In all seriousness.'

'Yes, Nikolai Nikolaievich.'

'I think I need some strong coffee,' said Nikolas. 'Maybe some brandy too.' He poured out coffee while the two women watched him in silence; he added a dollop of brandy, then leaned his back against the sink and faced them. 'Tell me something? Are silk shirts really what it takes to provoke Svetlana's love?'

'The point is delicate,' said Amelia. 'Your jacket is also fine. But I assure you my daughter is earnest.'

'My jacket.'

'Yes, Nikolai Nikolaievich.'

'Anything else?'

'All else is ordinary. Nice, you understand – I intend no offence – but ordinary.'

He turned away again and peered out through the kitchen window to the weedy yard and ramshackle garage beyond – and felt as bemused as Svetlana's smile. But he could not deny a sense of enchantment too, of fairy tales and ogres, of sleeping beauty, of awakening fresh to a new world where nobody – not even the sleeper – remembered why the sleep had been so long or who was responsible for it. There is serious magic in bridges thoroughly, irrevocably burned.

'Whose van is that?' he said.

'What do you say?'

'The vehicle in the drive. Don't you call it a van? Whose is it?'

'It is delivery truck, Nikolasha. I use it for work.'

'What do you say to the idea that Svetlana takes my shirts and I take the truck?'

'Nikolai Nikolaievich, you must not make jokes with me.' Amelia's cigarette jiggled up and down in her mouth as she talked. 'Such values are not equal. She must have shirts and legal papers of marrying. I speak to you of my only daughter's future. I insist on legal papers because she likes your body, and she never does this before. This is risky – to like man's body.'

'Um,' he said. 'What sort of mileage does the truck get?'

'Fifteen per gallon. But I need this delivery truck. I will not bargain with it.'

'No truck, no deal.'

'Then no deal,' Svetlana said.

'Quiet, Sveta,' said her mother. 'Why you ask for this truck, Nikolasha?'

'*I* need it.'

'I give you television set instead.'

'I want the truck.'

'I have gold icons.'

'Oh, come on, they're only gold paint.'

'You consider nothing without truck?'

'What does she want with my shirts, anyway?' Nikolas burst out, feeling trapped in gossamer – a fairy-tale sleeper again, tangled in silken threads – and so at the queerest of disadvantages. 'What good are they to her? They're too big for her.'

Smoke spiralled up past Amelia's cheeks; she squinted at him through it. 'I am sorry to tell you', she said, 'that pleasure in man's body is not so wonderful like men think. It is very little. Also, it dies quickly. This truth you do not know.' She shrugged. 'Men are vain. This is good. God bless America, if men have no vanity, they do not pay so high. Silk is different. Silk lasts. And design? Design lasts more than silk. These shirts are very, very fine. You do not understand such subtle things.'

'If she gets the shirts, I get the truck.'

'Forget it, Mama,' said Svetlana. 'He ain't worth it.'

'Quiet.' Amelia's voice was sharper than before. She took in an uneven breath. 'You do not know what you ask. You say to me, "Give your heart for your daughter's happiness." I do it. I do it with love. It is hard for me, but it is – '

'No, Mama. No!'

'It is done, my Firefly. To cement this union, Nikolai Nikolaievich takes delivery truck. But look you what I say, Nikolich. You take truck: she gets jacket also. The automobiles of this country are not yet known to you. Fifteen miles per gallon is good for truck.'

'I keep the jacket.'

'Sveta *must* have jacket. The stitching is rare.'

'She gets the shirts. I keep the jacket.'

Amelia sighed. 'You drive hard bargain, Nikki. OK. OK. You keep jacket. But when you marry, you let us look. Yes? We look jacket. Then give back. OK? Is good? We shake on it? Now we must have flour and vodka. I call Gairman. You pick up groceries. We must have ring also. This is America: we must have engagement ring.'

After all, if a matter's settled, why not celebrate tonight? Why wait for tomorrow? Amelia telephoned a pawnshop she knew in a nearby town – an old client happy to open on a Sunday for such a special occasion – and Nikolas went to choose a ring. He spent all he had on it, all twenty-five dollars left over from his morning's shopping; then he drove back to the Supermarket to show it to Herman and to collect Amelia's groceries.

'I suppose it ain't bad for twenty-five bucks – specially on a Sunday,' Herman said, holding the ring up to the light. He handed it back to Nikolas. 'How'd you get that girl anyhow? Guys around here been flocking after her since she was six. She sells them a piece of cake, then slams the door in their faces. You? You come along out of nowhere – and then buy her a grubby ring that isn't even gold.'

'Of course it's gold.'

'You think I'm colour blind?'

'It's white gold.'

'Yeah?'

'Yeah.'

Nikolas studied the ring while Herman studied him. 'It's what's called an Illusion setting,' Nikolas said. What could be better suited to a fairy-tale marriage than an illusion of a ring? If the black markets of Europe had taught him nothing else, they'd taught him about diamonds. 'White gold makes the stone seem bigger.'

'You mean it's even crappier than it looks? Jesus, some guys – '

'Herman, it's so filthy – and the gold is so scratched – that you can't tell anything about it. I have a feeling about it. I really do.'

'Yeah?'

'Yeah.'

'You behave yourself with Sveta – hear me? – or I'll come after you with a shotgun.'

By the time Nikolas got back to the clapboard house, Amelia, Svetlana and Mamochka were already working so hard they barely noticed him. Throughout the day they measured, sifted, mixed; they sliced, minced, rolled; they baked, boiled, fried. Towards evening they opened up the door to the lodger's room, which lay beyond the one they sat in and ate in themselves. It wasn't very spacious either, but with the bed curtains raised, the bed pushed against the wall and the bureau pressed into service as a sideboard, it made a cheerful enough spot for a celebration. They up set the card table there. They spread Amelia's best lace cloth on it.

And what a feast they laid out: *zakuski* and *pirozhki* – some with vegetables, some with meat, some with fish – cold *borscht* and *kasha croûtons*, squab soaked in wine and a salad of beans with celery seed, a cake called a *kulich*, shaped like a dome and decorated with artificial roses (even though Easter was long gone); they'd even made *paskha* from raisins, almonds, lemon peel and three cheeses pounded in a mortar.

At eight, Herman arrived with a case of wine. He kissed Amelia, right cheek, left cheek, right cheek. He kissed Svetlana. He kissed Mamochka. He kissed Nikolas too. Can this be? An American man in an American town kissing another man after the Russian fashion? At the height of the Communist scare? Nikolas surveyed his new-found family with a new-found respect. Rip Sullivan of Sullivan's Materials and Cloth arrived next with half a bolt of white satin and half a bolt of silk tulle for Svetlana's wedding dress. He kissed everybody, even Herman. Last came Yorkel, owner of the pool hall down the street, his arms full of lilies.

Amelia poured out frozen vodka as thick as corn syrup. They toasted the bride. They toasted the groom. They toasted Amelia, Mamochka and the three tradesmen. They toasted Mother Russia, the memory of the Tsar and Tsarina, the icons on the mantel – even the cheeses in Herman's refrigerator. Not until the fourth bottle, did the pace begin to slow.

'We can't give up now,' said Nikolas. 'Let me – I got one. I got one. Here's to the delivery truck.'

And at once the merriment snapped shut. The change was so abrupt that Nikolas felt giddy. 'What's wrong?' he said, looking from one to the other of the company. 'What have I done?'

Amelia avoided his eyes. Herman stared out the window at the dark. Rip Sullivan and the pool hall owner gazed down at their feet, invisible under the table. Even Mamochka bowed her head.

Svetlana drummed her fingers on the table. 'We can't toast the delivery truck, you jerk,' she said. 'You gotta know that.'

'Do I?'

'Ah, come on you guys, lemme just screw him. Whaddya say, Mamochka? Nothing's worth this.'

Amelia patted her daughter's cheek. 'No, Duckling. You have chosen.'

Svetlana reached for the remaining *pirozhki*. She studied it, turning it this way and that. Then she took a bite. 'Why do you suppose just looking at him makes me feel so fucking weird?'

While she chewed, she kept her glance on Nikolas, which he felt as well as saw, although he wasn't certain whether it was his flesh or his shirt that gave her such a glow. What a strange amalgam she was. With her mouth shut, there was a deep sense of quiet about her, a sense of waiting, of stillness over a springtime meadow before a battle begins, an aching transience – bloom on plum, down on peach. Her face was heart-shaped and slope-eyed. Her chin had a dimple in it. But then she opened her mouth; and at once the battle had not only begun, it was already fought and lost. The living were already back at base camp; what was left were vultures wheeling and screeching over half-rotten carrion in a field.

She sighed, stuck the rest of the *pirozhki* into her mouth (which curled at the corners). Then she giggled suddenly. 'Hey, Mama, what about the fucking orgasm? Whaddya think, huh?'

Rip and Herman, already pink from vodka, turned an alarming red. Yorkel sniggered.

'Who knows?' said Amelia with a shrug. 'You can do this, Nikki?'

'Do what?' Nikolas said, a little dazed. That's a lot of vodka to put away in a very short time.

'These men, look at them – like little boys,' said Amelia. 'They will not speak. I ask, what is orgasm? They snicker. I think maybe they cannot do.'

Nikolas cleared his throat. 'It's, eh, something some people have,' he said, feeling charmed and idiotic both.

'Do I have it?'

The three tradesmen spluttered.

'It's when – Well, let's see,' Nikolas said. 'It's when you lose control.'

'Lose control? Oh, you mean man.'

'Women too.'

'No!'

'Yes.'

Amelia burst out laughing. She laughed as hard as the men who were choking by now, helpless with mirth, clutching the table, their sides, each other, anything nearby. 'Is good joke. Is very funny. Man who makes joke will make excellent husband.'

'I'm not joking,' Nikolas protested, but he could not hold back his own laughter.

'Lose control?' cried Amelia. She slapped her thighs. Tears streamed from her eyes. 'Woman? Ha, ha, ha. Who will do business if woman loses control?'

'But what's it got to do with the delivery truck?' Nikolas said.

And Amelia's hilarity died again, as abruptly as it had only moments before. This time the silence was the silence of a tomb. Not even Svetlana seemed prepared to break it. Nikolas tried to stand and sat down again, too drunk to keep his balance in so restricted a space – too drunk to keep his mind from slipping back to London and Priscilla, to the way she walked:

coltish, a little awkward, a little clumsy despite her intense schooling and her rigid self-possession.

He buried his face in his hands. 'What will I do if you don't help me?' he said wretchedly. 'Why can't I just wash away the past? just forget it? I've done it before. Why not now?'

The point was real. Teresa Lopez-Vega? who'd changed his life? Forgotten. His father, sisters, inheritance? Forgotten. His first wife? fellow conspirator in the theft of a matching set of dildoes from a Mayfair whorehouse? Forgotten. He drew in a ragged breath. 'Take pity on me, Svetlana. What I wish with all my heart is that when you wear this ring, the world will order itself as it should be. I wish this for you. I wish it for me. I wish it for us both.'

He set the diamond on the table in front of her. She kept her face averted, but she'd heard the misery in his voice – she could not doubt its passion – and she was not by any means unmoved. 'Svetlana?' he said. 'Won't you even look at it?'

Herman leaned forward and studied the stone. 'I'll be damned,' he said. 'That did clean up nice, didn't it?'

And so it had. The diamond flashed and sparkled. It scintillated from all fifty-eight facets, pavilion reflecting, crown dispersing, white gold magnifying. Svetlana tried to keep her face turned away from it – and from Nikolas – but the unfamiliar ache in her body wouldn't let her. Despite herself she found the ring on her finger, just as she found her hand in his. This first touch, these two, hand in hand in the company of their elders, as proper as any Victorian couple, his hand a little damp from tears – what difference does it make in the scheme of things that she misinterpreted them? – her hand alive in his as it never had been before and a delicious puzzlement on her lovely face. That warmth she'd thought was the warmth of silk: it wasn't the silk after all, was it?

'Is it right to keep secrets from me now?' Nikolas went on. 'If a delivery truck can take away so much pleasure from an evening – and because of me – why should I be the only one who can't know the reason for it? Don't I commit myself to a new life here and now? Doesn't this commitment make me a member of the family? entitled to my family's trust?'

A short silence followed.

Then Rip Sullivan said, 'He has a point, Mellie.'

'You think this, Rip?'

'Yeah.'

'Yorkel?'

'Family's family.'

'Gairman too? You agree? Yes?' Amelia lit a fresh cigarette from the butt of the one she hadn't quite finished. 'Well, you see, Nikolas Nikolaievich, it is matter of business.'

For many years now, as Amelia explained, she had provided a full range of amenities: bed, bidet, mirrors and equipment to enhance the pleasures of the common appetite (as well as a perversity or two). Like Herman and Rip Sullivan in this small American town, she made her service available door-to-door for those who had no transport of their own or who were too busy to come to her. In recent years she'd used the truck less because something in her right hip made crawling in and out painful. Just as well that her clients had grown older and less agile with her. Only a week or so before this, she'd heard about a Volkswagen beetle at a very reasonable price.

'If you're not going to use the delivery truck any more – ' Nikolas began.

'Just listen,' said Rip Sullivan.

Amelia's clients were getting fatter as well as less agile. Look at Herman's little paunch. Look at Rip's plump thighs and Yorkel's many chins. A fat man in a tight jacket needs the seams letting out. And what about his wife? What about Ladies' Night at the Kiwanis? Why not surprise curtains for her birthday? Or a new cover for the sofa?

And yet there was no tailor for miles around Manhassat.

Amelia longed to fill the gap. Who was more qualified? Who knew these bodies more minutely? Besides, she had a real gift for cloth. She'd inherited it from Mamochka; she'd passed it on to Svetlana. She sewed with stitches so tiny that nobody could see them. She could smock, tat, pleat. There was no buttonhole she could not make, no flower she could not embroider. But to sew everything by hand is not economic; a tailor needs a sewing machine – and a Volkswagen beetle to broaden her catchment area.

Amelia's only saleable asset was the delivery truck. Where else was she to find the money for down-payments on such expensive items?

'That's it?' said Nikolas. 'That's all that's worrying you? Are you sure? Why didn't you say so?'

'You do not understand,' said Amelia.

'Sure, I do. Sell the ring.'

'Aw, come on, kid,' said Herman. 'You paid only twenty-five bucks for it.'

Nikolas held Svetlana's hand to the light. 'All you have to do is look at it,' he said, taken aback now, just as he'd been when he'd first washed it. 'To the right buyer it's got to be worth – God, I don't know. It doesn't draw any colour at all. I've never seen one like it. It must be worth at least three times as much as the delivery truck.'

Svetlana pulled her hand – still in his – to her breast. Amelia shook her head.

'You don't believe me?' Nikolas said.

'It does not matter if I believe you or not, Nikolasha. I cannot sell my daughter's engagement ring.'

'I'll buy her another one.'

'It will not be as before.'

'Why not?'

'No.'

'OK. OK,' said Nikolas, shifting from one scheme to another

as easily as Herman shifted beans on his shelves (and this despite the interesting placement of his hand on his bride-to-be). 'You searched my suitcase, didn't you? the lining? the envelope with the earrings in it?'

'This question is not polite.'

'What has politeness got to do with it?'

'You let us use those diamonds?'

Nikolas hesitated, then shook his head. 'I'd rather you didn't use the earrings. But come to think of it, why didn't you just take them? and the paperwork?'

'I do not steal from guests,' said Amelia primly. Then she laughed. 'We thought you dressed up to be girl sometimes.'

'I wish I could,' he said simply. 'I just don't think I can get away with it. What I had in mind was you dressing up instead.'

'Me?'

'You'd make a fine countess, don't you think? In exchange, let's say, for an item or two of your own choosing? I'd planned to ask you to have a go at it anyway. There's plenty of money for us both. I just wasn't sure how to make the request. I'll come along and help you carry.'

'You mean this?' There was a hush of awe in Amelia's voice. 'Ah, Nikki, for this I marry you myself.' She took up the hand that Svetlana had not claimed; she clasped it to her; she kissed it. 'Mamochka too. She marry you as well. All three of us marry you. We marry Gairman. We marry Rip, Yorkel. We even marry Countess of Carmarth, poor plain girl.' Then she said, her tone pensive, 'Who is this Countess of Carmarth, do you think?'

'Search me,' said Nikolas.

But if he slept in the lodger's room with any woman that night, he slept with the memory of his Countess. Maybe Svetlana cost a punter $25, but Nikolas was no ordinary punter. Amelia knew what was right for her daughter: A gown. A ceremony. A wedding feast. And, God bless America, a proper, old-fashioned nuptial night. There are virgins and virgins; and in this, Svetlana was just the kind of virgin Nikolas had been before he met Priscilla. No male creature before him had touched Svetlana's heart, much less penetrated it. For this reason she needed her mother's most exquisite protection. Nikolas had not been so lucky himself. Who can say? Perhaps things would have been different if Elizabeth had lived. Perhaps he would not have suffered so much already – and have so much more suffering yet to come.

Communications weren't then what they are now, but stolen cheques have never had a long life. Early the next morning, Nikolas and Amelia set out for the supremely ugly city of Cleveland in her delivery truck. Pittsburgh was a little closer, but the prudence of crossing a state line hardly called for discussion. Three hours' driving took them to a vast mall; there, on a dais in the middle of a cavernous store with a ceiling of metal struts and neon lights stood a Singer sewing machine more magnificent than any Amelia had ever dreamed of.

Nikolas took the prim and tidy clerk by the arm (grey hair neat against her scalp, grey cardigan buttoned to the top, glasses around her neck on a discreet chain). He whispered into her ear.

'What's that supposed to mean?' she said, pulling a little away from him, glancing nervously at Amelia, as lush as ever and elegantly debauched without her pancake.

Nikolas whispered again into the clerk's ear.

'Gawd!' the clerk said. 'You're kidding me. Oh, boy, wait'll I tell my husband. What'd you say I'm supposed to call her?'

'M'Lady.'

'I got to curtsy or something?'

'It's not strictly necessary.'

'You her son?'

'Oh, no, no.' Nikolas bowed his head. 'I am Her Ladyship's secretary. Now, perhaps, I think we might . . .'

He led the clerk to Amelia, who stood transfixed in front of the Singer sewing machine.

'I can try?' she said to the clerk. Her voice trembled with excitement.

'Sure you can,' said the clerk, and then added hurriedly, 'm'Lady. Ever worked one before? No? Want some help?'

Amelia nodded.

What an extraordinary idea a sewing machine is: cogs and ratchets plugged into a wall and driven round and round: magnificent chunk-chunk-chunk of metal through material. Amelia's heart leaped in her chest as the clerk sewed. Then came the moment when she sat down herself, positioned the swatch of buckram, lowered the presser foot, needle and – after all those years of waiting and dreaming – put her own foot on the pedal.

'Hey, you're going to be good,' said the clerk. 'I never saw anybody run a first seam as straight and easy as that. Try another.'

The Singer went backwards and forwards; it could baste, hem, gather. One attachment did embroidery; another made buttonholes.

But when the clerk disappeared with the Countess of Carmarth's Swiss cheques, her Letter of Credit with its wax seal and her passport (on which Nikolas had done a little deft remedial work), Amelia suffered an attack of panic so severe that Nikolas could not calm her. The clerk, returning with a form for her to sign, pushed him aside. 'Go away,' she said. 'What do you know about it?' She put her arm around Amelia's shoulders. 'Don't worry, honey. I mean, um, m'Lady. I know how it is.'

Amelia had difficulty focusing on the words. 'You say what?'

'I get hot flashes too.'

That was all – an assumed hot flush and appropriate sympathy. No questions. No doubts about the cheques or the passport. Amelia took possession of the machine, and the long-awaited future was hers.

She and Nikolas went to a ship's outfitter of such elegance

that the salesman wore a tuxedo and gave them sherry; Amelia hardly noticed. She was already so preoccupied with Svetlana's wedding dress that she signed forms without a tremor, only half aware that she'd bought a ship's bed for Nikolas to fold up against one wall of the delivery truck, a purser's desk with brass handles, a sink, stove, refrigerator and a round ship's mirror in brass. In some other shop – where? buying what? – she had no idea – at the precise moment she wrote the name 'The Countess of Carmarth', the full design of the gown came to her. It would probably take Rip Sullivan's entire half-bolt of satin and the entire half-bolt of silk tulle as well. The question, though, was how to put such a magnificence together.

Not even a glimmer of the solution came to her until they reached the Volkswagen dealer. As they opened the door to the showroom she realized how dauntingly complex the details of construction would have to be if she was to achieve the extraordinary simplicity she sought. The gatherings of cloth about Svetlana's waist and under her arms – under the arms is always difficult –

'M'Lady?' Nikolas said. He had to say it twice.

'What you want now?' she said. 'You cannot deal with this yourself?'

'I cannot sign your cheques, m'Lady.'

'OK. OK. Give it. Where is? This is very boring.'

'When do you want to pick it up?' said the salesman.

'You ask me what?'

'The car, m'Lady. You just bought yourself a car. You want it tomorrow?'

'I take it now.'

She was as indifferent and as imperious as God. Even Nikolas admitted later that it was her manner, rather than his machinations, that accounted for the salesman's unquestioning acceptance of this final, very expensive purchase, to be removed from his showroom at once with only the assurance of a foreign passport.

Despite her preoccupation, she drove the beetle back to Manhassat (her gifts extended to all machines); as soon as she got inside the door to the little clapboard house, she cleared the photographs off the mahogany table, unpacked the machine and sat down to it with its manual, even though it was past eight o'clock of an exhausting day after a night of drunken celebration. She sewed seams and ripped them out, oblivious to Nikolas, Svetlana and Mamochka. At midnight she staggered to bed with spots in front of her eyes, only to wake half an hour later – muscles of her neck twitching – in a state of abject terror.

Maybe people don't really want what they think they want, just as Beatrice says. But for somebody who really does want what she wants – somebody who's willing to take the necessary risks – the fear afterwards can be terrible. Amelia tossed and turned. She sweated and ached. She got up, went down to the living room and brought the bobbin case back to bed with her. Half an hour later, she fetched the embroidery attachment. By the early hours of the morning, the entire machine was asleep in her arms, a privilege she never allowed her clients.

But the terrors stayed with her. Her stomach flip-flopped the next morning even as she reassembled the machine on the mahogany table and set to work. She began to lose track of the details of the wedding dress; she snapped at Svetlana, who sat beside her reading a *Captain Marvel* comic book.

As for Nikolas, she could not bring herself to look at him.

'You don't need that ancient mattress any more, do you?' he said, coming into the living room just before lunch. He was clearing her things out of the delivery truck. 'What shall I do with it? Shall I take it to the dump?'

'No,' she said through her teeth.

After lunch he rushed into the living room, dangling a metal contraption. 'What *are* these things?' he cried happily. 'Handcuffs I know about. Leg irons I've heard about. But what do you with this? I can't even figure out where it's supposed to go.

149

Arm? Neck? Oh no, don't tell me it's – '

'Glumph,' cried Amelia, revealing her genetic inheritance from Mamochka.

Towards evening, he threw himself down in the chair beside Svetlana.

'There's a lot of rust on the floor of that truck, Amelia Semyonovna,' he said. 'It's going to cost a hell of a lot of money to take care of it. Do you have any cash left over?'

And she could bear it no longer.

She swung around. She leapt to her feet. 'Money? Cash? What money? How do you talk of such things? I know you. I know your heart. Stay two minutes. Do orgasm with Sveta. Then finish. Gone. This I accept. But to destroy her: this I do not accept. What is to become of my baby butterfly? Who is to tend her when *I* am gone? Who will feed Mamochka? You bargain. You bargain. But care? You do not care. Find me rope. I need rope. I hang myself at once. This very moment. You hear me? I cannot stop myself.'

Nikolas shrank back into his chair under the onslaught. 'It was you who arranged this marriage,' he said. Well, he didn't say it, he shouted it because otherwise he'd never have made her hear him. 'If you don't like the idea any more – '

'Marriage? Marriage?' screamed Amelia. 'There must be word evil enough to pronounce you. I have friend in St Tropez. He is lawyer. Will he take my case? Yes, he will – but for profit. Where is profit for my kitling in this? Where is profit for Mamochka? I know him. I think he will let me clean his floors. Because of you, my pretty squirrel is outcast. Weep for Mamochka. Because of you she starves. Because of you Amelia spends the rest of her life on her knees.'

'I thought you were going to hang yourself,' said Nikolas.

'Hang myself? How can I do such things? You see, Svetlana? Now he wants to kill me. I do not allow. First I cut out my own heart. Where is knife? I do it right now. I get knife at once.'

Amelia ran to the kitchen. She slammed the door behind her.

Nikolas stared after her. Svetlana went on reading *Captain Marvel* as fixedly as ever, one leg folded under her, the other dandling, one hand in a half-eaten packet of potato chips, the other gently poking at a bubble of gum – a magnificent bubble, pale pink, wonderfully translucent, immense and growing bigger. Nikolas focused on what little he could see of her face beyond it.

'What's your mother talking about?' he said. 'What is all this about a lawyer in St Tropez? What case? Is she really in some sort of legal trouble?'

'Naw,' said Svetlana, popping the bubble.

From the kitchen came sounds of water and a manic clatter of pans. 'Is she going to hurt herself in there?' Nikolas said.

'Naw.'

'Naw?'

'She always says stuff like that.'

'How can you eat potato crisps and chew gum at the same time?'

Svetlana shrugged her pretty shoulders. 'She's scared she's going to lose her sewing machine.'

'Her what?'

'Her sewing machine, stupid.'

'This is about a sewing machine?'

'Yeah.'

'She just got it. How can she lose it?'

Amelia burst back into the room with a saucepan full of water. This she upturned over Nikolas's head and raged off again while he sat there dripping.

Svetlana gave him a sideways glance, giggled, blew another bubble, popped it. 'She thinks the cops are gonna come.'

'Cops? The police? Why?'

'To take away her sewing machine.'

'What do they want with a sewing machine?' Svetlana flipped

a page of *Captain Marvel*. 'The Swiss cheques – Did she give her address or something? while I wasn't looking? She wouldn't do that, would she?'

'Naw.'

Amelia appeared with a second saucepan of water. Nikolas caught her wrist, wrestled with her, took possession of the saucepan, set it down. She grabbed at it. He twisted her arm behind her back and held it there. 'Listen to me, Amelia Semyonovna. Nobody is going to take your sewing machine away from you. Do you hear? Nobody. Now, will you talk sensibly if I let you go?'

She glared at him. Slowly he loosened his grip. 'What do you know about Americans?' she hissed. 'They hate Russians. I am Russian, so I am Soviet. I am Soviet, so I am spy. The police: they knock at door any minute now. They set out tracing me, it won't take them half an hour.'

'Who would set out to trace you? Why would anybody bother? Trust me. There is no danger. None at all.'

'Trust you? Trust *you*?' Her face worked. 'Trust you? You? Ha, ha, ha. Trust *you*? He, he, he.'

'Help me, Svetlana,' he said in alarm. 'She's making herself ill.'

Svetlana sighed, took the bubblegum out of her mouth, put her arms around her mother and rocked her from side to side as gently as she might have rocked a new-born baby. Amelia wept, hiccuped, shook herself and blew her nose into a handkerchief. 'Your English Countess, she calls cops. How many Russians you think live in this country? They send out description. They send out FBI.'

'You don't understand, Amelia Semyonovna. Let me try – '

'Understand? Me, I understand. I understand more than you know. You will run away. I will go to prison.'

'Listen to me, damn you,' Nikolas cried. 'When my English Countess realizes what's happened, she'll forget it as fast as she can. She doesn't have a choice in the matter.'

'You steal from her,' Amelia spat out. 'Money. Passport. Passport is very, very serious. She is not stupid.'

'She wouldn't dare call the police. She's invulnerable. If you *know* you're invulnerable, how can you admit how foolish you've been? What's more foolish than getting conned by the likes of me?'

Amelia quietened at once. There had been rich Englishmen in Monte Carlo. All the whores vied to roll them because they ran away at once and never complained. She eyed Nikolas up and down, good strong body, tall, straight, but that multi-layered expression on the face – smile bawdy and louche at the same time – who could trust such a man? She wouldn't dream it herself. But a titled English girl? with a big nose?

She shrugged. 'OK,' she said.

There was no Orthodox church for miles. Even if there had been, Amelia could not have guaranteed her reception in it. The local church – Presbyterian, I think – was a pretty clapboard building, white with an old spire and a bell, and the pastor was one of her regulars. But she was Russian Orthodox. Or at least she had been. Or at least, that's the way she remembered it. Anyhow, there was a matter of religion involved somewhere – and if not a matter of religion, then a matter of business: she made it a rule not to embarrass clients.

Besides, Yorkel had already offered.

Yorkel's Pool Hall took up the entire floor above the Pair-a-Dice Bar & Grill. On the morning of the wedding, Yorkel, Herman from the Supermarket and Rip Sullivan – all three of them stripped to the waist (acres of pink belly on display on this humid August day) – realigned the pool tables to form an aisle. Amelia's best lace tablecloth, her icons and her candelabra turned the bar into an altar. The town's undertaker, another regular client, filled the room with white freesias. At three o'clock, the wedding guests gathered, perhaps twenty of them including the

153

pawnshop owner who'd sold Nikolas the engagement ring, a retired professor of Greek from Harvard, the driver of Manhassat's only garbage truck, and the pitiable lad who'd come to visit Svetlana on the night Nikolas first arrived in town. Mamochka was bridesmaid. Amelia was matron of honour. Yorkel was best man. Rip Sullivan, in his youth an important figure – runner-up vocalist at the Akron Country Fair – sang the Te Deum in a voice that had matured without losing any of its charm.

Then came a hush. Then – oh, then – Svetlana appeared on Herman's arm. To a man, the wedding guests gasped at the beauty of the sight.

Of course Svetlana was beautiful to begin with, and of course she'd given up bubblegum for this most important half-hour of her life. But, dear God, the dress: who could have guessed at such a marvel? How right Amelia had been to risk so much for a Singer sewing machine. Svetlana was afloat in satin and silk. She was ethereal, blessed, haloed, as noble a bride as any wedding ever saw. I don't mean ruffles and fluffles. Nothing like that. There was softness, yes, but Amelia's complex pattern had produced the very effect she'd sought: extreme simplicity. This gown warmed and highlighted its wearer the way sun warms and highlights a meadow on a summer's morning. The veil was a mist that clings to rye grass before the day gets hot. Its folds passed and repassed as Svetlana walked – and there! See that? Could it be? Isn't it a rainbow?

Nikolas gazed in awe. Melville Katz, town registrar, was so stunned that he had to clear his throat several times before he could begin. The wedding guests held their breath throughout the ceremony as though they were a single body. The pool hall hadn't been this silent since a professional hustler on his way to Boston took a place at one of the pool tables that made up today's wedding aisle – and that was five years ago.

Melville Katz had a deep, resonant voice. 'You may kiss the bride,' he said at last.

And the deed was done.

The congregation let out a collective sigh; a cheer went up, and everybody ran downstairs together to the Pair-a-Dice, where the jukebox played, where vodka waited in frozen bottles, alongside herring and pickle and black Russian bread. The reception was boisterous, drunken, long and – to the delight of everybody – crashed towards evening by a company of Svetlana's girlfriends bringing a fresh supply of vodka.

The nuptial night that followed? A public marriage ought to entitle a bride and groom to privacy in their wedding bed; but for the sake of the Strakhan spiderwort (after all, its power is central to my story), I must reveal this much: the following morning Svetlana made a puzzling – and puzzled – comment to Amelia about the word that had caused such hilarity at her engagement party. Not that Amelia was taken in. Loss of control? Svetlana? Amelia roared with laughter as before. She was touched, though, and pleased as well. Married couples who share jokes, especially jokes against the world beyond their bed, are happier than married couples who don't; and she did so very much want Svetlana's marriage to be happy.

For one whole month, it was too. For one whole month, Svetlana puzzled her puzzlement. Whenever her eyes strayed near her new husband – which they did almost constantly – a frown creased her brow, her bubblegum stopped in her cheek, and her breath came a little faster. For one whole month Nikolas was as drunk on love as he had been on vodka at the reception. But, as everybody knows, one of the joys of a night of vodka, however wild, is that it leaves no hangover the next morning – the lack of congeners, they say – and every day Nikolas left his wedding bed without a hint of the inexplicable pain he'd suffered throughout his time with Priscilla.

At the end of the month, on a Sunday afternoon while Svetlana worked behind the counter of the Supermarket, he and Amelia lifted a final glass and drank a final toast. He kissed her fondly; he said he'd be back in a year or so. She didn't believe this any more than she believed Svetlana's tales of orgasm. But there were no tears or recriminations; they both knew that she was as anxious to see him on his way as he was to be gone. After all, she had a business to get up and running; and while Svetlana was so preoccupied, everything had to stay on hold.

So it was that Nikolas set out to continue along the road that had bought him to Manhassat scarcely three months before.

PART III

The Third Week in September

CHAPTER 10

During my first few days in Overton I'd yearned for just such an escape as Nikolas made from Manhassat. You wouldn't have caught me lingering on for a final glass or a final toast either. Right at the start, while Canfield hummed and Violette pretended humming was a perfectly normal way to entertain guests, I'd begun to count the hours. Oh, dear God, I'd said to myself, three hundred and fourteen to go. The next evening – hum-de-hum-de-de-hum – would I ever survive it? Two hundred and ninety hours? Was it humanly possible?

But by the time Beatrice told me about Nikolas's departure from Manhassat, I was counting only the hours to the next instalment of her story. My life as house guest had settled into a pattern. Early breakfast with the Canfield hum. Then a crossword puzzle while Harry read the papers and made notes on one of his ever-present notepads. I have to admit that the puzzle was only pretend, only a time-filler. How could I concentrate on a crossword? My mind was on nine o'clock because at nine o'clock I could go and see Beatrice.

'You don't have to call on her every day, you know,' Harry said, putting down his paper as I got up to leave. 'I thought we were going to get to know each other here, and we've hardly had a chance to talk.'

'Harry, we've lived together for six months. If that hasn't done it, what hope is there for two weeks at your parents' house?'

'You always learn about people when they're on your own turf.'

'You make me feel like a bug on a pin.'

'Hey, wait a minute.' He jumped out of his chair (I was backing towards the door). 'Come back here.' He pulled me into his arms.

I started to disentangle myself at once. Only that morning I'd awakened from a dream of young Nikolas. I'd never dreamed about a man before.

There's a poem called 'A Virginal' – I can't remember who wrote it – but it begins, 'Go from me: I've just left him.' Young Nikolas had been there beside me when I woke, really there, just for a split second maybe, but there. No, not *there*. Here. Right here, as near as Harry. (How had Harry suddenly grown so many arms? The moment I plucked one off, another sprouted. Arms everywhere. Harry the octopus.) By this time I knew so many intimate things about Nikolas – more than I knew about practically anybody else – that I should have guessed I'd waken one day knowing the way he smelled, the warmth of his breath, the texture of his flesh, things I couldn't possibly know.

But Harry – I'd never liked the hair that stuck out at the side of his neck, and here I was with my face jammed in it. 'You've spent so much time with Grandma that you haven't met any of my friends,' he said, petulant now. 'Hey, relax, will you? Come with me this morning. I want you to meet – '

'How about tomorrow? No, um, how about – ?' I pried the last of him off me and ducked mid-sentence through the back door, which swung shut before I could hear another word he said; I waved at him through the glass, then turned and ran across the lawn, through the trees to Beatrice's house.

She'd already prepared the tray of coffee and cookies. I carried it into Nikolas's beautiful room as I had each day for the last few days – this was a sunny, bright morning, not too hot – and basked in the unsettling elegance of his design. I ought to have been able to understand everything about the man just from looking at what he'd conceived and Beatrice had built. But for all I knew about him – this room and all the stories I'd heard – I caught only glimpses beyond the surface, only a hint here, a suspicion there. I couldn't catch hold of the man himself. I still could not see why he'd run away from Priscilla Carmarth, from her money, from power, position. And from his music too. And to what? Svetlana? a delivery truck?

'There's a story about a bird,' Beatrice said.

'Tell me.'

'I don't think I'm very good at rabbi stories. It's one of those rabbi stories.'

'Oh, please tell me.'

She put a lump of sugar in her coffee and stirred it with a clink-clink of her spoon. 'There's a rabbi who's famous for his wisdom. A boy comes to him – hands cupped to make a little cage – and says, "Tell me if this bird in my hands is dead or alive." Do you see, dear? If the rabbi says the bird is alive, the boy will squeeze it to death. If he says it's dead, the boy will let it free.' Beatrice paused, frowned. 'It's an old story.'

'What happened?'

She looked down at her feet, which were as distorted with arthritis as her hands; swollen joints bulged through velvet slippers. 'The rabbi says to the boy, "Whatever you will. Whatever you will."' She sighed then. 'A responsible rabbi would have said, "Let that bird go, you little sadist." But this rabbi was so busy being smart that he forgot to be responsible.'

'You think Nikolas is just devious.'

'No, no.' She stopped herself at once. 'Oh, my, of course I do,

161

dear. Who's more devious than Nikolas? But not just devious. Not just that.'

'I saw a whole flock of birds once,' I said.

They flew above San Francisco Bay. They were so high up, black-backed sea birds, hundreds of them. They wheeled in formation on the wind currents. Then – a wink, a blink, how had I missed it? – they disappeared. Just like that. The entire flock gone and an empty sky above me. I'll never forget it. Suddenly they appeared again, again all at once – the most magical sleight-of-hand I'd ever seen. I watched and watched. Knowing how magic works is as exciting as magic itself. I was only a child. 'Oh, looky, looky, it's two sides of a coin,' I cried, skipping beside my Uncle Phineas, who aimed his camera at the flock. 'Black wings in the sky' – I banked and wheeled, arms out the way kids do, aeroplane, bird, whatever – 'then white breasts only – whoosh! – no birds at all.'

'Poor Uncle Phineas,' I said to Beatrice, 'how could a snapshot get the birds and an empty sky both? He was very unhappy. The boy's like that, isn't he? Choose – it doesn't matter who does it, the rabbi, the boy himself – and the excitement's finished. That's what you mean, isn't it? The boy's caught. He's got to do it – something or nothing – whatever it is.'

Beatrice nodded. 'My, there is pleasure in a man's zest, isn't there, dear? especially when he's wicked?'

'You mean to tell me Nikolas doesn't go back to Priscilla? not even now? just because – '

'Love is such a very tight straitjacket. If he's wholly absorbed in her, he can't seek out another. How could he bear it?'

Beatrice leaned forward, picked up her coffee cup and smiled, a trifle impishly (which looked very odd: she was so old for an imp).

CHAPTER 11

Nobody can escape all restriction, though. Not even Nikolas. Maybe a flesh and blood woman couldn't hold him, but a fairy tale could. It did too. When he was little his mother Elizabeth used to make up fairy tales for him, just as my Aunt Peggy did for me. One of them – his favourite – was about an itinerant medicine man in the Midwest of the olden days, when America was a strange and terrifying place with wild Indians and malaria everywhere. This medicine man had a horse-drawn caravan full of bottles and potions; he had a silken moustache that reached all the way to the lapels of his coat and wafted in the wind. On the outside of his caravan he'd painted this sign:

PANACEAS for all PEOPLE
BALMS for all BEASTS

Dropsy, cancer, ladies' sickness, the shakes, fever, etc. cured for 50 cents

Sore teats, bot flies, worms, hoof & horn, etc. cured for a dollar

All manner of surgery 2 dollars

On the caravan's shelves there were bottles with heads of babies preserved in alcohol and strange chunks of meat pickled in salt; there were potions that banished fevers, balms that took away pain and a special ointment that grew whole new arms for farmers who'd fed their hands into threshers along with the sheaves of grain.

And hidden away beneath the driver's seat − only for the most special customers who knew the secret and were willing to pay the price − the medicine man kept a powder that exploded in billows of smoke and fire.

The medicine man could conjure the devil himself up from hell. The devil has dreams on offer.

'Any dream?' Nikolas would ask.

'Anything your heart desires,' Elizabeth used to say, dandling him on her lap, enchanted by the greed that small children don't yet know how to hide.

'I want to be − '

'Remember the price.'

'I want to be the Josef Hofmann of − '

'If you ask for something, you must give up whatever you love the most.'

'My mama?' he would say, laughing happily.

'Mama first of all.'

'I want to be Rachmaninov. I want to be Busoni. I want raisin cake for tea. I want . . .'

Again and again Nikolas begged to hear the story and play out the narrative. Again and again his greed shifted from music to some indulgence and back again before the game was played out. This old story is what had come to him as he stood in Amelia's kitchen; it's why he'd bargained so hard for her delivery truck in exchange for his marriage vows and his silk shirts.

He needed the medicine man's entire stock: potion for fever, balm for pain, ointment that grows new hands. Most of all he needed another interview with the Lord of the Morning.

During the weeks before the wedding, while Amelia worked

at her sewing machine, Nikolas had fitted the truck out with the nautical furniture that Priscilla's Swiss cheques bought for him in Cleveland. (Furniture for campers and caravans is so ugly.) He screwed a small upright piano to the truck's floor and packed a record player, a carefully selected library of records and several chess sets – items bought on the same outing, while Amelia was so preoccupied with dress design that she paid no attention to the wonders her signature secured for him.

When at last the delivery truck was a home on wheels just as the medicine man's caravan had been, Nikolas painted his own advertisement on its sides:

Nikolas Strakhan
Piano & Chess

Performances of music, Matches & demonstrations (blindfold, multiple opponent)

Winner: Chopin Competition, Warsaw; Queen Elisabeth of Belgium Competition, Joseph Hofmann Competition, Cracow, etc.

Chess Grandmaster

Well, perhaps he wasn't a grandmaster. Perhaps he hadn't *won* the competitions either. What medicine man's potions really cure everything that ails man and beast? And perhaps (if you're going to be pedantic about it), Cracow doesn't even run a piano competition, much less acknowledge winners. But Nikolas had placed at Warsaw, which after all is the most important of the competitions. He'd done so under great adversity too.

God knows, performance is bad enough. But competition! If you fail to make your mark, your entire life is likely to fail with you. Not just your artistic ambitions either. I'm talking money. I'm talking financial future. After all, think of the investment so far. Who can get as far as competition without a life of privilege? a fine instrument? years and years of lessons? time off to take them? to practise? to prepare for competition? time off to compete? even such dull items as the right clothes and a travel ticket? Performers have always come in two parts: talent and money. Maybe the proportions vary, but the one is no good without the other. Which is to say that, one way or another, any devil's gift must cover both.

Nikolas had grabbed the talent – the seductive sound he hadn't been able to produce all on his own. But when his father's Lear-like stupidity offered funding in exchange for a mere grovel, what happened? He turned petty thief and ran off, thereby tossing away an inheritance that was rightly his anyhow. Worse, he ran away to a place where nobody knew him, where he had to grub for a living, and so had little hope of establishing himself despite a highly saleable talent.

You see? He'd let a little melting go on near his heart: he hadn't cherished his gift above all else. I doubt the devil even shrugged; outcomes like this are so common. How stupid pride is though. By the time Priscilla entered the scene, the devil – a thrifty fellow – was already in the process of reclaiming the ill-used gift. He'd taken note of the family history that was to produce Beatrice's gnarled hands; perhaps he was amused that Nikolas's background fitted in so neatly with Teresa Lopez-Vega's curse.

The books say rheumatoid arthritis is probably due to some sort of auto-immune disturbance, one of those queer diseases in which the body attacks its own substance. There is no absolute prognosis; the ailment can go anywhere – clear up entirely, cripple entirely, settle down half-way between – and there is no known cure. Swelling usually begins in the small joints of the hands, especially the fingers. There's inflammation and a lot of pain.

When Nikolas played at Warsaw he was ill. If it hadn't been for a shipment of morphine he'd handled – from which he'd taken his profit in kind – he wouldn't have had a chance of competing. But compete he did. He placed too. For this he paid heavily. After the fever left him, his hands hurt whenever he lifted suitcases or tried to shift heavy furniture. This was bad enough. But far worse was the pain that came when he practised for longer than about an hour a day. He went to consultant after consultant. He tried rest, diet, splints, wax baths, diathermy; he took courses of aspirin, salts of gold, cortisone. He went to homoeopaths, Chinese herbalists, acupuncturists. Nothing helped.

A pattern did emerge, though. If he left the piano as soon as the hour or so was up, he suffered no attack. If he played longer, an attack was certain; and with each attack he could play a minute or two less.

This is to say that his already jeopardized career was at an end before it had begun, and he knew it. This is why he hadn't bothered to head toward the Mecca of New York when he found himself so unexpectedly in the United States. What could New York hold for him now? He drove along a road that twisted south and west out of Manhassat, more or less towards Illinois and cousin Canfield. He wasn't particularly anxious to see Canfield; but Illinois seemed as good a direction to head in as any, and he had almost no money. He figured his cousin might be good for a touch.

Eight hours later – the road by now straight and endless – a squad car appeared out of nowhere and screamed in his wake; he pulled on to the hard shoulder and rolled down the window. A policeman ambled over, billy stick, gun and handcuffs clanking as he walked. He leaned his substantial bulk against the side of the delivery truck, glanced at Nikolas, leaned sideways to read the sign, then turned to a study of his fingernails.

'Chess, huh?'

'Yes, officer,' Nikolas said politely.

'Licence.'

Nikolas handed him an English driving licence.

Even in those days a US licence was plastic, cold, hard, a

police state's internal passport as much as a permit to drive; it took skill and special equipment to forge one. Nikolas had never liked the idea of tying himself into a system like that, even fraudulently. English licences were little red books, usually tatty at the edges, with a pretty gold seal embossed on the cover: something for an Edwardian schoolgirl to keep pressed flowers in. You could use them in the United States for a year after your arrival; this meant Nikolas's depended only on the modest housekeeping he'd already undertaken on his British passport.

The policeman – face impassive – took the licence from him, opened it tenderly and studied each of its pages one by one. He shut it, tapped it with his fingers, took in his breath, opened it and again studied the pages.

'Well, well, well, whaddya know,' he said. 'First one of these I seen all day.'

Nikolas laughed. 'It's English,' he said.

'You from England?'

'Switzerland.'

'Whaddya doing with this here, um' – the cop turned the little red book this way and that in the evening sunshine – 'English licence?'

'I was educated in England.' It was mid-September, hot, humid. Nikolas wondered in a vague sort of way just *where* he might have gone to school in England. Eton? Harrow? They all sounded so unpleasant.

'You were speedin'.'

'I'm terribly sorry. I really am. I arrived only two days ago. Would I still be jet-lagged, do you think? It's odd driving on the wrong side of the road. How fast can I go?'

The policeman leaned back, looked down the road, up it again. There was nobody to be seen. 'You were *really* speedin'.'

'I'm a journalist,' Nikolas said, although he'd never in his life had any interest in writing. 'I've come to America to do a series for the *Sunday Times* – the London *Sunday Times*' – he didn't

168

even pause for breath – 'on the American response to the arts. The *Sunday Times* is particularly interested in what students in small college towns here think about music and such intellectual pursuits as chess. But I'm in something of a quandary because I don't know how to find a college that would serve my purpose. Have you any ideas?'

The policeman's face was blank.

'In Britain only a tiny minority go on to higher education. What the *Sunday Times* wants me to investigate is what effect an education has on widening the horizons of young people who would have ended up in blue-collar jobs at home.' Nikolas sensed a flaw in the logic of this tale. He rushed on, seeking safer ground. 'The arts editor is an American himself. When I left London, he told me that if I ever wanted information, all I had to do was ask an American policeman. And here you are, right when I need you.'

By now the policeman's face was a void, a vacuum.

Nikolas smiled and started again. 'Well,' he said, 'until now I'd thought of just tootling – '

'Nanapeewuck College down the road a hundred miles and a bit.'

'Nana-what College?'

'Nanapeewuck. Like I say.' The cop jerked his head in the direction of the road in front of them. 'They got a basketball team.'

'What goes on there?'

'They got a basketball team. Like I say.'

'So you did. So you did. I'm sorry. It sounds like the very place for me. Just where is it?'

The policeman spoke slowly to make sure Nikolas understood. 'Like I say. Down the road a hundred miles and a bit.'

'So close? Really? Oh, that's wonderful. I'll go there at once. How can I ever repay your kindness? I know. I know. I'll start my article with this very encounter. Tell you what, I'll send you a copy. Would you like a copy? Do give me your address so I can send you one.'

The policeman stared at Nikolas a moment, then slapped the side of the delivery truck. 'I catch you doing over sixty-three again, I dock you, no matter what funny little book you got. Understand me?' With this, he turned, clanked back to the squad car, climbed into it and started up the engine.

Nikolas called out his gratitude once more. He meant it too. Until this very moment, he hadn't had any idea what he was going to do in his delivery truck or how he was going to support himself in the weeks to come; he certainly had no wish to stay with Canfield long, if at all. He drove at a precise sixty-three miles an hour across the border and into Illinois.

There was a time when Nanapeewuck's Main Street was a boulevard of beech and elm where starlings clustered. But townspeople didn't like the starlings. 'Rats with wings,' they said. They cut down the trees, and treelessness turned Nanapeewuck into a hell-hole. Without trees, there was nothing to soften the wink, the blink, the squint of neon on filling station, motel, honky-tonk, Ma and Pa eatery. Besides, starlings don't care where they roost. Iridescent scavengers clustered as thick as blackfly on raw telephone wires above the fiercely hot, semi-molten tar of the streets.

If it hadn't been so late in the day, Nikolas would never have stopped, but he was tired. Also he was intrigued by the idea he'd cooked up for the policeman. He attempted a meal at the Ma and Pa eatery. To wash out his mouth he spent the last of his money at the honky-tonk. The following morning (after a first night in his delivery truck) he presented himself to the Student Entertainments Committee of the Community College.

The fall term had started only a week before, and the Committee were already running out of events. They took

170

Nikolas on at once. They made the arrangements. They put up posters around the school's quadrangles of burned grass:

EASY PICKINGS!!!

Win yourself a delivery truck
worth more than $2,000!!!
TONIGHT at the **RAILROAD BAR**
Nikolas Strakhan of London, England
challenges you:

**How many AMERICANS
does it take to beat this
ENGLISHMAN at his own
game? two? six? eight?
Can it be done at all?
Suppose you blindfold him?**

The Railroad Bar was a substitute student union of cheap booze and french fries in catsup. The Entertainments Committee pushed together a couple of tables; Nikolas set up six chessboards.

One of the magical qualities of the young – any young, anywhere – is their unbounded faith in themselves. Tell them about a problem that has puzzled generations of scholars, and they figure they might work it out in their lunch hour. So here sits this kid with a funny accent and foreign ways, and they say to themselves (and each other): you trying to tell me this jerk-off can beat six of us all at once at *anything*? Nikolas charged first-comers a dollar apiece; he let them blindfold him.

He beat the lot of them in an hour.

Of course, anybody who plays chess knows this isn't all that much of a trick. Harry played Bobby Fischer once. It was a prize he won – the opportunity to play Fischer. He was one of thirty, all playing the great man at the same time. He said Fischer walked from board to board as fast as he could go, momentarily pausing over perhaps a couple of moves – no more. Nikolas wasn't any Bobby Fischer, but he was a good, book-trained player. No country punter has a chance against such a person; no beginner has a hope in hell. By the time the bar closed, he'd made twenty dollars. He'd managed to drink most of the students under the table too; for this feat – and because his ebullience made them laugh even while he took their money – they obliged him by buying a couple dozen tickets to his recital the next evening.

Back in their lodgings, they told their tale to friends, roommates, landladies; by morning, half the town and all the student body wanted to hear Nikolas play. He'd been a fetching performer even as a little boy in Princess Andreyevna's salon; and the pain in his hands hadn't diminished his easy melodic line or the delicious threat – always present in his work – of slipping over into something, well, not quite polite. Besides, by now he could not play for more than about forty-five minutes, so his audience didn't have to sit through much music. He talked to them instead: why he'd chosen the pieces he'd chosen, a bit of their history, his own history in regard to them.

When he counted up his takings, he'd cleared almost $400.

Three days was enough of Nanapeewuck, but now he knew he didn't have to go on to cousin Canfield – at least not yet. He headed east again and south into the Yew Mountains, the Cheat Mountains, the Alleghenies. From there he went to the national forests of Kentucky and the Smokies of Georgia. Whenever his money ran low, he spent a few days at an agricultural college, an afternoon at a town carnival, three-quarters of an hour at the piano for a private party.

By the end of April, though, he found himself with only $100 in pocket and little further interest in this new profession; so he turned west again towards Illinois and the house on Rifferman Avenue that he'd visited when he was only five years old.

While Nikolas travelled American mountain ranges, Priscilla Carmarth readied herself for a dynastic marriage. He'd suffered. I don't deny it. But her suffering – and its continuation – was greater than his, if more conventional in its workings out. She'd spent the first semi-hysterical hours after he jilted her with a razor blade poised over her wrist; she held back only because she wasn't sure where her arteries were.

When she emerged from her private apartments a few days later, she was not the girl who'd locked herself in. Her friends said to each other, 'What *is* she playing at?' And then they said, 'Oh, of course, she's playing at being Priscilla.' Most of them hadn't seen her during the fortnight of her affair; they had no idea what had caused this blip in her behaviour. All they saw was an actress playing the part of the girl they'd known before her critical encounter in the rain outside Harrods: pale, prim, obedient.

This new Priscilla passed her time just as the old Priscilla had. She shopped. She went to lunch. She made chit-chat over tea. Why resist? What difference does it make? What difference does anything make? Not that she spoke these thoughts out loud. Not to anybody. They solidified inside her, though; and as the weeks wore into months – as the agony dulled – the old, pre-Nikolas boredom fluffed its feathers and settled down over her again: hen upon its hapless chick.

The only person who gave her solace during this terrible period was her grandfather.

William Nevill-Leach had grown sweeter with sickness. It's the last thing anybody would have guessed for him; after all, most people get nastier when they become ill – or, at least, more remote – and William, the father of the Dowager Countess of Carmarth, grandfather of the Countess herself, was a sharp-tongued, vain, self-centred man to begin with. His friends hissed over their teacups that he was, you see, not so very outgoing sometimes because, you understand, some people don't suffer fools gladly.

Phooey. What has suffering fools got to do with it? Most of the time he was just fickle. It's true that photographs of him as a child show an angel with a Dutch boy bob; thereafter, he'd rationed his charms like sugar in wartime, a lump here, a few lumps there. People adored him or hated him in precise accordance to their allotment. He'd lived a life of aimless indulgence in the pastimes of the very rich, and he was as profoundly and as despairingly bored as his granddaughter – as most such people are. Only a good fight gave him real pleasure; he loved to corner, thrash, humiliate and then extract apology like a Nazi dentist at work without anaesthetic. And yet, when he decided on loyalty, he was wholly loyal – a rare and endearing quality. He'd never betrayed Priscilla.

They sat together – he and Priscilla – in what he referred to as his study, although he'd never studied anything. It was a smallish room, comparatively speaking, a branch off the library, where the shelves were filled with books bought in job lots more than a hundred years before. A coal fire burned in the grate. William's windows looked across a greensward, past a fine, spreading oak and on to a lake in the distance.

It was a cold December day midway in the year that separated Nikolas's desertion from her marriage to Eddie Waltham, scheduled for the following May. She sat at her grandfather's feet, her cheek resting against his knees, his ancient, thin fingers in her hair. He'd come to have that opaque-paper look of the very ill – a stooped, drooped, fanfold of a man, bony knees jutting out, back hunched over so far that his jaw settled down on his belt. Only a hint remained of the old crystalline elegance, only enough to terrify his private nurse when the woolly blanket slipped off his lap and left him shivering.

'Your mother told me about this entanglement,' he said to Priscilla. They hadn't spoken of it directly before.

Even sitting at his feet like this – even at her ease – she was ill at ease. 'What entanglement is that?' she asked.

'I've heard all about your adventurer in Hackney.'

'My adventurer?'

'Your con man, little Priscilla. But Hackney, my dear. Couldn't you at least have lifted yourself, as it were, to the King's Road? How fascinating that my darling girl should get herself fucked by a con man the first time around. I didn't know you had it in you.'

The primness slipped a notch and she smiled. (With Nikolas gone, the only person for whom she managed a smile was her grandfather.) 'I quite enjoyed myself.'

'Delighted to hear it, my dear. Delighted. Why break it off? One denies oneself too many pleasures as it is.'

'I'm afraid he walked out on me.'

'Did he indeed?' Her grandfather cocked his head. The crystalline elegance flickered in his features again. 'How much did he take you for?'

'He didn't,' Priscilla lied.

'Now, now, confess to dear old grandpa. "Fess up." Isn't that what Nanny O'Malley used to say? What a fool the woman was. He accepted your mother's fifty quid happily enough.'

'Fifty pounds? For what?'

'You didn't know?'

'No.'

'That's what it took to buy him off.'

She shrugged, a delicate gesture. As Nikolas himself had noticed, all her movements were delicate. 'He'd have taken whatever was offered. He wasn't Nanny O'Malley.'

'Good-looking, was he?'

'I don't know. Actually I don't know what he was. Every time I think about him, I feel empty – almost dizzy – right here.' She tapped her breastbone with her knuckles. 'He was so – I wish I could pinpoint it – So alive.'

'When I was young . . .'

'Did you know somebody like that?'

'A boy.'

'A boy?' she prompted.

'They say, "A woman for duty, a boy for pleasure, a melon for ecstasy." It is not entirely accurate. This boy . . .'

'Tell me.'

'I loved him.'

'Me too.'

'He did not love me, Priscilla.' She said nothing. William stroked her hair. 'You think he loved you, don't you?' She took in a shuddering breath. 'Priscilla?' She let out the breath, and he began to chuckle. 'You think your Hackney man loved you?' Still she said nothing. 'Oh, dear. You're going to make me cry with laughter, and it's not good for an ailing old man to laugh so hard. A Hackney man? You think he – ?'

'It doesn't matter what he felt,' she interrupted, her voice calm, matter of fact. 'What matters is what *I* feel.'

'Don't spoil my fun. Tell me how much he got out of you beyond the fifty. Come on, tell old grandpa. One needs amusement in one's life. A hundred? Two? Less? You don't mean it. Nothing? You can't mean that. What about your chequebook?'

I'm sorry to say she denied it. She lied. I'm sorry to say – I really am – that she acted precisely as Nikolas had told Amelia she would act. In general, she preferred telling the truth because she'd discovered early that lying is rarely necessary. Correctly presented, facts reveal little of importance. But while the first blinding agony had dissipated, she still ached. She was still raw, exposed, afraid of her own intensities. She had not slept well since her last sleep beside him. Hour after hour – still – she thrashed in her bed. Every night – still – she pleaded with God. She pleaded with the absent Nikolas. She pleaded with his old creditor, the devil. Answer came there none.

But the more ingeniously she evaded questions about Nikolas's theft, the harder William laughed. Already doubled over, he doubled even further. His woolly blanket fell to the ground in a heap. He rolled about like a beach ball in a swimming pool. Priscilla waited. She was patient. She'd always been patient. There was a weak sun on this December day, nothing worth bothering with, more an enervation of the landscape than a lighting of it. Suddenly it drained William just as it drained the force from the vast stretch of lawn outside.

He sighed, sniffled, sighed again. 'Does Edward know about him?' She shook her head. 'How can one commit oneself to Edward Waltham? He is, as it were, the dullest man in Wales.' William sighed once more. 'Is this wise, Priscilla?'

'Is what wise?'

'Marrying Edward.'

'All in all, I think it is. I'm getting used to boredom again. I've always been good at it. With practice I may even come to enjoy it. Besides, he looks dashing in a hat. It's not an accomplishment all men can claim.'

'I look bloody glorious in a hat. Or I did once. Long time ago now. Or it seems long ago.'

'You know what I dislike most about Edward?' Priscilla said. The old man stroked her hair. 'His upper lip sweats when he gambles. Why do you suppose that annoys me so? It's probably the only evidence of passion I'll ever find in him.'

'I remember passion.'

'It's good, isn't it?'

'It takes up so much time.'

'Yes.'

'One always seemed to have too much time – far too much,'

William said dreamily. His energy was fading fast; he sank deeper into the chair. 'And yet one didn't, you know. Even as a little boy I wanted to whip the hounds. Don't know why I never got around to it. Now it's too late. I can't even tie my own shoelaces. Odd. I can't get near enough to them.' He brought down his papery eyelids over his eyes. 'Halloo-oo-oo there, feet. Can you read me? Halloo-oo-oo, shoelaces. Is my message getting – ?' And mid-sentence, he began to snore.

Priscilla got up quietly. She rearranged the blanket over his knees, touched his faded cheek and set off to arrange the flowers in the Great Hall.

The marriage of Priscilla Griffiths, Countess of Carmarth, to Mr Edward Waltham, the dullest man in Wales, was the wedding of the year. The Queen herself sat in the front pew for the ceremony, little German dumpling with her Jack Sprat beside her. Anne, a strapping, horsey eleven-year-old, was one of the children who carried Priscilla's train. These details splashed their way across the front pages of every newspaper in Britain. Detailed reports, both plum-vowelled and glottal-stopped, of Priscilla's underclothes, the cost of her veil, Edward's gambling debts and his womanizing: these dominated British tea tables in Harvey Nichols and Lyons' Corner Houses for at least three days.

With all this splendour I hate to criticize, but I have to say that Priscilla's dress wasn't a patch on Svetlana Buddyovna's. True, Svetlana's was the product of a whore's imagination, created from a john's spare bolt of cloth and put together on a Singer sewing machine from an American mall. Whereas, Priscilla's was the best money and prestige could buy: fiercely uncomfortable, made from cloth woven specially in Japan, designed for her by somebody so eminent in the trade that I dare not mention the name. It weighed a ton and cost enough to feed and house a family of six.

Even so, it wasn't a patch on Svetlana's. Nobody gasped when Priscilla started down the aisle of the ancient chapel in the country seat of Carmarth where Carmarths had married for generations. There were endless fiddly details; the overall effect was of one of those lady-panty things that my aunt Peggy hangs in cupboards to keep moths away – just like the lampshades in the flat in Brighton where Harry and I lived.

Nor was the food at the feast afterwards as good as Svetlana's Russian herring and frozen vodka, even though there were lords and ladies aplenty, even though Dukes of This toasted Baronesses That with Dom Pérignon, even though chat of horses, dogs and baccarat tinkled its way into the wee hours of the morning. And the wedding night? Oh well. Ho hum. Never mind.

But Priscilla did get pregnant in her wedding bed, however dully. In the proper course of things, she gave birth to a dull little son, who looked (even when he was only two hours old) precisely like Edward. William Nevill-Leach, dying anyway, died of simple boredom the moment he cast his tired eyes over this first great-grandchild's face – dropped dead, just like that, right there and then. The baby tumbled to the floor and screamed.

Two years later, by which time Priscilla was the richest woman in Wales and the richest in Britain apart from the Queen, she gave birth to another son, a clone of the first and of Edward.

CHAPTER 12

Harry's branch of the family were lawyers in Overton long before Illinois became a state in 1818. Wheelock, Merchant & Merchant gave Abraham Lincoln his first job in a law office; precisely what he did – well, Harry once said (imitating his father's scowl), 'That, young lady, is on a level of detail that need not concern us.' Then Harry, being Harry, laughed happily and told me that Lincoln swept out the place. I guess the firm were pretty good to their sweepers, though, because a Merchant was on Lincoln's White House Staff; and Wheelocks and Merchants have been consultants to practically every US president since then – as well as every governor.

Harry's father Canfield became a partner in the firm at only twenty-six; he was already a stuffed shirt then. When the telephone call came, he was thirty-one and teetering on the crotchety. People forgave him because he had the family's beauty, the wide-set eyes, the broad brow, the clear-cut features; people forgive almost anything in men who look like this.

'Who?' he said into the receiver. He didn't recognize the voice; he couldn't place the accent either – too clipped for New York, not flat enough for Boston, not quite English.

'Nikolas Strakhan. I'm your cousin.'

'A name from the distant past. Not the overly beloved past, I'd say. What are you doing here? *Are* you here?'

'I'm not wholly sure where I am. This town's nothing but bomb-sites. Why does the Midwest have to be so aggressively ugly? It's been a long time, Canfield. Fifteen years? Twenty?'

'A pity we don't meet with your approval.'

Nikolas laughed. 'Can I come to dinner tonight?' The pause that followed was a trifle too long, but Nikolas had only ten dollars left – and three bottles of Margaux. He waited.

'Sure, sure. Everybody's got to eat. I'll get hold of Violette and –'

'You're married? I got married once. Twice in fact – once to a whore and once to a whore's chambermaid. Maybe even – Is this Violette a good cook?'

'She's my wife.'

'Most Americans can't cook.'

Canfield thought of the little velvet jacket (he hadn't thought of it in years); he thought of the patent leather shoes and the click of the heels. 'Violette's father was Russian. Just like yours,' he said irritably. 'If you don't want – '

'He wasn't! Was he really? What kind of pans does she use?'

'What?'

'What kind of pans does she use?'

'What possible – '

'Aluminium pans are a health hazard.'

'A what?'

'They're very bad for you.'

Canfield's fragile patience broke. 'Nikolas, if you're up to risking Violette's cooking and her pans, come to dinner. If you aren't, don't. But get on with it. I have a client waiting.'

'I'm not allowed to eat out of aluminium pans.'

'In that case, stay home, wherever that is. Cook what – '

'Don't be so touchy. I'll bring my own pans. I'll be at your house at seven. Goodbye.'

181

Violette and Canfield were already living on Rifferman Avenue with little Fred, who was only a baby in those days; the family house had been a wedding present, lock, stock and asparagus patch. The beech trees already blocked off the ground where Beatrice Wheelock's house was to be built, but they were young trees then, slender and slight, orderly and matched, not anywhere near as interesting as they were to become. A well-tended vegetable plot took up the land along the side of the house. Violette gathered asparagus for dinner. She was a delicate woman – easily startled, often afraid. She'd been married for eight years; she'd taken tranquillizers for seven of them.

Over the telephone Canfield told her about the aluminium pans, and he didn't hide his annoyance. She knew – because he'd said so again and again – that he was annoyed *for* her rather than *at* her (he went out of his way to protect her whether she needed it or not), but in the end annoyance is annoyance; it spoils everything. The evening stretched out ahead of her, one long disaster. She emptied her mother-in-law's cupboards one by one and laid out on the floor a formidable array of casseroles, pressure cookers, saucepans, sauté pans, crêpe pans – God knows what-all else. Were they aluminium? She didn't know. This one, for example? She pinged it with her fingernail. If it wasn't aluminium, what else might it be?

She'd brought one pan with her when she married, only the one (she'd never been much interested in cooking), but she knew for certain it was cast iron. She decided to roast a chicken in it, figuring that a man who carried around his own pots might not eat red meat. She could do the asparagus in one of Nikolas's pots. The thought suddenly struck her: suppose she burned it? She'd never burned vegetables before, but then she'd never had to cook in a strange man's pots before.

She bathed little Fred and got him to bed by six-thirty. At a quarter to seven, when she was reading *Jack and the Beanstalk* to him, the doorbell rang. She peeked out of the nursery window, which overlooked the front porch. She could see the top of a man's head – she was directly above him – the spread of his shoulders and an array of pots in his arms. She stood frozen for a moment, caught between the immediate terror of Nikolas and the terror of Canfield's contempt if she pretended she hadn't heard him ring. She sometimes had nightmares about Canfield's contempt. She crept down the stairs and opened the door.

The sun was behind Nikolas, low in the sky; pots stuck out from him like –

She frowned. Like what? Of course, she thought then, like a tree-trunk with sprays of flowers around its middle. When she was small her Russian father had told her about wood sprites called *Ljeschie* which appeared in human shape but altered their form at their pleasure. A *Ljeschi* who walks in the woods is as tall as the trees; when he walks in the meadow, the grass hides him entirely. In springtime young husbands cut down fir trees, wrapped them in flowers and set them up before the marital bed, living trees of living wood, *Ljeschie* to ensure that their wives were fruitful and bore them many children.

'My God, you're so pretty,' Nikolas said in his intriguing transatlantic accent. 'Why didn't Canfield tell me? Oh, lucky Canfield.' He paused and Violette stared at him. 'I'm sorry. I know I'm early. It's awkward of me to be early, isn't it? I'm afraid I'm inconsiderate sometimes. I expect Canfield told you, but I don't mean to be. Really I don't. I'll make it up to you, I promise. Can I come in?'

She stood back. Perhaps she wasn't quite as pretty as he'd first thought, but in that shaft of evening sun there was an old-world delicacy to her, large eyes, pale skin, small mouth with little china teeth inside like one of those baby dolls that people's great-grandmothers played with.

'Where can I put these pots?' he went on, passing by her and walking into the house, through the living room, straight into the dining room. 'I hope I haven't offended you by bringing them. It's my doctors, you see. They are absolutely adamant. Isn't the kitchen through here? How amazing: this house is exactly as it used to be.' He pushed open the swing door that separated dining room from kitchen. 'No, it isn't. You've moved the sink. Why'd you do that? You can't look out into the garden any more. Oh, poor Violette, you must hate it. Let's move it back.'

Violette was used to rudeness – Canfield was often rude to her – but she wasn't used to strangers who made themselves completely at home at once and without leave. She was sure this explained the flutter in her chest. It had to, didn't it? Or could it have been what he'd said about the sink? The sink was Canfield's. He always called it *his* sink. '*My* sink' stood in '*my* kitchen', which was in '*my* house'. Canfield was very, very proud of his house and everything in it. 'My house was my father's house and my grandfather's. We go back five generations here.' He was the one who'd insisted they move the sink away from the window. Sunlight fades Wedgwood. '*My* Wedgwood.' She'd resented the change. She'd even, well, yes, she'd even hated it, just as Nikolas said. (Perhaps there was something magical about him after all.)

'Asparagus!' Nikolas cried, bending over her wicker basket and setting his clatter of pots on the kitchen table. He picked up a spear and inspected it. 'I've got just the right pot for asparagus. I'll cook it myself. What else are we having? I've brought a couple bottles of wine with me. Canfield is a barbarian. What does a man who lives in Illinois know of the finer things of life?' He stopped short, turned to her, smiled. 'Except there's you, of course. I can't fault him when it comes to you. There must be an aesthete lurking inside him somewhere. Oh God, I'm talking too much. I'm sorry. Speak to me. Say something.'

'I hardly know what to say.'

'Say you forgive me. I hate blabbermouths.'

Violette laughed. 'You're quite right about Canfield. He says wine has a terrible wine taste.'

'He's angry about the pots too, isn't he?' She nodded. 'Never mind. This too will pass. I've brought three bottles of a 1953 Margaux. They make an education all of their own.' He opened the door of the refrigerator and began to examine the contents. 'Canfield's always been prickly, even as a little – Oh good, are we going to have chicken? You haven't got any leeks here, have you? We could have leeks first – and grated carrots. Have you got a grater?'

Violette laughed again (and again felt that flutter in her chest). There just might be virtues to guests who dispensed with the preliminaries. And how young this guest was. The hair at the nape of his neck curled like little Fred's. She was thirty-one, as old as Canfield. They'd been high school sweethearts, lead couple at their graduation ball, married while he was still in law school (with never so much as a lovers' tumble in the hay). There'd never been anybody else in her life, not really, and yet looking at this boy, his wood sprite of a cousin, she felt – how to express it? Well, maybe no more than that the evening wasn't spoiled after all.

What could be nicer than that?

Canfield's Oldsmobile stalled on the way home from his office that evening. The engine boiled over. Why? Why do you think? Design faults, slipshod manufacture, corrupt mechanics. What half-adequate car demands attention in the middle of the rush hour? What excuse is there for a dashboard that withholds vital data? He had to fetch water from a gas station. He had to carry it himself. He had to open the hood, fill the tank, close the hood, start up again. His hands got dirty. Rounding the corner into Rifferman Avenue he wrenched into third: what a provocation is the grinding of metal on metal to a man already aggrieved. The gear slipped. No wonder either. Violette had driven the car once when it wasn't yet run in. He thought of the aluminium pots – and ground fiercely into second. He

185

thought of that velvet suit and the brown-wimpled nanny.

As if this wasn't enough, he reached his house only to find a delivery truck in the drive. His cheeks flushed. People have their own driveways to park in. They have the street. But no, they choose to make a direct assault on Canfield Wheelock's property instead, on his rights of ownership, on his dignity as a householder and a human being. By the time he opened the front door to see Nikolas and Violette, each with a glass in hand, both looking comfortable and at ease, he was shaking with fury.

'There's some snivelling moron in my – '

'Oh good. You're home at last,' Violette said, interrupting him, jumping up with a gaiety he hadn't seen in her in years.

He turned his rage from the ill-placed delivery truck to Nikolas. 'Decided to risk it, eh?' he said. He recognized Nikolas at once. He couldn't have said why; he'd never seen a picture.

Nikolas got to his feet. 'I'm accustomed to taking risks.'

'Are you indeed?'

'Can't you say hello?' Violette said, teasing Canfield much as his mother had teased him all those years ago. Violette hadn't done anything like this in a very long time either.

'Hello, Nikolas.' Canfield's voice was icy.

And Nikolas? Well, what do you expect? He clicked his heels and bowed from the waist. Of course he did.

But I have to say for Canfield that his irritation exploded into laughter. He laughed so hard he had to sit down. Nikolas poured out a glass of wine and handed it to him.

'Who taught you to do that?' Canfield said, taking the glass.

'Do what?'

'That – that confounded bowing stuff.' He collapsed into laughter again. 'Time was when I'd have begged to kill you for it.'

'You were a very ill-dressed and a very, very ill-mannered small boy, you know,' Nikolas said. 'My nanny was shocked. I loved my nanny.'

186

Just then Canfield noticed the glass in his hand. 'Get me a Scotch, Violette. Can't drink this stuff.'

'How do you know?' Nikolas said. 'You haven't even tasted it. Come on, drink to your beautiful wife and your little boy. I don't think Fred looks like me, you know.' Violette hadn't told him that Fred was adopted. 'But the next one will. You mark my words. I bet it's a girl. Can I be her godfather? I'd make a lousy father but a wonderful godfather. None better. What do you say? Let's have a ceremony with a priest and a font. I've always wanted a ceremony with a priest and a font.'

Canfield looked at the glass in distaste. 'Ugh.'

'Try,' said Nikolas.

'Try,' said Violette.

Canfield screwed up his face, sipped, swallowed. Margaux is a lovely wine, a profound wine. There's truth in it; there's warmth as well as breadth. A fleeting confusion crossed his brow. Then he smiled delightedly. 'Wine? You call this wine? This is something altogether − Nikolas, that your truck outside? You made me park in the street. Don't you know better than to park in front of somebody's garage?'

'You're not somebody. You're my cousin.'

'What's the sign mean? Piano? Chess? What's that about?'

'I travel,' said Nikolas.

A brief silence fell, and Canfield − his doggish temper alert to a bit of leverage − began the humming that so unnerved me during my stay in Overton. 'Hum-de-de-hum − '

'What's that?' Nikolas interrupted.

'What's what?'

'The noise you're making.'

'I'm not making a noise.'

'He can't hear it,' Nikolas said to Violette, a half-worried frown struggling to dominate the amusement on his face. 'Do you think he's going deaf? Our grandpa went deaf. He used to have a huge ear horn to − '

'I am *not* going deaf.' Canfield ruffled his shoulders. He took out a cigarette, lit it, drew on it. 'I get bored easily.'

'Is it a brain lesion?'

'A what?'

'I played chess with a kid who said his mother had a brain lesion. It was right here in Illinois. He said that people whose minds wander often have them. I'm not quite sure what a brain lesion is – I never met the kid's mother. Do you suppose such things run in families? The kid couldn't keep his mind on the board at all.'

Nikolas launched into an animated telling of the story of Nanapeewuck Community College, where he'd met the kid in that very first blindfold bout. What a good storyteller he was. Violette listened transfixed; even Canfield was drawn in, against his best intentions and despite the deep affronts he'd suffered. Canfield told a story himself – a pretty good story too. He laughed at a joke of Violette's. He drank a second glass of wine.

But the respite didn't hold. Dinner began with Nikolas's leeks, whole, blanched, in a vinaigrette. Whole leeks aren't easy for the uninitiated to eat. They dissolve into strings when you try to cut them. Canfield attacked with stabs of his knife. The dining table shook.

Then came the chicken, accompanied by the asparagus in one of Nikolas's pretty copper pots. Canfield rose to carve, a fine old custom handed down from Wheelock father to Wheelock son. The table swayed. It lurched.

'The trouble with cheap Danish furniture like this', Nikolas said, peering down to study the table's underside, 'is that the materials are so fucking shoddy. There's no way to strengthen the framework.'

There was a moment when Canfield wasn't sure he could breathe. This table – ? There are affronts and there are – This table was made from blond wood. This table was imported from Denmark itself. From *Denmark*. The expense of shipment?

188

Crippling. Customs? A Herculean test of endurance. All had been overcome by sheer willpower, because this was *my* table. *My* table was the prize possession of *my* household.

My *Danish* table.

The affront was compounded — doubled, trebled — at once when neither Nikolas nor Violette seemed to notice the malevolent (if humless) silence that followed it. Canfield retired to his study as soon as he'd served himself. He said (his voice grated through clenched teeth) that he had several big cases on. He stayed there all evening, went to bed early and was angrily, furiously, rigidly asleep when Violette undressed and climbed in beside him.

About three in the morning, she awoke and found him gone. He wasn't in the bathroom; he wasn't in little Fred's room.

'Canfield?' she said. She put on a robe and went downstairs. 'Are you there? Canfield?'

Light shone from the dining room.

'That stinking shit,' she heard him say as she reached the door. 'That goddamned, miserable — '

Canfield never, never swore. 'What's the matter?' she cried in alarm, running into the room.

There he lay on his back underneath the dining table, his face contorted with fury, his hands gripping the table's legs.

'That unmitigated motherfucker. It *is* cheap Danish furniture. That — ' He gave the table a vicious shake. 'You keep him away from me, Violette. Hear? He comes near me: I'm going to strangle him. I don't care what it takes. Just keep him away from me.'

She did as he said. She always did as he said.

She took Nikolas to see Beatrice Wheelock, and so it was that he began work on the designs for the house she lives in now — the one I so much admired as she told me these very stories about him. One evening he made *zakuski* from what he remembered of his engagement party siftings and rollings. He

189

shared a bottle of frozen vodka with Violette – Canfield took his plate to his study as usual – and when it was finished, she told him she couldn't have children – that's why they'd adopted Fred.

'Are you infertile?' Nikolas said.

The phrasing of the question took her breath away, but she nodded. 'Canfield's had tests and things. It has to be me.'

'No tests for you?'

She shook her head, and her large eyes filled with tears. 'He wants children more than anything on earth – we both do – but he can hardly bring himself to look at Fred.'

'Do you really believe this?'

'Even little Fred knows, and – '

'I don't mean that. I mean the test results. Have you seen them?' She shook her head again. 'Then how can you be sure? My mother's American husband couldn't impregnate her either. There's something wrong with the men in this country. Do you suppose it's the aluminium pots? Why don't you have tests yourself? I'll bet Canfield has a low sperm – '

But by now she was shaking her head so vigorously – and the tears streamed down her face so piteously – that he reached across the table and touched her fingertips.

'Please don't cry,' he said. 'Let's open another bottle. That'll help. It will, won't it? Vodka's the water of life. It's an old spell and an old enchantment for the growth of blossoms and fruit. Things will change. They'll be better. I promise. Don't cry. I can't bear to see you cry. Violette?'

The next day she took him for a drive and showed him where the Sangamon River is dammed to make Lake Decatur. There are pecans, pawpaws, persimmons here; there's spruce and balsam and Scotch pine. In spring everything is so fresh. Violette carried Fred; Nikolas carried sandwiches, lemonade, a blanket to sit on. They walked through brush, stopping here and there to let the baby investigate; Fred was just learning to crawl, a solemn child given to intense study of bugs on the ground. Quite by chance they came across a dale beside the lake. They unrolled the blanket beneath a massive fir tree with wild clematis snaking through its branches. They ate the sandwiches. They drank the lemonade. Fred slept and Nikolas and Violette –

Well, after all, what she'd seen in him was a wood sprite, a *Ljeschi* who'd made Russian wives fertile for thousands of years. Who would suggest that a mere mortal deny herself such magic?

By the time Nikolas left the house on Rifferman Avenue two weeks after he arrived, Beatrice Wheelock had full plans for the most unexpected house in Illinois; she also noted – not without a certain satisfaction (she'd never really liked her son Canfield) – that her daughter-in-law glowed in ways she'd never glowed before. She was not surprised when Violette began to suffer bouts of sickness towards the middle of summer.

In fact, it was she who first told Violette that what ailed her was pregnancy, not summer stomach upset. And Nikolas's predictions? a girl who looked like him? Not quite, but fifty-fifty isn't a bad score in the prediction game. He got the sex wrong. The baby was a boy, not a girl. But he was right about the looks. The child turned out to have blue eyes that change to purple as you watch. Nikolas's eyes. Tradescant eyes.

My Harry.

CHAPTER 13

During the last few days of my stay in Overton, this self-same Harry was growing increasingly suspicious – and, I think, somewhat jealous – of his granny. I adored my long visits with her, plainly I did; I thought about little else beyond the stories she told me. As for the rest of the Wheelocks, they were delighted they didn't have to spend so much time with me. They didn't seem to dislike me or even disapprove of me, but I'm afraid it was plain to everybody – except Harry, that is – that I was an increasingly reluctant girlfriend as well as a blurter out of what shouldn't be blurted out.

Harry frowned at Beatrice. His eyes flicked between her and me over fried chicken and iced water on my second and final Sunday lunch with the clan. After apple pie, he took her aside and had a tense, whispered conversation with her; then he insisted I go with him to Lake Decatur for the same reason Violette had taken Nikolas there, although what he said was that he wanted to show me one of the prettiest spots for miles around. That's Harry for you. He's always saying, 'Why don't people say what they mean?' and yet he hardly ever says what he means. I suppose what he wanted was pretty obvious, though.

His parents had put us in separate bedrooms at opposite ends of the house. I didn't mind at all, but Harry loves to sleep next to a warm body. Not that he wants anything much beyond the warmth; most of the time a dog would do fine. I guess you'd call him self-sufficient. I don't mean to be snide about this. It's just that for the most part he prefers himself, sexually speaking, to anybody else, male or female. Not always. Just for the most part. I suppose this was one of the reasons I seemed so right for him. I wasn't much experienced at bed. Not so much lack of opportunity as lack of interest. These stories of Nikolas and my dreams about him as a young man made up the first persuasive evidence I'd had that there might be a point to the fuss after all. Not that I was certain. A dream is only a dream. And yet every time I thought about him –

Anyhow, Harry and I walked nearly a mile through the pecan trees, the persimmons and the pawpaws that had bloomed for Nikolas and Violette and were now ripening (Harry plainly ripening a little with them). Suddenly he dropped to his knees.

'What's the matter?' I cried. 'Are you all right?'

'I want to give you something,' he said, rummaging around in his pocket. And right there and then he handed me the ugliest ring I ever saw.

'What's this for?'

'What do you think?'

'Oh Jesus, is that why you're on your knees?' I was cold and indignant. 'Get up at once. I don't want this ring. It's absurd. I hate the whole idea. People don't get engaged any more. How can you be so ridiculous? I don't want to marry anybody, especially some idiot on his knees. I don't – '

He leaped to his feet, face red and shamed – I shouldn't have said that (I know I shouldn't) – with such a violent jerk that he promptly fell over again. This time he let out a screech.

'Now what?' I said icily.

'I think – ' he gasped. 'I've hurt my knee or something.'

'How can you do this to me? First you bribe me into two weeks of purgatory, then you try to corner me with hideous rings and now – ' He *had* fallen at a queer angle, though. No doubt about it. There'd been a queer noise too. 'Have you really hurt yourself? How are we going to get you out of here if you have?'

He shrugged pitifully from his position on the ground.

After a few minutes the colour came back to his face, but a minor struggle to get him upright made it plain that the leg was going to need support for the long trek out of the woods to the car. I did what I could. The stumble-hobble back to the road, though – I can't bear to think about it even now. I drove him to Emergency in Overton, where he acquired a plaster cast, ankle to groin, and a pair of crutches.

That evening, while Harry lay exhausted and in his mother's care, Beatrice told me how Nikolas had become his father. But as she talked, I began to feel – how to put a finger on it? – that there was something not altogether straightforward about the story. Oh, not in the story itself or in her telling of it. But why this particular story? Why now? By the time she finished, I'd decided it had more to do with Harry's post-lunch whisperings than with my insatiable appetite for tales of Nikolas.

'Is this the deep, dark secret Harry's so worried about?' I said. We were drinking Cointreau out of jade saki cups that she said Nikolas had given her while he was working on the designs for her house. They were very beautiful, these cups, pure jade, delicate shades of green, translucent, with a streak or two of black in them. 'I bet he's ashamed of having Nikolas for a father, isn't he?'

'Oh my, I don't want to leave you with that impression. He isn't ashamed, dear. He can't be: he knows nothing about Nikolas and his mother. You mustn't tell him. He loves that stiff old dog Canfield, and he's a wonderfully loyal son.' She sighed; the weight of those Soviet curls of hers inclined her neck

194

eastwards. 'Nikolas doesn't know about it either. I would so much love to see – Don't you think this makes him a little more interesting?'

'Nikolas? He's fascinating already. He doesn't need – '

'I mean Harry.'

'Harry? Interesting?'

She nodded and watched me so intently that I nodded back, despite myself. She sighed then. 'Harry's a far better person than Nikolas will ever be – or Canfield either – and such an unexpected background does set him apart a little. You'd have to agree with that, wouldn't you? He's very much in love.' I lowered my gaze. I avoided her eye. 'Don't you care for him at all, Eve?' I could feel myself blushing. 'Won't you tell me, dear?'

'It's just that . . .' I trailed off ineffectually.

'What is it, sweetheart?'

'Oh, Beatrice, I don't know what to say. Harry's a wonderful friend – nicer than anybody. I'd love to be in love with him. Really I would. He's enthusiastic, warm-hearted, gentle. He'd never, never hurt me. I'd never again have to compute error margins for an explosives manufacturer, but . . .' I trailed off again.

'He says your uncle is a schools' inspector, very strict.'

'Uncle Phineas? I've never said so. Perhaps he is. He has very fierce jowls.'

'You see, there was an old indiscretion.'

'Uncle Phineas wouldn't care.'

'Plainly Harry doesn't know that. He thinks you're reluctant to marry him because of your uncle's high principles, and he thinks if I can explain the circumstances to you – '

'You can't mean this. It doesn't make sense. Some sort of derring-do is only going to intrigue me, not put me off.'

'That's what I told him.' She studied me a moment. 'Now you tell me, Eve Holland, is what you really want a man like Nikolas?'

I was up out of my chair before I thought. I don't know why. So I sat down again at once, feeling a bit sheepish.

'Is he the kind of man you want?' she repeated gently.

'This cup – ' I began and then went on in a rush, 'Oh, why doesn't anything make sense? These cups are so beautiful they make me ache. They just – But to carve a set of cups from jade? The waste – think of it. Why should such extravagance – such totally irresponsible extravagance – be so exhilarating? Why do I go weak at the knees because some guy in a story tosses away what everybody else wants? Oh, if only I did know. If only I understood something. Almost anything. If only – I can certainly tell you this much. If I'd had a chance at the young Nikolas you describe, he'd have had to run to get away from me.'

The pained play of expression across Beatrice's face took me by abrupt surprise, and the words were out before I had time to stop myself. 'You too,' I cried. 'That's it, isn't it? That's how you know so much about all this. Nikolas told you because – '

'He wasn't particularly interested in me, dear. I was just there. He wasn't particularly interested in Violette either.'

'But both at once? Whatever's in reach? Does he stop at nothing?'

'I wasn't always this old,' she said tartly.

'I didn't mean – Oh, why can't I keep my mouth shut?'

'It's so long ago now that sometimes I think I made it up to amuse myself. But I only have to look around at this house – ' She gave an involuntary shiver of pleasure, unexpected, shocking in so withered and distorted a frame. 'Canfield's father was an impatient man, as impatient as Canfield.' She glanced down at her feet and back up at me, then reached out and patted my hand. 'You are a foolish girl, though, aren't you? Is it just old-fashioned wickedness that intrigues you? Is this why Harry seems pale?'

'Oh Beatrice, no. I don't think – '

'Isn't it possible? You're a scientist, dear. You know about things like possibilities. It can't be absolutely *im*possible, can it?'

'Well, I suppose nobody can ever say – '

'Harry has a prison record.'

'Harry does? You mean there's a bit of Strakhan in him after all? I can't believe it. He never has trouble at airports or anything. Oh, poor Harry, he'll die of shame if he has a prison record. Is it true? All right, you have got me interested. A wicked Harry's got to be a step up from a righteous Harry, hasn't he?'

She laughed. 'I only wish the indiscretion were bigger.'

'Go on, go on. I can't wait. An indiscretion. Harry!'

'How puzzled he'd be,' she said half under her breath, 'if he knew the very secret he fears is the only hope he has left.'

CHAPTER 14

As soon as Canfield knew Violette was pregnant, he'd fallen hopelessly, stupidly, irrevocably in love with this baby-to-be that was Nikolas's child; he slept with his ear to her swelling belly. He read books on child rearing, every one he could find – cover to cover and back again – the very ones he'd mocked her for reading when Fred had first come to them. Holding the newborn in his arms he was Paul on the road to Damascus.

He carried pictures of baby Harry in his wallet. First smile. First step. First word. He recounted tales of Harry's kindergarten precocity to exhausted ladies at parties. He charted height and weight throughout primary school and gloated over adolescent escapades at America's Eton, Choate. Harry was a fine American boy – no doubt about it – but fine American boys have faults, and Canfield could find no fault in him at all. Not one. He saw his son as charming when he was callow, imaginative when he was lying, virtuous when he was priggish, manly when he was truculent, brilliant when he was slick.

By the time Harry graduated from Choate at seventeen, he was suffocating.

He laid his plans and took himself off to visit Nikolas, whom he'd never met, whom Canfield called Junior-that-crook, hyphenated, all in one word, a name to conjure with – a name Harry had conjured with ever since he was little. He'd spent hours daydreaming about Junior-that-crook. He'd turned snippets of family lore into tales of high adventure and tales of shady dealings into monumental epics. Nobody seemed more exciting or more exotic, not Spiderman or Superman or Batman. Nobody was less like Canfield and, by this token alone, nobody was more what Harry wanted to be.

The year was 1979, the year that Margaret Thatcher became Prime Minister of Great Britain. Which may mean something. Anyhow, a lot of time had passed in Nikolas's life as well as in Harry's, and the place teenage Harry ran off to was Paris because that's where Nikolas was living by now.

Harry had only the name of the town – oh, imagine it: Paris, France – and a telephone number. He ran to a telephone box the moment he got through customs at Orly.

'*Oui*?' said the indifferent voice over the telephone.

Harry could hardly contain himself. 'Are you Nikolas Strakhan?' he said.

'Who wants to know?'

'Harry Wheelock. I'm your nephew.'

'I don't have a nephew called Harry.'

'I'm Canfield's younger son.'

'Oh, God, what a bore. Tracked me down, have you? Are you as stuffy as your father?'

A delighted laugh bubbled up in Harry. He couldn't have held it back if he'd had to die for it – and he didn't want to hold it back. 'I've run away.'

'To me?' said Nikolas, shifting abruptly from boredom to curiosity. 'I forgive you everything. Take a taxi. Have you got the address? Ring outside, push hard. Top floor – five flights up. I'll see you in an hour.'

Right behind St-Sulpice in the sixth arrondissement Harry found the house: stone façade, iron railing of balconies above, huge, arched double-door in a dirty green with lion's head knobs – a secret, magical corner of the square, the very place to find adventure of a kind undreamed of on Rifferman Avenue. He rang the battered bell, dashed past an evil-looking hag in a black hole, ran up flights of dark stairs, knocked at the door.

Nikolas opened it at once. 'Harry?' he said. 'You're Harry?' He stared at him in wonder. 'Are you sure you're Canfield's son? You look just like me. Amazing. Absolutely amazing. You're a bit short, though, aren't you? Never mind, maybe you'll grow. Come in. Come in. I told your mother and father their next child would look like me. Did you know that?'

Of course Nikolas didn't know that Harry was his own son, not Canfield's at all, but it *is* amazing that Canfield had never noticed the similarity. As I've said, Harry's eyes weren't Wheelock eyes at all; they were Strakhan eyes. Anybody can see that. Wheelock eyes never change from blue to purple, no matter how long you look into them. There's never a wash of opalescence.

Beyond the eyes, though, the resemblance is hard to pin down. The volatility of Nikolas's face is such a distraction that I decided to study the two of them in photographs. Harry is entirely regular – clean lines, balanced features. He hadn't yet acquired that fetching scar on his cheek. Nikolas was flawed from the beginning; there's an irregularity about the mouth and an unevenness to the eyebrows and the dimples that gives his face an anarchic lilt. All faces are so much alike when you think of it – one mouth, one nose, two eyes – that it's doubly odd when such minuscule variations make one person into a mass-market consumer durable and the other into a wanton. Harry is what a plastic surgeon might have made of Nikolas had Nikolas gone for a facelift. Not that he needed it. In his middle forties, he looked – as a surprising number of men that age do –

practically as young as the teenage Harry. He was still fit in those days, still a fine male animal.

Harry gazed around him. On this top floor, the unpromising building had opened up precisely as it should have into a comic-book hero's hideaway – a very aesthetically minded comic-book hero at that. The room was immense, so large that the Bechstein (it had once belonged to Artur Schnabel) took up only a tiny proportion of the raw wood floor. Heavy beams supported an arched, skylighted ceiling. There were few furnishings: a massive bed, four Eames chairs at corners of a bright square of carpet, a refectory table. Graduated copper pots, from butter melter to lobster boiler, hung over the kitchen area next to a wide, red-flowered balcony that faced on to a cobbled inner courtyard – and beyond it, along the delicate curve of rue du Vieux Colombier to a roofscape of the sort no other city on earth can provide. Windows on the other side of the space, far away, looked straight into one pock-marked wall of St-Sulpice.

'What'll you have to drink?' Nikolas said. 'Are you old enough to drink? Wine? Whisky?'

'Wine,' said Harry. 'This is the most beautiful place I've ever seen. Can I sleep here tonight?'

'Of course you can. Stay as long as you like. Are you sure you want wine? Canfield hates it. Sit. Sit. How long are you here for? Do you speak French?'

'*Double-vay-say*. That's my entire vocabulary. I did know how to say "please" once. But I can't remember it any more. Hey, and *mercy*. That's "thank-you", isn't it?'

'Not really.'

'How should I say it?'

'*Merci.*'

'Isn't that what I said?'

'You're going to have to take some lessons, you know. You can't go around speaking like that. Think of my reputation. How did you manage to find your way here?'

'A friend. I'm not alone – or, rather, I wasn't alone. This girl got on in London. She knows all about France and she put – '

'Is she here?' Nikolas said, looking around as though a strange girl might appear out of nowhere. 'Where is she? What have you done with her? You haven't left her out on the street, have you?'

'She's come for a vacation with her father. She hardly knows him – except that he's rich. I think she's in love with him.'

'Rich? That sounds promising. Where's he staying?'

'Sixteenth something, she said. I don't know. I can't remember. She said a lot of things. Is there a sixteen-something? Does that make sense?'

'Money,' said Nikolas. 'Aristocrats and money. What's her name?'

'Mickie Wall.'

'Ugh. One of those boy's names. I hate that. Why does she do that? Doesn't she have a proper name?'

Harry shrugged. His laugh bubbled up in him again; it fizzed. 'I love being here,' he said. 'I never want to go home.'

'Wall,' Nikolas mused. He inserted a corkscrew into a bottle of Bordeaux. 'London. You did say London, didn't you? Hmm. Wall,' he said again, drawing the cork and pouring wine into two water glasses. Then he said, 'Wall. England. Of course. My God, that is money. Well, well, you old dog. And not yet eighteen either, I bet. Call her at once. I'll drive the two of you into the country for lunch tomorrow. We haven't a moment to lose. You did get her telephone number, didn't you? You haven't lost it or anything? Go on then. What are you waiting for?'

That evening Nikolas took Harry out to dinner at La Coupole, a restaurant as vast as Paddington station, packed with tables and waiters hurrying over colourful mosaic floors. There must be literally hundreds of eaters on the dining floor at any one time, writers (so they say), artists, poets – trainloads of them. There's a train-arrival bustle too, chattering and chewing, knives and forks clinking, glass tinkling. Chandeliers hang from ceilings high enough for birds to nest in. A platter of *moules*, goose *cassoulet*, salad, bread, a bottle of St-Estèphe, then another bottle – and yet another with cheese and wild strawberries.

Genes know each other. I'm certain it's not just a myth. They love each other or hate each other, Narcissus-like, the way only self loves self or hates it. Harry had been more than half in love with Nikolas for years; by the time this evening was over, he was besotted with everything Nikolas was and many things he was not. Everything Nikolas did, everything he said, even the sound of his voice: all this was pure enchantment.

The next day, as Nikolas drove out of Paris and into the countryside beyond, Harry dozed in the back seat, exhausted by yesterday's flight and last night's excitements – to say nothing of last night's wine – listening vaguely to Nikolas and Mickie Wall.

Mickie was not a pretty girl, eyes too close together, nose too large, expression irritable; but there was a solidity to her, strong arms, strong back, a reassuring bedrock – no nonsense. She needed her strength too. She'd just discovered passion – only hours after she'd landed in Paris with Harry – and passion is a nasty shock, especially the first time around. Mickie had been one of those little girls who was going to marry her Daddy when she grew up. Which is sweet in a little girl. It's cute. But she was a big girl now; everybody thought she'd grown out of it. She thought so herself. Yet even though she'd arrived to find a woman installed in Daddy's bed, the power of her own emotions had frightened her.

This was no childish snit of jealousy. This was a lust so primitive, so visceral, so agonizing that she knew she'd never be able to control it. Her mind skidded from side to side. Suppose she tried to seduce Daddy. Suppose – But he'd laugh at her, wouldn't he? Of course he would. She had to leave, get out. But how could she bear it? What was life without him? What was she to do? Kill herself? Kill Daddy?

Little wonder that Nikolas's professional efforts failed to hold her attention; conversation lagged and ground to a halt again and again.

'I've never seen a blouse like that,' Nikolas said, casting about for something – anything – that might get her to talk. Her blouse was heavily embroidered and sleeveless.

'Daddy bought it for me,' she said. She sat in front, staring straight ahead, her voice tense, distant; even so innocuous a subject as her blouse lay among foothills she was prepared to soak with blood – at least until she knew what else to do with them. She'd gone to Roedean; her vowels were diphthonged and plummy.

Nikolas glanced at her (still she kept her eyes straight ahead). 'A little draughty, isn't it?'

'It's comfortable. Daddy likes it.'

'You love your daddy, don't you? He must be quite a man.'

'I'm not at all certain why I feel as I do – or why you should ask about it – but the answer to your question is yes. Any objections?'

'Not a one. No, no, not a single one. I approve – wholly, absolutely – of girls who love their daddies.'

Harry dozed for another couple of miles; then he heard Nikolas say, 'When I first met Harry, he was only six years old.'

'Hey,' Harry protested, pleased for no reason he could think of, bemused too, still half asleep. 'What is this? What makes you say a thing like that? We never met at all until – '

'Shut up, Harry. You just don't remember. Anyhow, he said to me – it was the funniest thing – he said to me, "I have always admired the English pork pie." Now isn't that a strange thing for a little boy to say?'

'I couldn't have said that,' Harry said. 'What is a pork pie, anyhow? Is it a hat?'

'Don't be silly,' Mickie said.

Nikolas laughed indulgently. 'There's no man in the world who loves a meat pie the way he does.'

'What is this with the meat pies?' Harry said, profoundly puzzled. 'You've never – '

'I don't know anybody with a subtler sense of humour, either,' Nikolas interrupted. 'We're going to have to educate him, Mickie.'

'We are?' she said.

'We must introduce him to Paris, show him a thing or two – *saucisse de Toulouse, andouillettes, pâté en* – '

'*Andouillettes?*' Mickie said. For the first time her voice showed animation. Nikolas glanced at her again; the irritability of her face had lifted. *Jolie-laide:* trust the French to catch a puzzle in features like hers, pretty and ugly at the same time, light and shade, Ariel and Caliban. 'In America they're chitlins,' she said, 'a great delicacy in the south, so Daddy says, but I don't think I'd like the black-eyed peas that are supposed to go with them. Turnip greens sound delicious, though. I tried to get some in London. No luck, I'm afraid. Daddy once bought chitlins in a paper bucket in Los Angeles.'

'He's educated you well,' Nikolas said.

'I love food.'

'Do you? Really? So do I. What's sex when you can eat? Did Harry tell you that my mother's first husband was Courtney Milligan, the sausage king of Chicago? No? Harry's mother is the one who supplied him with the recipe that made the first American meat – '

'Nikolas, my mother never – '

' – the very first one.' Nikolas raised his voice to cover Harry's. 'Can you imagine that? The first meat pie in Illinois?'

'It is singular,' said Mickie. She looked at Nikolas a little askance, amused – and saw him for the first time. She frowned. She squinted. She caught her breath. Because this chap, this Nikolas – what was his surname? – perhaps he wasn't quite old enough. He wasn't anywhere near fat enough, but – She tilted her head. She squinted at him again – and again caught her breath. There! See it? Isn't that Daddy's shifty innocence? afloat above depths that had made him such a very, very rich man?

'I would have thought the idea of a meat pie much older than Harry's mother,' she said.

Harry opened his mouth to protest again, but Nikolas rushed on. 'Now if you look out to your left, Mickie,' he said, 'you'll see the bend in the Seine that houses one of the largest abattoirs in Europe. That's what everybody says. I prefer Paris to the countryside, don't you? You know the Left Bank at all? I've found a noble old hotel there – used to be a whore house – not far from the Luxembourg Gardens. The trouble is, I don't have the cash on hand to buy it.'

They stopped at a small restaurant in Auvers-sur-Oise, the town where Van Gogh painted out the last months of his life.

'They serve a *pâté à l'Anglaise* here that's not at all unlike the ones at home,' Nikolas said to Mickie as he handed her the menu. They sat in a garden in the shade of a big, dark tree; Van Gogh's squat church stood opposite with Gothic lace holding up its stained-glass windows. On the restaurant's patio an open charcoal fire flamed and crackled. The tablecloth was red-checked. The wine, poured out the moment they arrived, was fresh, tangy, clean the way French country wines so often are. 'A meat pie here can't be the same as one you'll get in London, but Harry wanted to do the best he could to make you feel at home. He called ahead and ordered for us.'

Harry stared at him in astonishment. Mickie said (the pleasure in her face deepened), 'How quickly his French has improved.'

Nikolas laughed. 'The thought was his. The execution mine.'

She studied him a moment. 'What did you say you did?'

'Me? Why? Did I say?'

'I know what Harry does.'

'I'm a musician.'

'What kind?'

'You don't really want to – '

'What kind?'

'Piano.'

'Are you any good?'

A flurry of emotions crossed Nikolas's face, and for the first time he told the truth of the matter. 'I was once,' he said.

Mickie nodded. 'If you'll excuse me,' she said, 'I must, er, powder my nose.'

As soon as she was out of sight, Nikolas leaned over the table and took Harry by the wrist. 'Now you listen here, Harry, I'm doing my damnedest to get you the money you need to stay on here in Europe for a while. That's what you want, isn't it? But you're going to have to show some enthusiasm about English meat products. I can't bring this off all alone.'

'What are you saying? I can't understand anything today. What've I done wrong? I don't think I've – '

'You don't have to. They're ghastly. But Mickie's father is not going to want a son-in-law who doesn't know anything about meat.'

'I'm going to get her to marry me? How? She thinks I'm a real dope. I was kind of babbling on the flight, and she plainly thought – She likes you, though. I can tell. What's meat got to do with it?'

Nikolas raised his glass and his eyebrows. 'The trouble with Americans', he said, 'is that they don't understand the important things in life. Wall is the biggest meat packer in the whole of England. I thought you knew the source of Daddy's millions. You said you did. Or did you just say you knew he had millions?'

'Mickie's American. Or French rather. Or both.'

'Come on, Harry. Just listen to her. Even you can hear she's English.'

'Her father's a banker. Stuff like that.'

'He can't be.'

'She says he's got the thickest Southern accent she's ever heard.' This time Harry struggled. But the zing – the zest of the wine, Van Gogh's church spire, the red-checked tablecloth – was too much for him, and he laughed with a delight he'd never known before, not even yesterday when he'd laughed so happily. 'There are always weddings in the – '

'She's not married already, is she? She should have told me at once. How dare she deceive me like that?'

'No, no,' Harry said, wiping his eyes, trying not to laugh again, failing. 'It's Mr Wall who keeps getting married. He's between wives at the moment. That's what she says. She says she's come to spend her vacation with him to keep him company. There's no meat anywhere.'

Nikolas was laughing almost as hard as he was. 'Not a sausage?'

'Banks. He's a speculator – margin buying, pyramiding – that sort of thing. That's what she said.'

'And here I am trying madly to enhance your reputation with a meat heiress. Garçon! Garçon! God, I hate meat pies. Even French meat pies. Why don't you have the biftek instead? I'm going to. It's superb here. For Mickie too? She doesn't really want that pie thing, does she?' He gave the order to an ancient waiter with a grizzled chin, drew in his breath and then said, 'Well, it's never too late. I'll start in on banks the minute she gets back. I know quite a bit about them. Why does she shave her armpits like that? It makes her look like she's got a man's beard under there. How come she knows so much about andouillettes?'

'I don't know. Hey, let me try.' Harry's eyes shone with the glorious absurdity of the idea.

'Try what?'

'To marry myself off to her. I can do it. I'm sure I can do it. I bet I know all kinds of things you don't know about banks and investment. Besides, how can I learn if I don't try? I want to make my own mistakes.'

Now I ask you, is there a stupider idea anywhere? If somebody else has already made a mistake, why do you have to blunder in and make it all over again? Despite the excellence of the beef steak and the shade of the big, dark tree, Mickie lost the animation Nikolas had provoked in her as soon as Harry took over the conversation. She fell silent and remained that way through the rest of the meal and throughout the ride back to Paris.

For the entirety of Harry's seventeen years, Nikolas had lived in Paris. He'd flown there from Chicago with a German industrialist's widow – a heavy-lidded, lush, languorous woman – whom he'd met in a bar on the East Side. He'd been procuring a sailor for a member of Sviatoslav Richter's entourage, an act of kindness (and of commerce) that was to have some importance later on.

The widow turned out to be a doctor, a specialist in rheumatoid arthritis. In those days, Nikolas still hoped – how could he do otherwise? he was so young – that he might somehow extend his time at the keyboard. His hands showed little of the disfigurement that's usual in victims of the disease. The widow examined him, assured him that hot mud, a year of rest in Paris – and herself – would make his hands viable again.

But when the year was up, the time limit was as unyielding as ever. Angry and despairing, he'd creamed enough money off her to invest in property on his own. So for most of the time Harry was growing up, Nikolas was a rich man in Paris. In the late Seventies, though – hard times for many people – he lost everything and so was back on the con when Harry arrived to stay with him. Harry was so enchanted with everything about Nikolas that when his ferreting around turned up details of the present venture – he went through pockets and desk drawers –

he decided at once to match it. He even tore up cheques from Canfield when Canfield at last located him.

'Are you out of your mind?' Nikolas said, aghast, for the first time sensing that Harry might mean trouble for him. 'Somebody offers you money, you take it.'

But money from Canfield was too easy. How could Harry prove himself worthy of his uncle's adventures if he took money from his father? Nikolas worked the commodities market? OK, that's what Harry would do. Besides, he had a serious feel for money, Harry did; he hadn't been kidding about his grasp of banking. Come September, he was to begin his Freshman year at Harvard Business School; he was one of only six Choate graduates in his class to make it.

So while Nikolas went off to a suite at the Carlton Tower in London, Harry stayed behind in Paris searching out an English-speaking computer; while Nikolas broadened his accent into an Illinois twang and passed himself off as a representative of the American Security Council in Washington, Harry set up a PDP 11 with an acoustic-coupled modem.

Nikolas's prospectus that summer consisted of what are called 'refundable booking deposits'. He had a shipload of sugar from Haiti on offer. He had eighty-eight million Camel cigarettes on their way to Peking and ten thousand tons of Pakistani cement. Risky? Investments like these? How could they be? Picard-Ogilvy et Cie of Geneva was the guarantor; the major investor was the American Security Council itself.

Pick your mark with care, and the money falls into your pocket of its own weight. Nikolas banked profits in an offshore account; funds went from there via Panama and Luxemburg to the Crédit Lyonnais near St-Sulpice.

And the refunds? Well, if depositors pressed him later, Nikolas would explain that the sugar had melted; the cement had solidified; rats had infested the cigarettes. It was a matter of wonder and delight to him that no investor questioned his word. Nor did any question the American Security Council, which didn't exist, or Picard-Ogilvy et Cie of Geneva, which had gone out of business years ago.

He returned to Paris in mid-August, flush with cash, to find Harry hard at work – and also flush with cash. Harry sat in front of an ancient VDU; a hank of rubber, sucking on the telephone receiver like some ill-tempered sex aid, reclined beside a big box with a black face and rows of red buttons.

'I'm playing at interest rates,' Harry said happily as he waved a greeting. 'The Cayman Islands started automated clearing only this spring. Convenient of them, don't you think? I'd hit the Seychelles too, but I can't seem to locate a number.'

That very afternoon, the police arrived to take Harry away.

'You're a thief?' Nikolas said. He was genuinely shocked. 'With those machines? Is that what you've been doing? Robbing people?'

'I guess so,' said Harry, who was really quite pleased with himself. 'Only banks though. They don't seem to have any idea –. They round down and keep the change in every transaction. Did you know that? I just take a little of it back from them. Like Robin Hood. I stole the PDP 11 too. That was harder, but you'd be surprised how lousy security is at French – '

'You stole the what?'

'The PDP 11. The computer. I couldn't afford to buy one myself. Well, I could now, I guess. But tracking down an acoustic – '

'How could you do this to me?' Nikolas burst out. 'Where's your sense of propriety? I don't know why I ever let you stay here in the first place. Canfield's son. I must have lost my touch. I thought I was pretty good at judging character. I hate people who foul their own nests.'

'It's not my nest. It's yours. I like it, though. I really do.'

'Idiot. Fool. How can you be so selfish? I suppose you think somebody's just going to pluck you out of this one, do you? Just make the charges go away? Pretend it never happened? How is your mother supposed to take this? pride? tears of joy? You're going to break her heart. What am I going to tell your father? Did you think about that?'

Harry laughed (perhaps a slightly wiser laugh than before). 'You sound exactly like him,' he said. He wore handcuffs by this time; two policemen stood patiently waiting, one on either side of him. 'Besides, I don't think I *can* get out of this.'

He lifted his hands. The manacles clanked.

Nikolas's anger deserted him at once. 'Aw, fuck it,' he said and drew Harry into his arms, embraced him, kissed him. 'Never mind, kid. Prison will do marvels for your French, and your French needs no less than that. I've never heard an accent as bad.' He considered a moment, then held Harry out at arms' length. 'You don't really mean that, though, do you? That I sound like Canfield? That's a terrible thing to say.'

A prison term? Harry? in some foul French hole? Certainly not. Canfield Wheelock was a lawyer and a good one. Stuffy as hell maybe – but as unscrupulous in his way as Nikolas. Not that he'd ever admit such a thing – or even recognize it in himself. And he was as proud of this little fling of Harry's as he'd been of all the exploits that had preceded it. It showed flair, didn't it? a touch of the devil? What man is a real man without a touch of the devil in him?

Canfield began negotiations at once and at once established that Harry had been arrested only for stealing the PDP 11 and the acoustic-coupled modem. Harry had done his damnedest to confess to his more important crimes, but the police understood nothing. His French was impenetrable, and Nikolas couldn't be reached. Besides, those were early days in computer fraud; hackers had to be very, very stupid to get caught at all.

The prison doctor diagnosed adolescent *crise*. Canfield

offered a generous settlement. A deal was struck. The *crise* was over.

Two weeks later – only a few days after classes started – Harry entered Harvard's prestigious Business School with a clean passport and a record as lily-white as any of America's most proficient spies might hope for. The only clue to his Paris adventure was a plaster on his face.

On the night of his arrest, *une garde a vue* in the chic little police station on the rue Bonaparte with half a dozen French villains (a couple of them ferociously drunk on some blind-pig brew), he got caught by a sideswipe in one of those sudden fights that blow up and die out before a cop on duty has a chance to get out the keys and open the cell. Harry burst open his cheek on the cell's wooden bench. Which is how he got the scar that alone lifts his face out of the ordinary.

The duty cop did his best with alcohol and sticking plaster, but by morning the cut was infected; and by the time Harry reached home, he'd have needed surgery to make his face as good as new. Trust an advertising man, though. Harry knows a good thing when he sees it; he refused to consult a plastic surgeon despite Canfield's rages and Violette's tears.

But what's really important to my story is the reason Nikolas never visited Harry in prison – the reason he wasn't on hand to translate Harry's confession, the reason he forgot Harry's existence less than an hour after policemen had bundled the manacled boy out of his flat.

CHAPTER 15

Maybe storms come from nowhere, but lightning? Don't let them kid you. Lightning is cautious. It foreshadows its strike, sends out an invisible tentacle of electrons, feels for its way on the sly. Then, only when its route is assured, comes the wham-crack, the jagged, brilliant, glorious dumping of charge that we all know. And yet, whose mind doesn't say – pulling back just a little from the beauty and the power of it – how can such things be? Why now? With all the time to work it out, why this route? Why not over there, where the trees are? Aren't trees what lightning is supposed to fancy?

The Midwest looks so smooth, so imperturbable, so dull. Overton's sky lowered and growled on the last morning of my stay there. (We were already packed for the trip to New York.) I ran to Beatrice's house with a newspaper over my head. I'd never seen a real, live Midwest storm – at least, I don't remember seeing one. From her window, while she talked, I watched clouds boil and curl and snake and spill. Rain slapped and retired, slapped and smacked, slapped and retired again.

The more she talked, the more I saw at last that the Nikolas of her story moved amongst people with something of this

214

storm's savage indifference. No wonder he was exhilarating. Isn't this just what most of us ache after in our secret dreams? Rage across the landscape. Take what you want. Forget the rest. Untamed, uncivilized, undomesticated. No guilt, no fear, no regrets. Nothing that ties the rest of piddling humanity to the dirt of the earth.

In majesty and turbulence of such magnitude only the mathematics of chaos can find islands of structure.

For the first time since I'd left Berkeley, I wished I hadn't left at all. I wished with all my soul that I'd had the guts to stay behind and study chaos myself. Why didn't I? I don't know. Money was a problem, but money can be borrowed. The job offer from Edison – with its promise of work on explosives – was flattering as well as tempting, but flattery and temptation can be evaded. Ulysses did it. Why not me? I kept thinking that all it comes down to is what I want. I, Eve Holland. What do *I* want?

If you want something badly enough, you'll find the guts to go out and take it. In the end, either you court the danger that allows you to achieve something or you pretend it doesn't exist. There's no in-between.

Except in fairy tales, of course.

CHAPTER 16

In any kind of story, opportunity must present itself before it can be taken advantage of. When it does, it's got to be powerful enough to drive everything else out of mind. Later, on the very afternoon of Harry's arrest, Nikolas attended a reception at the British Ambassador's in Paris. This was a grand affair for a visiting Minister in one of the finest townhouses in the city. The ballroom is an annexe; one wall is windows, vast, round-arched, ornate, Napoleonic. The ceiling is so high you can hardly see the plaster encrustations that decorate it.

Nikolas stood in a small group of British gentlemen of the sort who just might be interested in a quick profit on refundable booking deposits. A blimp in pinstripes was holding forth. Nikolas fidgeted, sighed irritably, and turned to grab a *canapé* off the tray of a passing waiter. It was then that he saw her. Or rather, it was then that he saw the dress. Clothes didn't interest him much, but this dress caught attention from all over the room.

The blimp followed his glance. 'Ah, that one,' he said. 'It *is* rather super, isn't it? A Dior?'

Nikolas stared. Dior? Of course it wasn't Dior. Amelia Semyonovna Johnson had made that dress. His own mother-in-law. He was certain of it. Who else could fashion something so simple? so bold? so elegant? It wrapped its wearer in light. Surprise almost made him drop his *canapé*. (I do say 'almost'. After all, it was smoked salmon and he was very fond of smoked salmon.)

'It's just a dress, Mr Strakhan,' laughed the blimp.

Nikolas swallowed the *canapé* and, without a word or a backward glance, plunged into the crowded ballroom. The dress took centre position in a group of gowns and tuxedos.

'*Excusez-moi, Madame,*' he began.

She turned then. And this time, if he hadn't eaten his *canapé*, he most certainly would have dropped it.

Poor God. He gets so bored. Sometimes, just for a moment's relief, He plays hide and seek with the devil. That's when absurd coincidences come about. Nikolas had forgotten Priscilla. Of course he had. Twenty years. Who can remember what happened twenty years ago? He'd forgotten her face, her stance, even that exquisite line that ran from her knee to her thigh. And yet the air itself went still. It cocooned him in quiet. All he heard was his own breathing.

He reached out for her in a dream, in a daze, asleep. He took her hand in his. He turned it palm down, then palm up. The dress had long, draping sleeves that ended at her fingers. He lifted the cloth aside and put his lips to the bare skin of her wrist.

'What's this?' hee-hawed one of Priscilla's companions, the Lady Catherine, a Lady of the Queen's Bedchamber (chandelier light glinted off her jewels). 'Hey, hey, there's something going on here that nobody's told us about. Aren't you going to introduce us, Priscilla?'

Neither Nikolas nor Priscilla moved. 'Shouldn't friends meet friends?' Lady Catherine said.

'What?' said Nikolas distractedly.

'My name – '

'I don't care who you are,' Nikolas said.

Lady Catherine was embarrassed, not a feeling she was overly familiar with.

'I hate these people,' Nikolas said to Priscilla, drawing her out from the astonished company – from Lady Catherine, from Mrs Montague Parsons, even from Mr Buffy Douglas, an ancient evil-looking man with an ear horn and the biggest gambling debts in Paris.

He drew her towards the huge doors, through the terrace room that runs all along the back of the annexe, through the drawing rooms of the house itself, into the hall and down the wide flight of stairs (her beautiful gown floated out behind her), to the gravel courtyard beyond and the high, wrought-iron gates to the street.

She said, 'Where are we going?'

'Fucking.'

'Oh, what a good idea.'

'How am I going to get all this cloth off you in under ten seconds without damaging something?'

'It's delicate, isn't it?'

'Oh, yes,' he said, 'there's a line between your knee and your thigh – Taxi! Taxi!'

'I meant the dress,' she said laughing.

'Dress? What dress?'

Taxis are impossible in the rue du Faubourg St Honoré – out of the question. Everybody knows this. And yet one pulled up and stopped for them in the crazed traffic as if dispatched there by the devil himself.

'St-Sulpice,' Nikolas said to the driver. 'And be quick. I'm in pain.'

'You're ill?' she cried in alarm.

'Don't you ever stop talking?'

They sat side by side on the battered leather seat. He touched her forehead. His hand trembled, and she saw it. He ran the tips of his fingers across the tips of her eyelashes, the right eyelash, then the left. He traced the line of her mouth, her chin, her ear, then along her jaw and down to the small dip at the base of her throat. It was summer, about seven o'clock in the evening, broad daylight still, still hot. The traffic, jammed at all hours, day and night, cleared at once.

'Nikolas?'

'Hush.'

Despite the years, the route his hand took was as familiar to him as the hand itself. Her collarbone and then that juncture with her shoulder. He reached her heart; he felt it beat. He bent his head against it. Oh, lucky Priscilla, who could always hear the beating of that heart. And he realized suddenly that every night, every single one for twenty years, he'd dreamt of the line that ran between her knee and her thigh.

There's a stall in a wintry French town on the coast of Brittany that sells oysters culled from a tiny cove nearby. They're piled high in willow baskets. You prise them open and eat them right there in the marketplace. There's nothing like them in all the world. They're better than American Chincoteagues, far better than the mild oysters from the bayous of Louisiana, better even than English Whitstables. These French oysters: they're firm to the tongue; their liquor has the faintest hint of metal to it, and their taste is the clear, clean taste of the sea.

Priscilla took her breath in gasps. 'Faster,' she cried to the driver. 'Hurry! Hurry! We're both in pain.'

Nikolas thrust the contents of his pockets at the driver as the taxi pulled to a stop beside the great church. Coins scattered to the pavement. The fine arched door of his apartment building refused to open. Just plain refused. He tried again. Really he did. He inserted his key, oh, so carefully. He pushed with – oh! – such great delicacy and such absolute attention. Who can explain how things like this come about?

It was not the door that took him in.

The woman who owned the *épicerie* across the street gasped in delight at what she saw and dropped a tray of beetroot into her *céleri-rave*. The baker next door to her worked his dough and floured his apron with an abandon that frightened his cat and set his dog howling. The *charcutier* on the corner stuffed his sausages double-time and so full that their skins burst the moment they hit the griddle of Mme Duclos, his most unforgiving customer, who was ever afterwards to buy her sausages in the sixteenth arrondissement – and never afterwards to eat sausages anywhere near as sweet.

So it was with a cheering audience that the lovers managed to stumble up the stairs to a bed.

They didn't surface until noon the next day. He dressed then, went out into the street and bought salads from the *épicerie*, bread from the baker, sausages from the *charcuterie*. Back at the apartment, he opened a bottle of wine and spread out a picnic. She wore one of his shirts; her long, slender legs were bare, and the weather changed as they ate. A smattering of rain hit the skylights in the ceiling, much like the smattering of rain that had hit her packages when he stood with her for the first time outside Harrods.

'Do you really have grown-up sons?' he said, spooning more egg mayonnaise on to plates. 'How did you manage that? Two of them? What are their names?'

'John is the older. Gerald's the younger. He's sixteen.'

'I never liked the name Gerald. Were both boys Caesarean?' She nodded. 'Why do you suppose a cut across the belly is so salacious? Metal through flesh. The thought makes you tingle all over, doesn't it? I saw a calf delivered by Caesarean once. In Utah, I think. Or was it Arizona?'

'You've done a lot of travelling since I saw you last.'

'I have a daughter,' he said then.

She glanced up at him, then glanced away. 'I know.'

'Do you? How? Because of the dress?'

'It's a long story.'

'Can't you shorten it?'

'You were right to leave me, Nikolas Strakhan,' she said. 'I loved you too much, didn't I? Nothing in such excess can be healthy.'

He got up, fetched his coat from the cupboard, fished in the pocket, then sat down again and laid his fist, knuckles up, on the table. She turned his hand over, prised open the fingers. In his palm lay the earrings he'd taken from her all those years ago, still as they were on the day, still broken as he'd broken them pulling her fiercely to him in the park.

'Sentiment? In you?' she said. 'How fascinating. Is it possible?'

'Tell me about the dress.'

She took his hand in both of hers, kissed the fingers and the palm – but shook her head. 'I don't know anything about it. Eddie bought it for me.'

'Who?'

'Eddie. My husband, Eddie.'

'No he didn't.'

'You think I'm lying?'

'Don't try to suck me into the tedium of your life, Priscilla. Cute and coy bores the shit out of me.'

She raised her eyebrows at him over her fork. What he'd attributed to some pettish whim of God's – Priscilla garbed by Amelia Johnson – was a far more earthly matter than he'd ever have guessed on his own. 'I rarely wear clothes by anyone else. I have the distinction of being the person who funded the first Semyonovna collection, and one of my privileges – '

'You funded the what?'

'Are you serious? You mean you actually don't know? Your mother-in-law's as famous as Lagerfeld. There are very few – '

'Who's Lagerfeld?'

'You're the most annoying man I've ever met. Are you going to make me grab for that bottle of wine or will you pour it for me? Why do you keep it so close to you? Couldn't it sit between us on the table?'

'I hate it when people meddle in my affairs.'

'I wouldn't dream of meddling in your affairs. Your daughter looks exactly like you, did you know that? It seems like magic – to see your features in a girl. I wish I had a daughter.'

'Tell me how you found these people.'

'A good private detective.'

'You don't call that meddling in my affairs?'

'Nikolas, my dearest, I call that meddling in my affairs. The Crédit Union cheques were *my* cheques. That passport was *my* passport. Amelia was easy to find, but you didn't stay with her long enough for me to get funds to you. Do you want some money now?'

'I always want money.'

'Cash or cheque?'

If you're good at refundable booking deposits, you can keep a fiddle going for several years. Nikolas was just back from that London trip; he was poised to put a down-payment on the old hotel near the Luxembourg Gardens that he'd wanted so badly. It had been a small family hotel once, and the moment he first saw it, he'd seen himself in it as paterfamilias. Studio on the top floor, kitchen and dining room on the third floor, children on the second. He'd never much cared for children before.

Which is to say he certainly didn't *need* money.

'What are you paying for, Priscilla? past services? future?'

'Both, I hope. You're quite a bargain, you know. I got you for a fifty per cent discount last time.'

'I don't remember that.'

'You insisted on cash and then didn't even bother to collect.' She shivered happily. 'I do so adore it when you steal from me. Oh dear, you'd better pour me some more wine since you won't let me pour it myself.'

She watched his eyes as she spoke. A trace of something –

perplexity? pain? – shifted its way through the amusement and then settled uneasily on insolence. 'Why don't you buy me this flat?' he said.

'You don't own it?' she cried. 'Oh, that's wonderful. You actually don't? Tell me it's true.'

'Nikolas Strakhan does not own this flat.'

'Who does?'

'Jean Fourier.'

Jean Fourier was the name Nikolas used on his Panamanian account. It was also the name he used whenever he purchased property; he'd used it for the first time when he'd bought this immense loft with money he'd creamed off the German industrialist's widow.

'I'll buy it from him this afternoon.'

'Maybe he's not available this afternoon.'

'Don't tease. I want him now. Please let me do this, Nikolas. I have so much money and so few real pleasures. Let me just unbutton your – '

'Uh-uh. In France there are no discounts before tea.'

She bit her lip, smiled. 'I'm more than willing to pay the full price. Tell me, do you still think of yourself as a musician?'

He pulled away abruptly. The past does repeat itself. It's boring that way. Intriguing too. Both at once. She'd said much the same thing all those years ago, and he'd reacted with the same indignant hurt. She'd just assumed he'd have got over such nonsense by now; she was enchanted to find it wasn't so. There's something endearing about hope. Something innocent, charming. Something vulnerable.

'Don't turn away, Nikolas. What about – '

'How dare you ask me that? Do I *think* of myself as a musician?'

She reached out, tentative, gentle, but drew back again without touching him. 'All I want is for you to take from me what is mine. I don't care how you do it as long as you do it.

223

I'm a limited person – and very badly educated. I can appreciate you – genuinely appreciate you – only as a taker of things, as a thief, not as a musician. Don't be angry with me. Please.'

But his back remained toward her. He stared out the window at the rain on the balcony, on the massed geraniums, on the roofs of Paris beyond. The sky cleared, clouded again. She got up, walked around the huge room, studied the graduated copper pots, the small meat locker he used as a refrigerator, the vast empty floor space: no piano.

The Bechstein had developed a crack in its sound board; its hammers were shredding. The body of it had gone off for analysis and repair just two days before – quite an operation too, because a concert grand is too large for a staircase as narrow as the one in this building. Special movers had lifted it out the windows with a crane and scaled it down the wall of St-Sulpice. Its legs leaned against a wall in the coat cupboard.

One way and another she knew this – or sensed it – just as she knew he owned the flat, just as she knew he had a more than adequate bank account. What's interesting is the lie she didn't anticipate and didn't identify. Or rather, the one crucial truth he omitted. Why didn't he tell her? Why didn't he say he couldn't play for more than a short time – by now reduced to twenty minutes – in any twenty-four hours? Come to think of it, why hadn't he told her the first time around, years ago? There's no one to whom this flaw in him could have mattered less.

'Nikolas?'

'What?'

'How do you practise without a piano?'

He sighed, irritable still, and chafed against a lie for the very first time in his life. 'I sold it.'

'Don't all pianists have to practise?'

'I don't want to talk about it.'

'Why not?'

'Because I don't.'

'Shouldn't we put this food away?'

'Do what you please.'

'Eddie told me that Paris is surprisingly short on recording studios,' she said then. 'I can't remember why the subject interested him. Nothing interests him. So I bought one. I can't even remember why I bought it. Do you want it? Will you take it from me? I haven't got the papers on me, I'm afraid. But I could get them in an hour.'

'I don't know anything about recording.'

'Neither do I.'

'Then what are we talking about?'

'Such a place is – obviously – musical. It's quite lucrative too.' She smiled at his sullen frown. 'You could also steal a night club from me if you want. It used to belong to some singer. I forget which. Josephine Baker maybe. I don't have those papers here either, but you'd be good at running a night club.'

How could she disconcert him so? How could anybody? He was used to control; most of the time, he let go only when it served him. But with her he was as helpless as he had been all those years before. She sat beside him as ready to be taken as the picnic on the table – more than ready, eager, avid, skin with a soft sheen to it – and yet, and yet – The edges of his mind quivered with an uncertainty as painful as the intensities of his body.

'Sometimes you disgust me,' he said.

Another spatter of rain hit the skylights. 'It's not all, Nikolas. You must not think purchase is all.'

He said nothing.

'I love the buying of you,' she went on. 'I love the triumph of it. But I also love you. No, no. That's wrong. I love you, and I also love how I got you and why I got you. They're trimmings – the how and why – important trimmings. But in the end, they are only trimmings. What's important is the need.' She reached out as she had before, hesitated once more, then took courage;

she stroked his neck, his throat. He tried to pull back. He wanted to but he couldn't. He just couldn't. 'I need you desperately – how can I explain it? – the way muscles need a skeleton. For all these years, that's what you've been to me: the skeleton that holds me upright. I think to myself, I can't go any further, then I think, oh, but somewhere in the world – somewhere – does it matter where? – somewhere there's Nikolas. And I'm all right. You can't leave me again. I won't let you. Oh please, Nikolas. Come to me. Take from me.'

Doesn't it seem that at long last the devil has granted Nikolas another interview? that things are possible now that were not possible before? Does it come as any surprise that this time, unlike the time those years before, Priscilla woke toward evening to find her lover still asleep beside her? his arm across his eyes to shut out the light that had already faded from the sky?

The formalities took only two weeks. At noon on the last day before the August exodus from Paris, Priscilla arrived with the papers that were to make Nikolas owner of a sound studio, a night club called Les Liaisons Dangereuses – and owner of his flat as well as seller of it, both at the same time. They were talking animatedly, the various documents spread out all over the table, when there was a hammering on the door.

If your livelihood involves risk and powerful people with lots of money, you're careful about giving out your address. Casual callers are rare and unlikely to be friends. Nikolas rose from his chair, paused, kissed the top of Priscilla's head.

'I think,' he said, then paused, squeezed her shoulder. 'It's probably best if you wait in the bathroom. I'm sorry about this. If you hear, eh, anything strange, lock the door, will you? Don't forget the telephone in there – ' More hammering. 'Go.'

'But, Nikolas, I think – '

'Go. Go. Go.'

He waited until she was out of sight before he went to the front door. As soon as he turned the knob, sheer weight propelled three gigantic men into the room.

'*Sang-mêle*,' one of them shouted at him. A deep voice, harsh, guttural. An insult of course. But why? A dare? He was black – this one who shouted – black moustache hardly visible against black, black skin. Not French born. An African. Nikolas could hear it in the voice. Mali maybe. Maybe Senegal. Not police. Not customs or immigration. Nobody official. They're a brutal lot, the Senegalese. They've cornered the market in hit men.

'I do apologize,' Nikolas said, exquisitely polite. 'I'm sure the trouble lies entirely with me, but I can't make out what you're saying. I'm afraid I don't speak any French – not a word. I can only assure you that whatever it is, it has nothing to do with me.'

'*Oui, oui. Stahnt-amay.*'

'You want somebody else. Down the stairs and to your left. That's the – '

'You!' Priscilla cried, emerging from the bathroom. Her voice was as sharp as any staff sergeant's thwack. She planted herself in front of the African. 'I told you not to come before six.'

The African quailed, and Nikolas's tension collapsed at once into laughter. 'What is this?' he spluttered.

'This poor little man' – she gestured at the immense African – 'is trying to say "Steinway".'

'Steinway?' said Nikolas on an intake of breath. 'A Steinway? What a terrifying woman you are. You've bought a Steinway? For me?'

'I didn't want them to deliver it until after I'd gone. I'm so sorry. I've embarrassed you.'

'Embarrassed me?' He took her into his arms, laughing still, and waltzed her around a step or two. 'How could you embarrass me? What size is it? *Entrez, entrez*,' he said to the men, abandoning the pretence that he spoke no French. '*Un verre de vin? Vous boirez du vin avec moi, n'est ce pas?*'

227

The three men refused the wine, but Nikolas drank a glass while they conferred in the animated way Frenchmen do; they decided the Steinway was too big for the stairs. They set up winches; they hoisted a blanketed piano over the balcony and through the windows, precisely reversing the route Nikolas's Bechstein with its cracked sounding board had taken only days before, precisely the route the Bechstein would be following itself as soon as its repairs were complete.

The tuner arrived – a scrawny blind man with a toolbox – and Nikolas drank another glass while they unwrapped the piano and set it up on its legs.

'A Steinway,' Nikolas was saying as the tuner worked. '*My* Steinway. Look at it, Priscilla. Don't you envy me? Isn't it a noble beast? I'm a man with a Steinway.' He was delighted, enchanted. A Bechstein, fine instrument though it is, isn't strung to produce such a big, rich sound; that's what they tell me anyhow. He lifted the piano's top and peered inside. He paced off the floor. There was space for two grand pianos if he got rid of the Eames chairs that were the only living-room furniture in the apartment. Plenty of space. What do people need chairs for?

The moment the tuner finished, Nikolas sat, picked out a few notes, a few chords, then began to play in earnest. Priscilla lounged, feet up, in one of the chairs already fated for disposal. She'd heard him play at Bressingham's, the London restaurant where he'd first seen her. That was a lifetime ago; she'd paid no attention then, and he hadn't played for her since. Bach, wasn't it? She'd heard Bach in church. She'd heard him in concerts too because people like her go to things like that; she'd always enjoyed music in a passive sort of way, the way my Uncle Phineas does – a comfort sound like the sound of a brook or the tides or rain on a corrugated roof.

My Aunt Peggy used to tap her feet, nod her head and say, 'It's "Poets and Peasants", isn't it?'

'No, Peggy. It's not the "Poet and Peasant Overture",' Uncle Phineas said. It never was.

None of us Hollands has much of an ear. My tin ear is as solid as Aunt Peggy's; however inadequate Priscilla's was, it was better than that. After she'd been listening for a while she decided something was different. She had that clean, cool mind; she knew it wasn't just the cloth stretching over Nikolas's shoulders that inclined her to bawdiness. The great Bach, that fierce intellect – could it be? – was he easing his knees together and apart, a little in, a little out, the way Nikolas himself sometimes did? just for the anticipatory tingle of it? Such a droll thought. Not the Bach she remembered from church.

He stopped abruptly.

'Why aren't you performing on a stage somewhere?' she said. 'You're a genius. I always thought you were. But this is – '

'The funniest thing happened yesterday.' He interrupted her as though the thought had just occurred to him; he'd played several minutes over the limit, and the pain in his fingers was sharp enough to make his breathing a little shallow.

'Oh?' she said. 'Is something wrong with your hands, Nikolas? Why are you – '

'Svetlana wants to divorce me. Why does she want to do a thing like that? I got the papers yesterday. We must have been married – I don't know – fifteen years or so – '

'Twenty.'

' – and suddenly she wants to divorce me. She's barely crossed my mind in all this time, and yet divorce makes me unhappy. I don't like being unhappy. She says I deserted her.' He sighed one of those abrupt, ironic sighs for which there seems to be no word in English. 'I'm surprised she even knows where I am. Jesus, how stupid of me. You told her, didn't you? But it was so long ago. Why bring up divorce now? I hate feeling unhappy.' He put the lid down over the keyboard. 'Why did you say you wanted the piano delivered after six? You didn't tell me you were going anywhere.'

'There are sometimes troubles in my life too.'

'Like what?'

'Eddie's dead.'

'Well, that's a step in the right direction.'

Two days before, across the Channel from this sunny French afternoon, not far out of Cardiff, Eddie Waltham, useless in life, had driven a long, low, slope-eyed car – a Jaguar, I think – into a holiday camper and died. The holiday family died too, mother, father, grandmother, three children. They were Greek.

'When do you leave?' Nikolas said.

'I've arranged a flight out of Le Bourget at six.'

'You could have told me, you know.'

'I did. Just now.'

He got up from the piano and went to look out the window at the pock-marked wall of St-Sulpice. Priscilla hadn't so much changed as clarified, solidified, strengthened. Which is to say she'd grown up. Some people do. She'd controlled a fortune and quadrupled it. There were respectful whispers in the City. Fear too. Nikolas sensed this about her, just as she sensed the truth about him. Doubtless it contributed something to what he felt. For the past fortnight he'd been in retreat, as from a swarm of bees whose sting he hungered for even as he fled. Why doesn't passion ever make sense? He ached to push her away, but he couldn't bear to let her out of his sight. He couldn't bear watching the small movements that told him her mind was already on airports and luggage. Tomorrow she'd sit down to breakfast in a life that excluded him entirely.

'What's the point of this exercise?' he said, throwing himself into a chair, feeling panicky, desolate, foolish – all at the same time.

'Don't be silly, Nikolas. There are formalities that must be dealt with. There are trusts – '

'I'm not talking about Eddie. Who gives a fuck about Eddie? I'm talking about life.'

'Life?'

'Yeah, life.'

'You mean life in general? I don't have time for a philosophical discussion. I never thought of you as the sort to go weak at the knees.'

'It's not my knees.'

'What then?' she said.

So he told her about his hands — to capture her pity, bind her to him — even though he feared that telling her was a terrible mistake, a disaster that would somehow bring disaster in its wake. She folded him in her arms. 'There, there,' she crooned to him as she'd crooned to her sons — Eddie's clones — when they were younger, when they'd skinned their knees or burned their mouths on pudding.

'There, there. Come, come. Don't cry. It isn't the end of the world.'

Eddie's death hadn't moved her. It was tiresome, that's all. There was a lot of detail to be got through, funerals, lawyers, gambling debts, banks, those trusts. This wasn't much different. She was touched that Nikolas had kept his secret so long. She understood its power for him — its iconic significance — better than he did (which wasn't difficult), but the problem itself didn't trouble her.

'There, there,' she said again. 'Why haven't you shifted your attention to some other area? one that doesn't call for so much pressure on the fingers? Another instrument for example? Or composing perhaps. What about composing?'

'For Christ's sake, Priscilla' — Nikolas's anger was immediate (and hardly distinguishable, she thought, from her sons' anger at just such a juncture in the comforting) — 'can't you see? Do I have to spell it out for you? Everything I touch outside the piano is dross. Sure, I can do light stuff. I can write crap. Aren't you pleased? It's workmanlike, saleable crap. I've sold a couple of film scores, a couple of songs. I even made the hit parade once. But as for the real stuff: forget it. I end up with little more than a tinkle. What I do has no heart. Doesn't that amuse you? Doesn't it make you laugh? Isn't it what you always said? that I have no heart?'

She stroked his brow. She stroked his neck. She whispered in his ear.

'What?' he said, pulling himself out of her arms, staring at her in astonishment.

'Marry me.'

'What for? What good is it going to do?'

'I didn't actually have *good* in mind – not as such. I thought you might marry me now that Eddie and Sveta are, well, more or less settled – '

'What is this? Pity? Or corporate takeover?'

'There, there. Never mind.' She reached out, patted his cheek. 'You haven't said anything about other instruments. What's wrong with trying to play another instrument? something that doesn't hurt your hands?'

He sighed irritably. 'I play the fiddle, the oboe, the clarinet. I can manage the cello. I've tried the flute and – Priscilla, I have no real affinity for anything but the piano. What do you want me to do? take up the triangle? spoons? I refuse to talk about this any more.'

'It won't go away just because you refuse to talk about it.'

She cocked her head. She bit her lip.

'What about conducting an orchestra?' she said. 'You haven't mentioned that. You wouldn't have to play anything if you conducted.'

'I imagine orchestras take a good deal of money too,' she went on, warming to her idea. (His objections seemed slow in coming, a lot slower than she'd expected.) 'I could help. We could do it together. Come now, Nikolas, don't pout.'

'You're going to drive me mad,' he said through his teeth.

'It looks so easy. A man just stands there and – '

'How can you say such dumb things?'

'Explain it to me.'

'I don't want to waste my time.'

He got up as he had before and stared again at the wall of the church; she fetched her purse, took out her chequebook, wrote a cheque and handed it to him.

'What's this for?'

'It's a cheque.'

'I can see that.'

'Nikolas, I'm buying a few minutes of your time so I can find out why you can't manage such a simple thing as conducting an orchestra. If I don't understand the situation, I can't possibly help. Go on, take the cheque. That's it. Put it in your pocket. There's a good boy. Now tell me.'

You see how right he'd been to keep his secret? The running was over. The nets were out for the capture now, the beast at bay. She waited.

'What I do, I do on my own,' he said and began to pace back and forth in front of the window. 'The controls – they're hidden, out of sight. Only I can work them, and even I don't know how I do it most of the time. What do you have in mind for me? the Salvation Army band? How do I get sixty other guys to feel the way I feel inside myself? How do I get them to work the controls the way I do? I can hold the field myself, but I can't get other people to do it.' He paced faster. 'What do you expect? You want me to turn myself inside out? metamorphose the moment *you* toss the idea in front of my face?'

'Aren't most umpires players first? That's the same sort of thing, isn't it? in principle?'

'You just don't listen. It's not that I'm unwilling. I'd love to conduct. Love to do it? To get a sound that big, my sound – If somebody said, "Strangle Priscilla and you can conduct," Priscilla would be on a slab at the morgue within the hour. But

233

I know my limitations. I have no talent. It's as simple as that.'

I saw a panther once in a cage that paced the way Nikolas was pacing now, back and forth, back and forth. The zoo keeper fed it with meat on the end of a long pole. 'I'd sell my soul to acquire the gift,' Nikolas laughed, as wildly as that panther laughed at the meat on the pole. 'But I've bargained with the devil before. I was too fucking young to realize what I'd got. Why should he give me another chance?'

'Perhaps he'll set new terms,' she said tartly. 'All this is rather up in the air, isn't it? Have you actually tried to conduct?'

He flung himself back into the chair and took a packet of cigarettes out of his pocket (his hands shook); he lit the cigarette, drew on it. 'Priscilla, Jesus, of course I haven't tried.'

She scanned the sprawl of him and the hang of his head. 'If you've decided you can't do what you want, why don't you marry me and be comfortable?'

'I don't want to marry you. I don't feel friendly. I'm going to screw somebody this time around.'

'The very thing I'm asking for.'

He said nothing.

'Don't go silent on me again, Nikolas. You over-employ that trick, and I've always hated it.'

'I don't know what more to say. I've said everything.'

'Allow me to announce our engagement, and I'll deposit a hundred thousand pounds in your name at the Crédit Lyonnais.'

There are times when the hardest, most mercenary whores don't want their trade shoved down their throats. Nikolas stubbed out his newly lit cigarette. 'I didn't hear that,' he said coldly.

'Two hundred thousand.'

Silence.

'Three hundred thousand.'

'A takeover after all, is it? A hostile takeover at that.'

'Four hundred thousand.'

'No!'

'Five hundred – '

'Done! Done!' he cried.

A week later, on the very day of Eddie's funeral, *The Times* ran a tiny item announcing the engagement of Priscilla, Countess of Carmarth, and M. Nikolas Strakhan of Paris. Not Count Strakhan. He would not concede her even this.

In early November, not six weeks after his engagement to Priscilla became public, Nikolas married Mickie Wall at a registry office in a small town outside Paris.

And Priscilla? Whatever did he think she'd do? Single-minded people are dangerous. But when she found out about Mickie, she said – there was a moment's hesitation (but scarcely more than that) – 'As far as I'm concerned, you're still engaged to me. What you do when you're out of my sight is your own business. See that she feeds you well. Promise me that, will you? It's all I ask. Little enough, wouldn't you say?'

Like Priscilla, Mickie had decided on Nikolas within minutes of meeting him; like Priscilla, she had iron in her soul. A week after that first lunch in the shade of Van Gogh's church in Auvers-sur-Oise, she'd followed him to London on his commodity-peddling trip, accosted him in the Carlton Tower and conceived their first child on the red plush sofa in his suite before he even remembered her name (much less that he didn't like it). She was hugely pregnant when they married; Daddy, the great Matthewson Wall, cut her out of his heart, out of the family – and out of its financial empire too. She wept bitterly. Nikolas didn't care. He had Priscilla's half million in the bank. He dried Mickie's tears for her and, comforted, Mickie was shrewd enough – and French enough – not to worry about a husband's mistress, especially one who paid so well for the privilege.

But what man doesn't dream of such a life? Two doting women. Two separate households, at home in both Paris and in

London: Priscilla stuffing him with money and with fiercely expensive delicacies; Mickie giving him children and a butter-based Normandy diet of the sort Daddy had always loved. He surveyed his realm like God.

He grew fat.

Oh, dear, how sad it is when a man gets fat. Soft layers close over dovetailed muscle; pink rolls peep out (how can he bear it?) between buttons and above belt. His jacket drapes tent-like from his belly instead of his chest. His sex – I know it's as silly a collection of dangling things as ever dangled, but I do so hate to see it disappear under all that glop as though it were eggbeaters sucked into a bowl of dough.

Worse, two years of adoration and domestic bliss brought complacency; Nikolas forgot the musical limitations he'd described with such passion. Priscilla didn't push him. She did what she was best at; she waited – and kept up a delicate but relentless pressure.

One day after a particularly fine lunch, he said to her, 'OK, I'll conduct, just for you.'

'What a good idea,' she said. She cupped her chin in her hands; her eyes shone with triumph. 'I suggest the Queen Elizabeth Hall and some very, very famous soloist.'

'You've thought about this, haven't you?'

'I've thought about little else. If you play at the Queen Elizabeth Hall people take you seriously. As for a soloist – '

'Richter.'

'He's so unreliable, Nikolas. What about – ?'

'Nikolas Strakhan conducts Sviatoslav Richter in the Queen Elizabeth Hall. I like it. I want it. The hall will be booked well in advance, probably a couple of years in advance. He'll keep a commitment to me. I know he will. Priscilla, this is going to be fun. Pick a date about two years from now.'

'Now, listen, Nikolas. Richter hardly plays any more, and he – '

'What a lot of homework you've done. Pick a date.'

'I really don't think – '

'Come on, come on.'

'Any date?' she said with a sigh.

'Any date.'

'The third of September 1984.'

Nikolas beamed. He took as much pleasure in his increasing size as Mickie did. She still loved her Daddy more than any person on earth. Nikolas? Her own children? OK. Sure. Why not? But Daddy was the one and Daddy had been very plump. Isn't more always better than less? Priscilla handed Nikolas a platter of chocolate truffles. 'Richter's Russian,' he said, 'and a sentimental Russian at that. I'm a fellow Russian who helped him out in a foreign country when he needed it.'

'Did you?'

Nikolas smiled, savouring the joke (and the truffle). 'He was on tour in America the year I was there. I procured a sailor for one of his minders in Chicago. The sailor beat the shit out of the minder and took every penny they had, tickets, cash, watches, everything. If I hadn't given him money, I don't know what they'd have done. Tell him – '

'You gave somebody *money*? You? I don't believe it. I can't believe it.'

'Not *somebody*. Richter. They literally didn't know where their next meal was coming from. Besides, I had my cut from the sailor. You tell Richter that Count Nikolas Strakhan Senior died twenty-five years ago on September 3rd, 1984. A proposal to Gosconcert and a personal letter from you, a heartfelt request on behalf of his old benefactor Nikolas Strakhan, the procurer of Chicago. The concert is to be a memorial for the twenty-fifth anniversary of my father's death.' Nikolas laughed. 'He's got to be dead by now, and it's about bloody time he did me a favour. Richter too, come to think of it. He's never gone back to America. Isn't it strange? There's nothing he loves more than a whiff of danger, and yet he hates America.'

So it was that the date was set, the hall booked and the soloist, well, hooked rather than booked.

Priscilla bought fifty forested acres of New York State so Nikolas could study the chummy Leonard Bernstein, who knew the names of his players' children. She bought an estate outside Berlin so he could study Bernstein's opposite as a leader of men, Herbert von Karajan, a living, breathing ex-Nazi with a ruthless ice-grip on command. Whatever else it is or is not, there is an element of tribute to Nikolas in these two allowing him to entertain them to dinner. He grew more complacent still.

When he reached the point of choosing players and decided to pick from the talent on show at the Brighton Festival, Priscilla invested in the Grand Hotel so that a suite would always be available there for him when he needed it.

PART IV

Reprise

CHAPTER 17

Richter Plays

nd   What a pity that the conductor had
en   to be Nikolas Strackhan; he hung
r   over the orchestra like a cloud.

Sitting over cappuccino with Harry the morning after the concert, I'd tried to imagine what it would be like to receive reviews like that. How could a person bear it? Just getting a couple of mediocre grades is enough to make me suicidal. This was the public pillory. One slip of the foot and the pack is at your throat: that's what Uncle Phineas says. But plainly I was letting my own limitations tweak the data. This may be excusable in a lover of fairy tales – but not in somebody who manipulated error margins for a manufacturer of arms and explosives.

So I'll make use of a mathematician's trick: I'll work from first principles. A con man's first principle is getting his foot in the door. If Nikolas was fighting to get his foot in the door, he wouldn't care what the reviewers said – except for the effect it had on his initial objective. If recording companies refused to sign him up, if they slammed the door in his face, he'd just have to rethink the approach. There's no need to get all emotional about it.

After a day on the telephone, he shrugged, returned to Paris with Mickie and the children – and began his rethinking. He'd been home only a couple of weeks when a cool little note arrived from Priscilla telling him to meet her that evening at Les Liaisons Dangereuses.

She'd been right about so many things. Amongst them was Nikolas's gift for night clubs. He'd cut up Les Liaisons Dangereuses into small rooms, installed a piano, chess tables, easy chairs, carpets. There was a sense of quiet, intimacy and old-fashioned grace; there was also a sense (largely justified) that here was a place where patrons could negotiate any pleasure they could imagine. It was very popular.

'Good evening, Nikolas,' she said. There was a resonance in her voice, nothing he'd ever heard in it before. Not worry. Not upset. She did not bend over to kiss him as she usually did.

'Sit down, for Christ's sake,' he said. 'You know I hate craning my neck like this.'

'An armagnac,' she called to a passing waiter.

'*Oui, Madame.*'

As he turned away, she added, 'Wait a minute, Marcel. I'll take it in a balloon glass this evening.'

Nikolas was abruptly on the alert. 'What is this? open rebellion?' He hated balloon glasses.

'I'm celebrating my – ' She broke off, laughed, sat down. 'I feel free for the first time in, oh, I don't know, nearly a quarter of a century. As soon as I get back to London I'll go to Harrods and have lunch at the Capitol. Then I'll go to Brighton. I've always liked Brighton.'

'Brighton, eh?' If Nikolas had been given to narrowing his

eyes, he'd certainly have narrowed them by this time.

'The Tory Conference opens quite soon. I've never gone to a party conference before. I've always wanted to, you know. I quite enjoy consolidating what's mine.' She held out her hand and admired the braid of white gold and diamonds he'd designed for her; he watched every move, every glint of light from the stones. 'You know, Nikolas, what you should have done in life is jewellery. And interior design. You're very good at arranging furniture. I suppose I ought to explain myself. Ah, Marcel, thank you.' She took the bowl-shaped glass from the waiter. 'No comment, Nikolas? Silence? Good. I've made you angry. Why do you always turn silent when you're angry? It's a silly way to exert an edge.

'Now let me see,' she went on, 'most of the contracts – the various properties in Berlin, New York, London – are worded so that I'll have no trouble regaining sole possession. The suite in the Grand Hotel in Brighton too. I admit I had some difficulty securing the paperwork for Mickie's house. That one surprises you, does it? It took some investigative work – and a hefty bribe. You've taught me a great deal, you know. Without you I'd never have known how pleased the authorities are to find money launderers on your scale. I've spent the last month insuring freezes on accounts in Panama, Luxemburg, London, Paris. That's the lot, isn't it? Unfortunately, I gave you the sound studio and Les Liaisons Dangereuses before the need for advance planning arose. I shall claim both in compensation for breach of contract. As for the St-Sulpice flat, it's a simple case of extortion.'

Nicholas said nothing.

'I'll give you until after the conference,' she said. 'Not for your sake. For the children's. I'm quite unaccountably sentimental about children, even my own dull boys. Three weeks should be time enough. Mickie's efficient. Perhaps with you out of the way, her father will help. Oh, Nikolas, I've had such *fun*. No wonder the Lord kept vengeance to himself: it's such a satisfying way to spend time. But I've left out the point, haven't I? You often remark on my tendency to leave out the point. Let's see. How can I state it best? Your concert was the culmination of years of work – work that you didn't even notice. But it changed my life. An impressive result for a musical indulgence, wouldn't you say? No, no, don't bother to tell me yet again how unmusical I am.'

Priscilla surveyed him. She stroked the curves of the balloon glass. She smiled at him over its rim. 'This is a beautiful shape for a glass. But for a man? Oh, dear, no. I told you when I first met you that I wouldn't like you fat. Remember? That was such a long time ago. When I decided I had to remove the feeling I had for you – rip it out entire – I could only hope I'd been right. I couldn't think of any other way.

'But a fat man in Paris wouldn't serve the purpose. You told me so yourself. Remember? "Snobbery is a public vice." That's what you said – those precise words. Publicans and butchers' wives are out on view where English people can see them. It had to be a fat man that the sort of people *I* know could see – and in London. I had to be able to hear the jeers myself.' She gave a girlish giggle. 'It worked too. You are a clever boy, aren't you? I was so bored in the Queen Elizabeth Hall, I went to sleep. You have no idea how wonderful the relief was.'

She shook her head, swirled her armagnac, shook her head again. 'A man who runs away a first time because his passion overwhelms him: this only increases a girl's obsession and rightly so. But twice – Twice and the obsession must be destroyed, whatever the cost. You shouldn't have married Mickie when you were formally engaged to me. It was illegal. It was unkind.'

She sat as she always had, a little awkward, a little uncertain, eland or wildebeest despite her wealth and power – and her newly found passion for revenge. A predator's eyes are still, as

Nikolas's were. Forget that panther though. He's a weakling, caught and caged. What we have here is a piranha – and not in some aquarium either.

'You set me up,' he said.

'Did I? Is that what it's called? I guess I did, now I come to think of it. I can see why you take pride in such matters. It's the sense of conquest, isn't it?'

'First you attend the Tory Conference. Then you destroy the love of your life. Is there a logic here?'

'Don't think you can outwit me, Nikolas. Any move on any of the various properties in any of the various names, and you'll be arrested at once. Actually, I'd rather not have that. I'd rather beggar you than gaol you. As of this precise moment, you don't have a single liquid asset left to manoeuvre with. Every account is frozen. Not that there was much to freeze. You have been spending freely, haven't you?'

She rose from her chair, tossed back the rest of her armagnac, set down the glass; then she cocked her head and scanned him quickly. She'd never encountered a piranha before – after all, they're South American fish – and perhaps what she saw was her own reflection in the water.

'You look quite odd,' she said. 'Could it be fright? What an unexpected pleasure. Have I frightened you? After all these years?'

His eyes glittered. 'You've always frightened me,' he said.

PART V

Late September and Early October

CHAPTER 18

By the time Priscilla left Nikolas sitting alone in Les Liaisons Dangereuses, Harry and I had been in New York for a couple of days. I loved New York, just as I'd expected to. So did he. It was dirty, ugly, smelly, noisy: as awful as everybody said it was, and we adored it for all the reasons everybody else adores it. We'd also defeated it in one small way, and there's nothing like victory to inflame love. The cast on Harry's leg, his crutches and his charming warrior-like scar seemed to make people feel just the right combination of guilt and pity; they helped us get taxis. One man even gave up his own taxi for us. Can you imagine that? a New Yorker giving up a taxi? We managed to keep our giggles back only long enough to accept the offer.

Anyhow, it was early evening on the East Coast of America when we got the telephone call from Nikolas; thinking it over now, I'm pretty sure he called us within an hour or so of Priscilla leaving him. For all her grasp of him, she must have missed out somewhere. The only way you can freeze *all* the liquid assets of a guy like that is to kill him outright.

'Where are you?' cried Harry.

'In Paris. I've got to talk to you.'

'In Paris? You're calling all the way from Paris?'

'I have to talk to you in person.'

'So talk to me. I'm right here.'

'Not over the telephone.'

'Hey, come on. Eve and I won't be back in Brighton for another – let's see, I guess it's just under ten days. We can't talk any other way.'

There was excitement in Nikolas's voice. 'I need your help. Do you have a guest bedroom where you are?'

'We don't have a bedroom at all – not even for us to sleep in.' We'd rented a tiny kitchen apartment in one of those old West End Avenue hotels. 'We have to crawl all over each other to brush our teeth. I have to keep my notepads in the refrigerator. You aren't thinking of coming here, are you? to New York? Hey, what's so important that you'd fly all the way here to talk about it?'

'I don't see what else I can do.' There was a pause. 'New York has the best sound equipment in the world.'

'I don't know anything about sound equipment.'

'I'll be there sometime tomorrow. You'll be at home, won't you? I'll be in touch as soon as I'm in and settled.'

Me? My reaction was extraordinary, stunning. I was practically faint with – Well, what? I don't know. I couldn't say. A child on Christmas Eve with the promise of Christmas morning ahead. Heart pounding, breath shallow, hands moist: all these things. I reprimanded myself severely, and yet – Coming here? Tomorrow? Nikolas? What would I think of him now? in the flesh? What would he think of me? He'd look different than he had in Swiss Cottage, wouldn't he? seem different? How could he help it? All the stories. All that intensity. Maybe he knew nothing about the affair I'd carried on with his younger self, but I knew. Oh, how I knew.

Harry and I fussed over the menu and decided at last to serve him lamb for dinner, just like the lamb that Mickie had made on the day I first met the Strakhans. Harry stayed at home the next afternoon waiting for the telephone call while I set out in search of *carré d'agneau*. I took longer than I'd expected because I might as well have been seeking some sort of gastronomic holy grail. I had to try half a dozen butchers before I found one who was willing to cut from a carcass after the French fashion.

The telephone rang just as I got back inside and began to unpack the groceries.

'Nikolas? You're here already? Where?' Harry said into the receiver. 'The Plaza? That's rather a shift, isn't it? Lousy bed with nephew exchanged for one of the snazziest hotels in town?'

'I'd rather stay with you,' Nikolas said to him, 'but if I can't be uncomfortable with you, I'll be comfortable somewhere else. Can I come to dinner? Is that convenient?'

'We've been planning on it ever since we heard from you. In fact, Eve's just back with – '

'No meat, please. You don't mind, do you? I can't eat meat – not today. Meat's bad for the nerves after a transatlantic flight. Can I come right now? I'll be there as soon as I find a cab.'

So I set out again.

Well, what the hell. I couldn't expect the man to turn polite, could I? easy? thoughtful? Who would have claimed Nikolas was nice? Besides, who wants nice? What good is that? Even so, I went on my search for fish without the enthusiasm I'd put into lamb. The A & P on Broadway had a special on shrimp. I bought three pounds.

By the time I got back with the makings of another dinner in a large paper sack, Nikolas had arrived.

Oh, dear, what is it about Christmas morning when you finally get to it? Why does it always disappoint? The midden of crumpled wrapping paper and scattered spoils – and nothing left to open. Who can settle for reality after weeks of imagined promise? Forget the dream. Forget young Nikolas. The reality in front of me was definitely, irrefutably the Nikolas of Swiss

Cottage – enormous, gigantic. He overwhelmed the place. The walls recoiled. He had to bow his head to fit himself beneath the ceiling. If he'd inhaled too deeply the front door would have burst off its hinges. He embraced me ebulliently within these confines, kissed both my cheeks, patted my back, but somehow managed to leave me still carrying my heavy grocery bag.

I struggled with it to what served as the kitchen: stove, sink, refrigerator and a few shelves in an alley off the main room. He eased his bulk after me.

'Are there cockroaches in here?' he said, looking around with curiosity.

'Armies of them,' I said.

'That's because of the bacon grease.' He picked up an old coffee can, part way full of the stuff. 'Why do you save bacon grease? I'd have thought England would have cured you of such a barbarism. Of course, the English don't know anything about food either. You should never cook with bacon grease. It ruins the flavours.'

As my Uncle Phineas says so often – as all we Hollands know so well – if you lose your temper, you lose your shield. I'd never lost my temper, not once in all my life; I wasn't even tempted to lose it this time. I went cold, as always before. How could I have expected so much from this vast intruder? What skew in my brain accounted for such a chimera?

'I do not cook with bacon grease,' I said coldly.

'Then what do you save it for?' said Nikolas. 'I'm going to throw it out at once.'

'I don't *save* it. This is New York. Don't do that.' I grabbed the can out of his hands. 'You can't pour bacon grease down a New York kitchen drain. It clogs. You have to – '

'What have you got in there?' he interrupted, opening the shopping, now safely perched in the sink.

'Shrimp.'

'I don't like shrimp.'

252

'That's too bad.'

'Americans overcook it.'

'Not me.'

'Really?'

'Really.'

'How are you going to cook it?'

'I'm going to poach it, Nikolas. What do you care, anyhow? If you don't like shrimp, what difference does it make how I prepare it?'

'My, you're touchy today. What is it? I've always meant to ask you, Eve, are you one of those women who suffers from PMT?'

'Nikolas!' Harry said sharply. He stood behind Nikolas, his crutches under his arms, which meant he was standing in the living room. 'Leave her alone. She's already had enough trouble because of you. You want a drink? What about you, Eve? Can't you come and have a drink too? Who cares what we eat. Let's hear what this big secret is all about. Nobody's ever flown across an ocean to consult me before. I'm all aquiver. What'll you have, Nikolas?'

'I bought a bottle at the airport,' Nikolas said, producing a litre of Glenlivet. 'Your whisky's never any good.'

Harry used to buy cheap whisky on the grounds that whisky is different only in the minds of people who read the advertising he writes; he held to his principle so strongly that he insisted we drink cheap stuff, however terrible, or drink none at all. Most of the time he didn't seem to notice, even though he adores really good whisky; but I do remember a bottle so awful that even he couldn't drink it straight. 'We'll portion it out,' he said. He bought a better bottle and poured a few ounces of the ghastly bottle into it. The result was as ghastly as the original; I poured both down the sink. Maybe Harry forgave me for refusing his hideous engagement ring. I know he forgave me for his broken leg. But the whisky I poured down the sink? Not quite. Not even now.

'Hey, Nikolas, what is this secret?' he said. He sat himself gingerly on a straight-backed chair – happy with a glass of Glenlivet – and balanced his crutches against the wall beside him. 'Why have you come all this way?'

'You're the only person I know who has a real understanding of politics, Harry,' Nikolas said, seating his immense rear on the sofa, filling it end to end.

Since Harry's politics are as slick as his advertising jingles, I figured Nikolas was teasing him. Which seemed strange. Fly the Atlantic to tease Harry? Very strange. Harry nodded sagely and looked pleased with himself. 'This is about politics?'

'I just heard about a programme of Ronald Reagan's called Star Wars. You ever heard of Star – ?'

'Of course I've heard of Star Wars,' Harry said. 'There's been almost nothing else in the papers for months.'

'This is very wrong, Harry. Do you know – ?'

'Yes, yes. I know all about it.'

'Nobody is doing anything to stop him. Nobody in industry or in the army is doing anything. The Mafia love him. Somebody must act. Who better than the artists of the world?'

Harry took a swallow of whisky and chortled. 'Artists aren't exactly known for political activism – not around here anyway. What sort of artists do you have in mind?'

'Me.'

'You?'

'That's right.'

'Nikolas Strakhan, political activist?'

'I've flown over here to kill Ronald Reagan.'

'You've what?'

'I'm here to kill Ronald Reagan,' Nikolas repeated.

Harry burst out laughing. 'You flew three thousand miles to tell me this? Why didn't you say so on the telephone? A month ago you'd never heard of the guy.'

'Harry, I am absolutely serious.'

254

'Couldn't you have been this – uh – serious over the telephone? You might have saved yourself an expensive trip.'

'Your telephone is bugged.'

'You're mad.'

'Somebody has to do it,' Nikolas said mildly.

'Bug my telephone? What for? This isn't even my telephone. Why would anybody bug it?'

'Who cares about your telephone, Harry? Somebody must take a moral stand. Somebody must show these people that they are not invulnerable. I need your help.'

Harry stared at Nikolas. 'You?' he cried. 'A moral stand?' Nikolas watched him, smiling. 'Come on. Tell me another. Nikolas Strakhan, the moral arm of the arts?' Harry giggled and gasped. 'The government thinks I'm so dangerous they bug my hotel telephone, and you think – I hate to tell you this, Nikolas, but I can't even kill spiders in the bath.'

Nikolas studied the glass in his hand. 'I thought of poisoning the air-conditioning system.'

Harry burst out laughing again. 'Where?'

'At the White House, I guess. That's where he lives, isn't it?'

'What do you mean, "you guess"? You can't do that. How are you going to get poison on to the grounds, much less into the system?' Harry rocked back and forth. 'If you managed to kill anybody at all, you'd end up killing guards, maids, tourists – '

'Are there tourists around? I hadn't thought of that.'

The brilliant sometimes mock their inferiors by playing the fool. So far as I could see that's what Nikolas's teasing amounted to. The joke wasn't particularly funny. Killing politicians is the sort of thing that tends to come at the end of an evening, when everybody's too drunk to think of anything interesting to say. 'Line 'em up and shoot the lot,' one drunkard says. 'Cyanide in their Weetabix,' crows another. I was embarrassed for Harry. Maybe he wasn't as bright as Nikolas, but he didn't deserve to be ridiculed in front of me this way, knowingly or unknowingly, for whatever obscure reason.

'Help me with the table, will you?' I interrupted. 'Let's eat the shrimp.'

I fetched knives, forks, plates; Harry got up and hobbled to the table to arrange them while I went back to the kitchen area. By the time I returned with wine and warmed garlic butter, Harry and Nikolas were seated.

Harry said, 'Hey, Eve, you'll be happy to know that Nikolas isn't going to poison Reagan after all.'

'How nice for Nikolas,' I said, laying out the table. 'How nice for Mr Reagan.'

Nikolas frowned. 'Harry explains that things might be even worse without Reagan,' he said, 'but I still think – ' He leaned over to the table and peered at the garlic butter. 'Is that for the shrimp? It looks good.'

'Listen here, Nikolas,' I said. 'I'm going to cook one meal. Only one. I'm not going to poach shrimp for Harry and me, and then go back and poach some for you just because you get a kick out of flexing your muscles. Make up your mind right now. Shrimp or no shrimp?'

'I'm going to tell Mickie you're not nice to me.'

'Shrimp or no shrimp?'

'If you don't cook them all, they'll go bad.'

'I'll put them in the freezer at once.'

'Freezing ruins the flavour.'

'Shrimp or no shrimp?'

'I've got to decide this very minute?'

'This very minute.'

'Shrimp.'

It *is* a pretty dish, my shrimp. I poach them in their shells with sprigs of parsley and some bay leaves. The eater shells them and dunks them in garlic butter, sopping up drips with a good, strong bread. Harry opened the wine.

'What kind of bread is this?' Nikolas said, peering at the loaf on the bread board.

'It's called corn bread,' I said.

'It doesn't look French.'

'That's because it isn't. New Yorkers make better bread than the French.'

'That's not true.'

'Yes, it is.'

'You don't know what you're talking about.'

'Neither do you.'

Nikolas studied me with a strange mixture of expression on his face. Shame? Victory? Could it be a dare? Why would he dare me? to do what? Then he turned his back on me and said to Harry, 'Maybe I could plant a bomb. Do you know anybody who can make a bomb?'

'No,' said Harry.

There was a slight pause, and a sense of pure delight – about time somebody gave this guy a taste of his own medicine – bubbled up in me. 'I can,' I said, smiling.

'Hey, come on, why do you say things like that, Eve?' Harry said in a half-whine. 'She only worked error margins at a computer, Nikolas.'

'You don't have any idea what I know,' I snapped. 'I said I can make a bomb. I meant it. Explosive, charge, detonator, a timing device maybe: there's nothing to it.'

Nikolas ate several shrimp in quick succession, paused, wiped his mouth. 'You sure you can do this?'

'If you doubt me, why bother to ask?'

'I've never doubted you. Hand me a piece of that bread, will you, Harry? I don't even know what explodes. Is it dynamite?'

'Plastic's more powerful. It's easier to ship. Or smuggle. But you wouldn't have to – '

'Plastic? Regular old plastic? like in this salad bowl? I hate plastic salad bowls.'

'Sheets rather than bowls. A hundred pounds would make quite a dent in the White House. You could line a foot locker with it.'

'How's it work?' Nikolas stuffed several more shrimp into his mouth. I saw with a sense of shock that he was eating the shells too; Aunt Peggy does that. A driblet of butter glistened on his chin. But it was all so puzzling. Why cross the Atlantic just to play some strange game of 'tease the nephew'? I didn't get it, even though I could see that he'd taken the bait I'd offered and upped the stakes – decided to tease me instead. Or dare me. Which was more puzzling still. A bomb? Nikolas? Don't be absurd. Just a dead horse to beat. Just a joke within a joke. I knew it. He knew I knew. So why the dare? I hate hidden premises; and somehow, despite my certainties, I feared what was to come.

'What's the point of asking?' I said. 'You don't really want to know, and I don't want to go on playing patsy for you.'

'What role do you prefer?'

'No role at all, thank you. I've had quite enough already.'

'Eve, I want you to tell me how to do this.'

I scanned his face and found such complexity there that I hardly knew how to answer. Harry looked from Nikolas to me and back again. 'Eve – '

'Here's your explosive.' I held up the pot of shrimp. I pulled a limp sprig of parsley from it. 'And here's your fuse. Tie an old-fashioned reef knot in the fuse and stick it into the explosive.' I draped the parsley over the lip of the pot to the lone shrimp on Nikolas's plate, all that remained of the dozen I'd put there only a moment before. 'This shrimp is your charge. Its tail is your detonator. This second sprig of parsley is the fuse that connects fish to fork.'

'What's the fork?' said Nikolas.

'A timing device of some sort. It goes off, triggers the detonator, which sets off the charge, which sends a shock wave to the – '

'What are you going to do with your life, Eve?' he interrupted. 'You ought to get a doctorate in mathematics.'

I have to admit – Well, I was completely off-balance. I hadn't mentioned mathematics to Nikolas, and computer operators aren't often fanciers of graduate courses. And then I thought – not thinking very clearly, snatching only at a level horizon – Harry must have mentioned something to him before I got back with the shrimp.

So I said, 'Women don't fare all that well in mathematics. Aspasia got torn apart by dogs. Look, Nikolas, I appreciate your interest, but there's no point in – '

'That's a stupid thing to say.' There was an abrupt ferocity in the words that was different from anything I'd ever heard from him – or from anybody else. 'How can somebody as smart as you talk about the *point*? Point? There is no point. Answers? There are no answers. Questions? There are no questions. You have talent. Use it. You're a coward if you don't. Fuck 'em all. If you've got the courage, that is. Otherwise, you'll crawl on your belly like practically everybody else in this sad old world. Ask me about it sometime. I know. I learned the hard way.'

There's an old Orson Welles film, one made after he himself got so grotesquely fat. You don't even realize he's playing the lead until about half-way through when the camera falls on his face from an oblique angle: lo! there's the young Welles, instantly recognizable. Nikolas's unexpected passion lit his face just like that camera's eye – and I saw the man from the stories I'd heard. I saw the phantom from my own bedchamber. For a moment I was too startled to speak.

I cleared my throat then and said – a little lamely – 'I don't have the money. Besides, I – '

'How much money does it take?'

'Who knows? Education is expensive.'

'Guess.'

'It's dangerous to put price tags on fantasies.'

259

'Guess, damn you.'

'Nikolas, the question is academic. The time for that sort of thing is past.'

'Sounds like cowardice to me.'

'Does it indeed?'

'Come on, admit it. Then you can move on, marry my nephew here, bake a pumpkin pie, teach kindergarten.'

'I don't have the slightest intention of – '

'Can't you bring yourself up to the present?'

Rage? It's blood-shot like Jupiter's great eye. That's it, isn't it? I'd never have guessed. Lakes of molten lava – that's what they used to say made up the eye. They said it was the belly of a planet ripped open to deliver a new moon. Right? Wrong? What difference does it make? Here's incomprehensible wildness: howling storms in red, blue, yellow that never –

'What the fuck do you care?' I cried.

'Eve, you shouldn't – ' Harry began.

'Shut up, Harry.' Was it Nikolas who spoke? Was it I?

'How–Much–Money–Do–You–Need?'

A maelstrom sucks you in, holds you there, won't let you go. 'I despise mathematics! I despise you!'

'How much money?'

'Get a good grade. Be a good girl, be nice, be tactful. Never say the wrong thing. Never lose your temper. Never – Why? Why do we do it? Nobody gives a shit. One small mistake, and you've got catastrophe. What about that? I bet you didn't know that, did you? That's the principle that unites error margins and chaos. What a joke – just what Uncle Phineas says. How could I have missed it for so long? They get you at home. They even get you in complex numbers. One slip of the foot, and the pack is at your throat. You came all the way across the Atlantic for a good joke? What's funnier than that? Why am I always the one who has to be good?'

'Maybe you'll outgrow it. How much?'

'Thousands. God, how should I know? Thousands and thousands.'

'How many thousands?'

'Ten. A hundred. What's an extra couple zeros? What difference does a zero make? It's more than I'll ever have.'

'A hundred thousand's a high price for a doctorate. Pounds or dollars?'

'You get what you pay for.'

'No you don't.'

'OK. Yeah,' I said, reining it in, hands trembling but at last tacked down to a pattern again. 'That's right. For once we agree. I don't want to spend my life shoving inclined planes down pimply teenagers, and I'm sure as hell not going to collate any more error margins for a living. So what good is the fine knowledge I'm going to acquire for this non-existent windfall in pounds or dollars? What am I supposed to do when I've finally got it?'

Nikolas shrugged. 'Come to me.'

'What's that supposed to mean?' Harry burst out. 'What would she come to you for?'

'I can give her some of what she wants,' said Nikolas. 'Not by any means all. But some. A great deal more than you ever will.'

Harry gasped. 'How can you say that? Right in front of me?'

'You want me to say it behind your back?'

'Shut up or get out,' Harry cried. His face went pale. It went red. His eyes watered.

'OK.' Nikolas shrugged again. 'Tell me, Eve. What's the consultation fee for an explosives expert like you?'

I stared at him a moment, then burst out laughing. 'Well, usually my financial advisers work out the details – '

'Eve! Stop this!' Harry's voice came out in a strangled groan.

' – but as near as I can recall, I never tell people how to blow up heads of government for less than, well, let me see, what was the figure? ten thousand? No, no, it was a hundred, wasn't it?'

'A hundred thousand, eh?' said Nikolas.

'That's right,' I said.

'A hundred thousand is pretty high.'

'As I say, education is expensive.'

'Dollars or pounds?'

'Pounds, of course, and in – '

'Haven't you had enough for one evening?' Harry cried. He was only twenty-three years old, but he was so enraged he looked – and sounded – as though he was going to have a stroke any minute.

Nikolas reached out and patted his cheek. Then he turned to me. 'You've got yourself a deal, Eve. You know, your shrimp is excellent. May I have some more?'

You wouldn't think such an evening could be anything short of disaster, would you? But another bottle of wine and it was as though no tempers had been lost, as though no jokes had been played, as though nothing had been said about my future, as though we were perfectly ordinary friends at the end of a perfectly ordinary evening.

As Nikolas was putting on his jacket, I couldn't resist saying to him (just for the dare of it), 'Are you still planning to blow up Reagan?'

He laughed. 'I'd love to let them know we could get at them if we really wanted to. But, what the hell, I'm a businessman with a business to run. I'd better leave the assassin's crown to somebody else. When are you going back to England? You're sailing on the *QE II*, aren't you?'

'I've always wanted to go by ship,' Harry said, opening the door to the hallway.

'When does it leave?' Nikolas said.

'Friday.'

'I'll go with you. Can I do that? You don't mind do you?'

He embraced Harry, who said, 'Just as long as you leave my girl alone.'

262

'OK,' said Nikolas.

'Promise?'

'I promise. Book me a cabin, will you, Eve?'

I should have said, 'Book it yourself.' But the evening hadn't been perfectly ordinary. I could still feel the shock of a lifetime's first tantrum; I could still feel the exhilaration. Hope? Is that what it was? And the one glimpse of Nikolas as he had once been – Suppose he lost the fat?

I said, 'You'd want to go First Class, wouldn't you?'

'Naw, I want to spend time with my favourite nephew. You're going Tourist, aren't you? I'll go Tourist so we can be together.'

I don't know why it hadn't occurred to me that the ship might not have any cabins left. There was less than a week to go before sailing. The Cunard clerk on the telephone was curt. Of course they had no cabins in Tourist. A shared cabin? What an absurd idea. First Class? Sold out months ago. There was not a single bed free on the entire ship; even the waiting list was endless. I rang Nikolas to tell him.

'Never mind,' he said. 'I'll work something out.'

'You can always fly back,' I said.

'Too much luggage.'

'You can't have too much luggage. You flew over here.'

'What time did you say you sail?'

'Three o'clock. But you don't have to – '

'I'll be there.'

But Nikolas wasn't at the docks when Harry and I went on board. We stayed on deck while the ship pulled out of New York Harbor; then we investigated our cabin and unpacked. In the last couple of days, Harry's leg had begun to hurt inside its cast, so he rested while I prowled the corridors. At eight I went to meet him for dinner.

'This way, Madam,' said the *maître d'hôtel* when I gave him my name.

'Wait a minute,' I said, after I'd followed him through the Second Class Dining Room. 'Shouldn't I be in here somewhere?'

'No, Madam.'

'I'm not – '

But then I saw Harry sitting at a large table. He wasn't alone either. There with him sat Nikolas, overflowing the chair, the table, even the room, huge though it was.

He rose to greet me. 'Hello, Eve.' He took my hand and bowed over it.

'How did you get here?' I cried, delighted to see him.

'In a taxi. Sorry I was late. I had some business to take care of at the last minute. I've got a present for you.'

'I mean how'd you get a berth on this ship? There weren't any. I tried every persuasion known to man, and my Uncle Phineas taught me all of them.'

Nikolas searched my face; he still held my hand. 'Maybe you didn't want it enough. Waiter! Waiter! Ah, here you are, boy,' he said, letting go of me, turning to the *sommelier*, who was young and blond with an upright carriage and an arrogant manner. Nikolas sat. 'You can pour the wine now. Go on, go on. This is my present to you, Eve. Margaux 1953. I bought a whole case on board specially for – No, no, boy. Not like that.'

The *sommelier* winced and straightened.

'If you want to get ahead in this business, you'll learn to pour the glass only half full.'

'Sir?'

'Only up to here. That's the boy. Now you're getting it.' He turned back to us. 'I figure we could make our way through a case of wine in the course of the trip. Don't you think? We'll hardly even need to work at it.'

'Isn't this the wine you served when I first met you?' I said, taking a sip. 'In Swiss Cottage?'

'Hey, come on. How could it be?' said Harry.

Nikolas shook his head. 'Good girl,' he said. 'I knew you had taste. It's rare in a woman – a taste for wine. But you are rare, aren't you? I'm not going to eat, so the least I can do is drink well. The food on the *QE II* is notoriously poor. Can you imagine what English food for English people on board ship turns out to be? I can't bring myself to eat such stuff, at least not this – ' He broke off. 'Waiter! Waiter!'

A waiter, plate of spinach aloft, wheeled in his tracks. 'Sir?' he said.

'That spinach looks good. Is it? Give me a bite. Um. It is good. Give me a little more. Well, more than that. God, you're stingy for a well-paid waiter. Just put the platter down. What's your favourite food, Eve?'

'Caviar,' I said.

'No hesitation there. What kind of caviar? Malossol?'

'Fresh if possible.'

'It's a signal.'

'What?'

'Like a flare. Fresh caviar. Remember that, will you?'

'What for?'

'Just remember it.'

I spent most of the journey in a deckchair, in a fog of sleep and wine, with an unopened book in my lap. Each night, Harry, Nikolas and I worked on the case of Margaux; on the fifth and final night we finished it. Nikolas suggested we go to his cabin for a farewell drink.

'Let's have it in the bar,' Harry said. 'The cabins are too small for three people.'

'I've got something to talk to you about,' Nikolas said. Harry and I exchanged martyred glances. We sighed. 'No, no,' Nikolas laughed. 'This is something quite practical. No more politics.'

Nikolas's cabin was a space as small as ours, way too cramped for a man as big as he was even though he had it all to himself. To this day I have no idea how he got himself a cabin on a ship that had no cabins to spare. Nor can I understand how he managed to fit his bulk on to that narrow berth at night. I sat cross-legged on the floor. Harry took the chair and slotted his leg in its plaster cast between bunk and door; the pain around his knee had increased steadily during the voyage, and he was becoming somewhat alarmed by it. Nikolas poured out water glasses of whisky – Glenlivet again – for each of us.

'I want you to do me a favour,' he said.

Harry and I spoke at once.

'Sure,' I said.

'No,' said Harry. I looked at him curiously. A pained smile played about his mouth, and his refusal was flat. Absolute.

Nikolas raised his eyebrows. 'Don't you even want to know what the favour is?'

'No.'

'This is the man who drank my Margaux so happily.'

'Whatever it is,' said Harry, 'we don't want to have anything to do with it.'

'I've just got too much luggage,' said Nikolas. 'I need a little help getting it off the ship.'

'And you couldn't talk about it in the dining room?' said Harry.

'I wanted to give you a drink.' Nikolas turned to me. 'Here's my favourite nephew refusing to help me get my luggage off a ship. Now does that sound friendly?'

'I don't want to sound friendly,' Harry said.

'All I need is a hand with a couple of speakers. You can deal with them along with your regular luggage. I'll have them sent to your cabin just before – '

'What kind of speakers?' Harry interrupted.

'Have another drink,' said Nikolas.

'I don't want another drink. I want to know what kind of speakers you've got.'

'You know anything about speakers?'

'Not much.'

'Then what difference does it make?'

'I don't know. Just tell me.'

'They're called JBLs,' Nikolas said with an airy dismissal. 'Satisfied?'

Harry's smile was suddenly brilliant. 'You are the limit. How could you ask me to do something like that?'

'What's a JBL?' I said.

'They're about six feet high,' Harry said.

'So you do know something about speakers?' Nikolas's grin was a touch sheepish now, but I can't say he sounded all broken up. He took a swallow of whisky and went on. 'Never mind. You can help me with these.' He pulled over two huge leather bags, beautiful leather, soft, with leather handles.

'What's in them?' said Harry.

'Nothing. Just clothes.'

'Let's see.'

'I can't manage these and the speakers at the same time. I can't carry luggage. You know that. It hurts my hands. It's just personal stuff, clothes, pyjamas. That sort of thing.'

'I want to see inside.'

'You're as nasty as British customs.'

Nikolas opened the bags. All I saw from where I sat was a disorderly heap of white material. 'See?' he said. 'Just pyjamas.'

Harry pulled one of the bags toward him, took out a bundle of cloth and tossed it on the floor. 'What are the components in here? mixers? amplifiers?'

Nikolas shrugged. 'New York has the best and by far the cheapest sound equipment in the world.'

'This is for the sound studio in Paris?' Harry said. 'Hey, this one's a video recorder, isn't it?'

'What do you want from me, kid?'

'Can't you get videos in Paris? I thought the French made good videos.'

267

'If I declare this stuff, it costs so much I might as well get Fedex to ship it. Nobody's going to stop a young couple like you with a broken leg and crutches. That scar makes you look like everybody's favourite war hero, Harry. Did you know that? Who's going to search a war hero?'

Harry struggled to his feet. 'The answer is no to speakers. No to stereo components. I won't do it. Eve won't. We won't. No. Come on, Eve, let's get out of here.'

'OK,' said Nikolas, no more disappointed this time than he had been before. 'So what about this?' He pulled a cloth bag out from beneath the bunk. It rattled. He opened it up to reveal a jumble of knives, forks and spoons. 'It's English silver anyway. You'd only be bringing it home.'

'No, no, no,' said Harry.

Nikolas thrust out the binoculars he wore around his neck. 'What about these? You'd only have to sling them over your shoulder. You'd never even notice they were there.'

As we made our way back toward the bar together, just Harry and I – minus the binoculars – I said, 'What was that all about?'

Harry shrugged. 'I don't know. All I know is that nobody in his right mind carries anything of Nikolas's across an international border.' He laughed then. 'Besides, he's nuts. A video recorder! Why bother with a video recorder? He couldn't be saving more than fifty bucks on the thing.'

Tourist Class passengers divide into two lines to disembark from the *QE II*. One is for those who can carry all their luggage, and one is for those who can't. Since Harry and I couldn't manage our three suitcases and his crutches, we joined the long, doubled-up line for people who couldn't carry all their luggage. Only a dozen or so stood in the line for those who could carry their luggage – the line that was to disembark first.

A few minutes before we docked, Nikolas appeared in a beautiful cashmere coat. By this time we stood about half-way back in our line; I said to him, 'Why don't you join us?'

'No, no,' he said. 'I've just come to say goodbye. I'm in the other line.'

Despite all my exposure to him, I hardly knew what to say. 'With six-foot-high speakers?'

'I hired a couple of porters to help me,' he said, and at just that moment, over his shoulder, I saw two liveried porters going down the ramp outside, each of them in charge of an immense black box on an industrial trolley.

I laughed. 'Are those what you were asking us to carry?'

Nikolas turned, glanced, nodded, but without much interest. 'I can't wait in a long line. I have this condition – '

'Is something wrong?' said Harry. 'What's the matter?'

Nikolas frowned and, for the first and only occasion in all the time I knew him, a look of pure sadness crossed his face. He patted the immense chest beneath his cashmere coat.

'My heart is too small,' he said.

CHAPTER 19

I always think of Brighton in the rain. Harry and I first arrived there in one of those very English drizzles, that clinging, bone-penetrating, nasal-dripping chill unknown anywhere else in the world. And the heaviest rain of the year slapped at our Hertz car all the way back from Southampton docks, hypnotic flick-flack, slish-slosh of wipers, and water so deep on the road that traffic slowed to a crawl to ford it. We drew up in front of our pretty flat in a downpour strong enough to rip leaves off trees along the road. The only cheer in the scene came from the row of spiderworts we grew, still vigorous despite a month's neglect, blue and purple against the low stone wall that separated our building from the pavement.

By the time we'd been back a few days and the weather had lapsed into its usual drizzle, Harry's leg hurt so much that I persuaded the local hospital to give him an emergency appointment. We ordered a taxi early – Hertz had picked up the rented car – in the hopes that evidence of the Tory Conference, just opening that morning, might take his mind off the pain. As he'd told me, a government conference was a gargantuan undertaking. A swarm, a horde, an army had descended on the town: some five thousand delegates plus press, staff, wives, mistresses, hangers on. The place just had to be jumping.

But we drove and drove, and the more we drove, the more his mood soured. 'Maybe we hate our politicians in Illinois,' he grumbled, 'but at least we admit it when they come to town.'

Not so in Brighton. Not one banner spanned any road or adorned any filigreed street lamp, neither 'Welcome Prime Minister' nor 'Go home Margaret Thatcher'. Not one shop-front sign hailed the government or reviled it. The marquee of the conference hall (poor, hideous heap of cement) announced the 'Conservative Party Annual Conference'. That's all. In ten days' time the very same plastic letters would perform the very same duty for a visiting pop star or an ice-skating road show. It's true that there were waist-high, crowd-control barriers in front of the Grand Hotel, but there wasn't any crowd. Nor was there any phalanx of police cars or squad of motorcycles. One lone bobby paced back and forth, clapping his hands to keep them warm.

While we waited in reception at the hospital, Harry read out the major conference story that had appeared in the previous day's *Evening Argus*: Mrs Thatcher had requested an extra telephone line for the Grand Hotel's Napoleon Suite; the BBC television crew were delighted with their rooms at the Sandpiper, a B & B tucked away behind the hotel. Such a pity really. Harry had so enjoyed the thought of a town grovelling at the feet of its reactionary head of state; there's nothing he loves more than a good, safe rant. The phlegmatic English – and his own leg, of course – had spoiled everything.

'Illinois? Where's that?' the orthopod said, turning Harry's cast delicately from side to side as though it were a piece of a mouldering Egyptian mummy. 'Are you certain there's such a place? Never mind. All Americans are mad. I suppose it's not their fault. Too much open space.' He stuck Harry's X-ray up on one of those scanner plates. 'What your leg needs is movement not restriction. I'm not surprised it hurts.'

They cut off the plaster and replaced it with a pressure bandage, which hurt more than ever at first. But over the next day or two the pain eased, and one morning Harry awoke rejuvenated. He got his motorcycle out of storage. He tinkered with it.

'A welcome-us-back party,' he said. 'At once. Tonight. You bake salmon. We'll celebrate.'

He'd gathered around him a small group of what I'd call the tremulous left; he called up a dozen of them, mostly graduate students at Sussex University. The little flat resounded with denunciations of Conservatives and corruption. The lady's-panty lamps jumped with the vigour of it, and the party broke up just after one in the morning only because everybody was too drunk to stay awake any longer.

As Harry and I washed the dishes in our little kitchen, he stopped, took me in his arms, said, 'Marry me.'

I disentangled myself at once and stuck my hands back in the soap suds. 'You look here, Harry Wheelock, another word – just *one* more word on this idiotic subject – and I'm on the next flight out of Gatwick. How can you bear these people? They're so pretentious.'

'They have principles.'

'They have principles like I have hair toner.'

'Don't say things like that. You don't really mean it.'

'Harry, damn you, I mean exactly what I say.'

'Hey, don't spoil things. Nobody gets along better than you and I do. Why can't we get married? It would be so much more convenient. Besides, you haven't got the money to fly anywhere tonight.'

I shook the suds off my hands. 'That's it.'

'Oh, no, don't let's fight. I don't want to – '

'I'm not fighting. I'm getting out of here. I've just spent the last four hours – no five – bored out of my wits, and now you start blabbering – '

'How can you say that? You're talking about my friends –'

Well, I guess I was the one who pushed him into a drunken spat this time. The to-ing and fro-ing went on for an hour or so, increasingly cold on my side, increasingly bitter on his, while I packed my bags to leave, and he drank himself into a stupor. He finally passed out on the floor and lay there snoring. I surveyed him for a moment, then got down on my knees and began to go through his pockets: a few pounds, a couple of credit cards and the keys to his motorcycle.

There was a knock at the door just as I was laying out this pitiful haul. Harry stirred, grunted and fell back to his snoring. Even with a party not long ended – and a security fanatic for a landlord – it probably doesn't make sense to fling open the door of a flat at such an hour in the morning without checking who might be on the other side, but that's just what I did.

One of those helmeted delivery people stood at the door, visor down, a faceless figure – scary-looking too, especially at such an hour, even if he was as short as Harry.

'Eve Holland? I've got a package for you.' Was the accent Irish? I'm really not sure. I'm lousy at accents. But there was something about the voice. A lilt. Something. 'Can I see your passport?'

'Why? What do you want my passport for? I thought people signed for packages. I don't think I want whatever it is. Get your foot out of the door.'

'Don't fuck with me, girlie. I got to see your passport.'

I fetched my passport.

He studied the photograph; he studied me; he studied my signature. Then he handed over a brown envelope. I remember thinking as he disappeared that the front door to this building had the biggest bolts on it I'd ever seen. Nobody unauthorized ever got in.

I ripped open the envelope.

So fairy godmothers come with wands and filmy dresses, do they? Isn't that what tiny Fred insisted? Here were cash and travellers' cheques. Here was everything I needed to get me out of Brighton this very night. More than that. Oh, much more. Bank notes spilled out on the floor, official-looking papers too, bonds of some sort, all of them in foreign languages, French mainly, some German.

A typed note floated down from my hand and settled atop the pile:

```
Herewith £100,000 in full payment
for   educational  services  ren-
dered. Check the Grand Hotel at
2:50, which should be about twenty
minutes from now, for a graduation
performance.

If the future ever presents a need
for a pound of fresh caviar, it
will be forthcoming at once. This
is a commitment as well as a
promise.
```

My watch said two-thirty.

It was stupid. I know it was stupid. But I grabbed Harry's helmet, his donkey jacket, the keys to his bike. He'd chained the thing to a lamp post outside the house. I'd driven it once or twice (he kept wanting to teach me), and I'd sat behind him often enough, moll-like, hating every street we covered, every pedestrian we roared past. The open road is just as open in a car; and when it rains you don't get wet.

Unlock the chain, kick back the stand, key in the ignition, teeter a little – not too bad – pick up a bit of speed. I can go up through the gearbox well enough. A straight line is OK.

But, oh dear God, that first corner – Screech out in a vast arc, up on the footpath, graze the chemist's plate-glass window, jolt sideways, lurch back, graze the Albion Pub's fine wood exterior, veer into the road, corkscrew wobble of pure terror. Then past Queen Victoria staring out to sea, as indifferent as God; from there out on to the Front, black Channel, glittering West Pier, string after string of street lamps; final swing-swerve down the long ramp to the Brighton Sailing Club.

A grassy open area stretches for a surprising distance in either direction in front of the sailing club; a promenade with lamps on it and a high wall – some twenty, maybe thirty feet – reaches up from water level, where I was standing, to Kings Road above and the Grand Hotel itself. It's quite a sight, the Grand Hotel at night, a brightly glowing birthday cake of a building, flood-lit, massive and elegant with that New Orleans-tainted, yet very English charm so characteristic of Brighton, wrap-around, wrought-iron balconies above an ornate, glass-house arcade: the whole as respectable and as solid as the statue of Queen Victoria I'd passed on my way here.

The minute hand on my watch crept up to 2:50. Nothing happened.

At 2:54, I said to myself, 'Well, if he's not going to blow it up, what's the point of – '

It's so delicate at first, just a mist of smoke, a tongue of flame and a second of silence: explosive takes in its breath like a singer. Then, Jesus, the glory of the whoomph-smash it lets loose. There's not always fire. After all, what does absolute power need of token force? A massive column of grey shot into the sky, switched off the birthday cake – instant total eclipse – and blew every pane from every window in a single clap of thunder. Whole sheets of frontage, tons of York and Portland stone hurtled out. An explosion like this reverberates in your heart and your entrails, rattles the bones in your legs and your neck.

If I hadn't been standing below the line of trajectory, the wild barrage of stone and glass would have killed me.

I've never in my life seen anything so awesome and so beautiful. I never expect to see anything like it again.

EPILOGUE

Nikolas is right. If you're lucky enough to have a talent – any talent, large or small – you're a coward if you don't use it. How could I allow myself to back away this time? especially now that I had money? more money than I needed? almost as much money as I wanted? Hours before Harry woke from his drunken stupor the next morning – about the time the English newspapers got their early editions on the street – I was on a flight from Gatwick to Luxemburg.

I read about the great Brighton bombing in the *International Herald Tribune* over breakfast in Esch-sur-Alzette.

ASSASSINATION ATTEMPT FAILS

There was a picture of the war-torn Grand Hotel. The story said that while Prime Minister Margaret Thatcher had survived, others had not been so lucky. This was early days. Nobody even knew how many had died.

The death of innocent people is a serious matter. I have no wish to make light of it. I hadn't thought about people, innocent

277

or otherwise – not in all the hours that separated me from Brighton – much less about them dying. In months to come I was to suffer emotional storms that arose without provocation, swept over me and left wreckage behind them. Unexpected noises shocked me back to the violence of the explosion itself. Sometimes I woke from sleep in a state of terror. But sitting in that riverside café with coffee and the *Tribune*, I felt only a queer kind of pride. I'd been there. I *knew*. I was slightly irked at the IRA's claim to the explosion. A visor-helmeted delivery boy: what right had he to such an event?

And if, even as I read, I doubted myself – if for a moment, I thought, 'Oh, come on, Eve, you're only imagining you were there' – the story's final sentence reassured me:

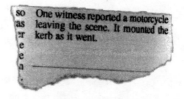

Every time I see a motorcycle, I hate them more. Mounting that kerb was the least of it. A couple of streets later, in a panic, I over-revved, lost the steering, careened too low and far too wide around a corner. The ungainly monster flopped over on its side. I slid out from under the back – skinned, bruised, trembling, but otherwise unhurt – and ran the rest of the way to the flat to collect my luggage.

The Luxembourgeoise are famous for their understanding of financial delicacy. I banked my bonds, flew to New York, entered Columbia's graduate school and took my doctorate in mathematics in under three years. My thesis was on fractals – it's a magnificent area of the field, gathering momentum at the time – and I had a contribution to make. Only the tiniest of contributions, to be sure, but a real one, and one that was to be published.

The let-down after the intense work, though: I didn't know what to do with myself. Uncle Phineas suggested a month of travel, so I went to London to see a few plays and wander the streets. On my very first evening – just off the plane, nothing planned but a walk and a night's sleep – I got caught in a crowd of concert-goers. Jostling my way through them (it was only the slimmest of chances), I saw a hoarding that said

---

The BRIGHTON PHILOMUSICA

Nikolas Strakhan, conductor

Rimsky-Korsakov: Russian Easter Overture
Elgar: *Enigma Variations*
Delius: *On hearing the first cuckoo in spring, Brigg Fair, Summer night on the river*
Liszt: *Les Préludes*

I'm no fonder of concerts than I ever was, but – What is it about danger that's so seductive? Fairgrounds, movies, books, circuses – even newspapers: scare people witless and you double your profits.

The house was a good deal smaller than the Queen Elizabeth Hall, and many seats were empty. The orchestra, smaller too, was already making its anarchic sounds when I took my seat. The lights dimmed a little.

Nikolas appeared on stage.

I hardly know how to describe my reaction. I'd expected to feel something. Certainly something, but not – I actually

279

gasped aloud. Speak of fairy tale. Here was the frog turned into a prince. Here was the man of Beatrice's stories, the man I'd glimpsed over shrimp in New York – young Nikolas, phantom Nikolas, make-believe Nikolas – lean and sinewy, enticing and forbidding at the same time, a half-run, half-walk for an entrance and a many-layered smile for his players. His greeting to us, his paying audience, was Caesar's open-handed salute to his foot soldiers and a curt nod of the head: a frisson swept through the theatre, sparsely filled though it was.

But then the music started. Look, I hate to admit to this. I hate being such a Philistine – and so changeable. Despite my intensities, despite the glory of this man reborn (no matter of what): despite all this – and within only a few minutes – I was as bored as ever. If my seat hadn't been close to the stage, I'd have left; I held back only because the audience was so small that a walk-out from the front would have been evident even to the orchestra.

As soon as the interval came I headed toward the nearest exit as fast as I could.

And ran smack into Harry Wheelock.

'Eve!' he cried, pulling me into his arms and kissing my forehead. 'What are you doing here?' I hadn't seen him or heard from him – or about him – since the night of the bombing.

'You do look well, Harry,' I said. 'Are you well? This is an amazing event: to find Nikolas conducting again.'

Harry laughed. 'Do you know, I was thinking of you just this very minute. I've missed you. I really, really have. And here you are – like magic. I bet you don't know that tonight is Nikolas's very first concert since the one you and I saw together.' I shook my head in wonder. He laughed again. 'What a night that was, huh?'

'Will you let me buy you a drink, Harry? It's the morning

280

after that still send shivers down my spine. Those ghastly reviews.'

'Nope,' he said firmly. '*I* get to buy *you* a drink.'

We fought our way to the bar. Despite the meagre number in the audience – or perhaps because of it – the crush was as mad as London interval crushes usually are. 'Whatever happened about Priscilla Carmarth?' I said. 'I've often wondered but – '

At just that moment, Harry was swept away amongst the drink-buyers with a look of perplexity on his face. He surfaced again a few minutes later, balancing a couple of whiskies.

We toasted each other, and then he said (reaching out and taking my hand to reassure me as he spoke), 'Don't be offended, will you? I've just got to ask. How did you manage to persuade some guy to buy my Katana in the – '

'Your what?'

'The motorbike. It was the middle of the night. Where'd you find anybody to buy it? Was it that blond guy at the party?'

I hardly knew what to say. Life with Harry seemed so remote, and I'd put it behind me so quickly, that I hadn't bothered with how he might have explained the loss of his motorcycle to himself. 'You never got it back?' He shook his head. 'I'm sorry, Harry.'

'I didn't know how unhappy you were. I just didn't realize. You do know that, don't you? You didn't have to sell a motorcycle to some Sussex University dork to escape. Don't look at me like that, Eve. OK. OK. Let's not – '

I withdrew my hand from his. 'I'll send you a cheque for it tomorrow.'

'Hey, no,' he cried. 'Please. Don't say that. It's not what I had in mind at – Let's change the subject. Tell me – '

'Why mention it then?' But he looked so crestfallen that I relented. 'Oh, Harry, I'm sorry. I don't know what's the matter with me. I'm a little tired, that's all. What about you?'

281

I smiled at him. 'Do you still love making products come out on top?'

Harry's brow knitted and unknitted. 'I'm Nikolas's manager.'

'No!'

'Product or person: there isn't any difference.'

'Harry Wheelock, you're going to shock me.'

'I'd like that,' he said. 'But you can't really mean you don't know what happened to Priscilla, can you? Didn't you see the papers? You know she's dead, don't you? Eve, she was in the Grand Hotel the night it blew up.'

I opened my mouth to say something, but no sound came out.

'You must have been on your way to Gatwick or Heathrow or whatever by the time it happened. Anyhow, the bomb was in her suite. That's why security didn't find it. You don't turn out the Countess of Carmarth's bathroom. We figured . . .'

The moment of the explosion, I'd known that Nikolas had lined those enormous JBL speakers with gelignite, that the collection of electronic stuff under his pyjamas had included detonators and wiring, that the video machine had served him as timing device. That was smart, using that video machine. Very smart.

But it's just that – the smartness itself – that made his trip to New York so hard to fathom. I'd thought and thought, and I could not figure it out. Why did the man go all that way? What possible advantage could there be? Any arms dealer in any country – certainly in Ireland – could have supplied materials for a bomb. At a pinch he could have used fertilizer. Why get involved in the hassle of an Atlantic crossing?

'What'd you say?' I said to Harry.

'It *is* noisy in here, isn't it? You'd think they could enlarge the bars in these – '

'What did you say about Nikolas? He had a breakdown? Is that what you said?'

Harry took a drink of whisky and shook his head in dismay. 'I've never seen anything like it. I visited him several times — Mickie carted him off to one of those Swiss mountain spas — and each time I saw him I came away quaking. The tortures of the damned. You know, I bet it was even worse than the breakdown he had when he was a kid. Hey, maybe knowing that suite of Priscilla's was really his — That makes sense, doesn't it?' He shook his head again. 'I had no idea people could go through such agony and live. He told me once that he longed to die and couldn't.'

This time the sense of danger — or was it evil? — was so strong that I actually felt a pricking on the back of my hands, if not my thumbs. 'Harry, tell me something. Is he better tonight?'

'What do you mean? Better than what?'

'Is Nikolas a better conductor? Better than he was when we saw him?'

'He doesn't have to be. Hey, just look at him. It hardly matters how a guy like that sounds.'

'Yes, yes, but the music. Is it better or isn't it?'

'You're kidding me. You can hear for — '

'I can't hear anything.'

'Nothing?'

'Nothing.'

He took in his breath. 'Eve, the difference is stunning. There's no comparison. None at all. Sexiest stuff I've ever heard. What's more seductive than corruption right at the heart of something pure? How often do you find a performer like this? Maybe the reviewers won't fall all over themselves, but they'll spend yards of column space trying to figure out just why he appeals to everybody. It's going to sell, Eve. Oh, boy, is it going to sell . . .'

Plainly — plainly — Nikolas had intended to kill Priscilla even before he flew to New York. Politics? Forget it. Without her money — quite a chunk of it, enough to overcome the disaster of that first concert (and to continue a way of life he had no intention of letting go) – he'd never have conducted again. This is more than smart, isn't it? This is brilliant. And can't you just smell the brimstone? Everybody's looking for an IRA bomber who wanted to blow up a Prime Minister, when in fact, the Prime Minister is cover-up for a musician who's killed a Countess.

'. . . and tomorrow,' Harry was saying, 'I'm going be fighting off record companies. I bet there are already – '

'Why did Nikolas fly all the way to New York?' I interrupted.

Now I really couldn't let go of it. New York – The risk was so terrible. And come to think of it, why let an outsider like me know that he was involved in such a dangerous plot? I could have rumbled him at any minute. And then there was the money he sent me. Bizarre. Just bizarre.

'When?' Harry said, puzzled. 'You mean to see us? you and me? on West End Avenue? Oh, that. That's no fun.'

'Isn't it?'

'Huh-uh. He came for you. Don't look so surprised. I've watched him in action before. I know you never liked him, but you have to admire him for sheer gall. I've never been so furious – '

'Came for me? Nikolas?'

'He just doesn't give up. What did you want out of life? How could he exploit whatever it was to get you? How much of a dare would it take? He always figures on a dare. He likes dares.'

I looked at Harry blankly.

'Hey, want to wait for tomorrow's papers with me?' he went on. 'For old times' sake? Nikolas says he's tied up tonight. Something deliciously secret, I gather.'

It's true that I was looking at Harry, but it wasn't Harry I saw. What I saw was a border of the Mandelbrot set. Fantastic riches? Is that what you want? Here are fields of jewels, a universe of them, one after another after another, glittering, scintillating, blinding. Dragons and magical creatures? Here they are, caught up in ripples, swirls, whirlpools, that are infinite, twisting, endlessly changing. This set is the most beautiful of mathematical entities – the devil's polymer, the most impossible of impossible quests – and one that lies at the heart of everything. They say God's a mathematician. Just like me. But God has seraphim to pleasure Him when He's dull after His work – as I was after mine. A seraph has six wings, six hands, six feet, a human voice; a seraph has no heart, but it's celestial – divine – when it practises love. Plainly not Harry.

But Nikolas – Something deliciously secret? Tonight?

'Have you got a piece of paper?' I said.

'Paper?'

'Paper. Paper. Harry, I must have paper at once. Right this minute.' He took a pad out of his pocket. 'Pencil? Pen?'

'Hey, what's the matter? Are you sick or something? You look feverish all of a sudden.'

'The pen. The pen.'

'Hey, come back here. You can't leave me like this. You haven't finished your drink. Hey! What about my pen?'

But I was already out of the bar, down the stairs, out into the street, round to the back of the theatre. I could hardly breathe as I scribbled the note:

> What I fancy is fresh caviar – although
> I'll settle for malossol if I can't have it.
> I'm at the Basil Street Hotel.

I left this at the stage door with strict – if stuttered – instructions that it was to be delivered to Nikolas immediately. Then I took a taxi back to Basil Street.

285

If you've ever doubted that the devil keeps his part of a bargain — that he has something deliciously secret on offer (and tonight) — what about this?

A reply was waiting for me at the porter's desk when I got to the hotel. I asked for my key, and the porter handed me a note there and then — as though Nikolas had written and dispatched it hours ago, as though he'd known all along that I would be in the audience, meet Harry in the interval, write to him at once, just as I had written.

After the concert. 12:30 tonight.
Carlton Tower. Malossol? Not on
your life. Fresh Beluga awaits by
the pound.